W9-BBE-890

The Secret Keepers of Old Depot Grocery

The Secret Keepers of Old Depot Grocery

Amanda Cox

THORNDIKE PRESS
A part of Gale, a Cengage Company

Thorndike Press® Large Print Christian Fiction.
The text of this Large Print edition is unabridged.
Other aspects of the book may vary from the original edition.
Set in 16 pt. Plantin.

**LIBRARY OF CONGRESS CIP DATA ON FILE.
CATALOGUING IN PUBLICATION FOR THIS BOOK
IS AVAILABLE FROM THE LIBRARY OF CONGRESS.**

ISBN-13: 978-1-4328-9465-8 (hardcover alk. paper)

Published in 2022 by arrangement with Revell Books, a division of Baker Publishing Group

Printed in Mexico
Print Number: 01 Print Year: 2022

For the real keepers of
Old Depot Grocery.
I hope I did Old Depot
justice in my little tale.
It certainly holds a fond place
in my childhood memories.

1

Present Day

Sarah nudged aside last night's puddle of clothes with her bare foot, the exposed designer label sticking out a bit too much. At the dresser in her childhood bedroom, she tugged open the drawer that without a doubt was just like she'd left it twelve years ago. The scent of lavender filled her nose.

The familiar sight of favorite T-shirts and the sachets Mom tucked into every drawer soothed the ache in Sarah's chest. Pain that followed her to her mother's front porch in Brighton, Tennessee.

She grabbed a T-shirt and a pair of cutoff shorts from the drawer and slipped them on in place of the borrowed nightshirt she'd been wearing, relieved that the old shorts still zipped and snapped without too much effort. Sarah stood in front of the full-length mirror in the corner and inspected her reflection. The faded Old Depot Grocery

T-shirt was a little tighter than she'd prefer, but it looked all right. Her gaze traveled downward to the large square bandages her mother had affixed to her knees, covering cuts that she hadn't even registered until Mom pointed out the dried blood last night.

The reflection in front of her was something of a time warp — this skinned-knee version of herself. If she could forget that the minor injuries to her knees weren't from a failed Rollerblading attempt.

The aroma of Mom's famous biscuits and gravy drifted under the bedroom door. Sarah's high school throwbacks might fit now, but not for long if Mom started feeding her like this.

Sarah padded down the hallway's worn beige carpet and entered the bathroom. She splashed cool water on her face. When she lifted her eyes, seeking the basket of hand towels Mom kept on the shelf beside the sink, Sarah spotted the large triton seashell from Aaron's and her honeymoon six years ago. A gift she'd sent back home to her parents.

Sarah held the shell to her ear, listening for the sound of waves. She'd walked that beach, hand in hand with her husband, an ocean of possibilities in front of them. She placed the shell back on the shelf and grabbed the towel.

Pressing her face into the terry cloth, she attempted to scrub away the memory. Was it possible to go back and get a redo on life? Pretend there'd never been a reality beyond this rural town and a little girl's dream to play shopkeeper for the rest of her life.

Following her nose, Sarah walked to the kitchen. Her mother faced the stove with a gingham apron tied around her waist, piling fluffy biscuits onto a platter. Overhead, Mom's hen collection adorned her cabinet tops, lined up in all shapes and sizes like they marched in a perpetual parade. Sarah smiled.

"Morning, Mom. Breakfast smells amazing. You shouldn't have gone to all that trouble though."

Her mother turned and flicked a glance over her, but her expression remained placid. Inscrutable. "It's not every day my only daughter shows up for an impromptu visit."

Sarah tried and failed to detect the emotion motivating that statement. Whether it was sadness or wariness, Sarah wasn't sure.

Though Mom had been roused from a deep sleep when Sarah arrived at two in the morning, you wouldn't have been able to tell from the way she'd ushered Sarah inside, cleaned her wounds, and served her a cup of herbal tea before leading Sarah to her old bedroom. Always a hostess, even when the guest was completely unexpected.

Or maybe Mom had expected Sarah to come these past two weeks, and the fact that it had taken her this long to seek her mother's comfort was the greater surprise.

Sarah sat and her mother poured her a cup of coffee. Once the cream and sugar were stirred in, Sarah took a sip, but the brew she normally found so comforting turned her stomach instead. She set the mug down on the pinewood table with a clunk.

"Something wrong with the coffee?"

Sarah swallowed back the nausea welling in her throat. She shook her head, afraid to open her mouth.

Mom placed a plate of biscuits and gravy in front of each of them. She never took her eyes off of her daughter, as if the constant eye contact could pull the answers to unspoken questions from Sarah's lips. "Are your knees feeling okay this morning? Do you think we got out all the bits of glass?"

Crystal. "Yeah. They feel fine. Thanks."

Sarah had felt strangely numb while she sat on the fuzzy pink toilet lid cover while Mom had inspected for grit embedded in her skin.

An accident, she'd said when Mom asked her what happened. But the shatter of delicate crystal on mahogany floors before she fled the silent house yesterday had been the most cathartic thing she'd experienced in quite some time. The destruction had been intentional, cutting herself on the mess she'd made, not so much.

"So . . ." Mom took a long drink of her coffee.

Sarah picked at the edge of her biscuit, bracing herself for the question that would follow that long pause.

Mom set her mug down and dabbed her chin with a napkin. "How long do you think you'll stay?"

She said the words with a gentle smile, but Mom wasn't asking how many days she should expect Sarah's visit to last. She was making sure Sarah knew better than to use her house as a permanent hideaway.

"When will Dad be back?"

Mom glanced at the wall calendar as though she didn't have her husband's trucking schedule memorized. "He'll be on leave in a week. He's supposed to get his usual seven-day break."

"Oh good. I'm looking forward to some quality father-daughter time." Hopefully that would be enough information to keep her mother from digging any deeper into Sarah's plans. And maybe two weeks would be long enough to ease her into the idea of turning the mother and daughter team that ran Old Depot Grocery, the store that had been in their family for decades, into a mother and daughter *and* granddaughter trio.

Sarah never should have left in the first place. "When are you headed to the store?"

"Not until closer to noon." Mom massaged her hands. "I have a doctor's appointment."

"Is something wrong?"

"Just a routine checkup."

Sarah pushed back from the table and wiped the crumbs from her hands. "I'm going to head to Old Depot to spend some time with Nan. Help out if she needs it."

"The only help she needs is in seeing reason." Mom muttered the words behind her mug.

"What did you say?" Sarah grabbed a Tupperware from the cabinet.

"Is that all you're going to eat? You're practically a toothpick as it is."

"Sorry. I'm feeling a little rocky this morning, is all." Sarah placed her nibbled biscuit in the plastic container for later. Wasting food around her mother's house was not an option. If her mother only knew how many casseroles Sarah had been given that were now untouched and molding in her refrigerator back home, she would have an apoplectic fit.

"Maybe you should stay in bed and get some rest."

The last thing Sarah needed was more time alone with her thoughts. "No. I think a day at Old Depot is just what the doctor ordered." She set her plate in the sink.

"Sarah . . ."

"Bye. I'll see you later." Sarah smiled through her forced chipper tone and then grabbed her purse and keys from the hall tree by the front door. She slid her feet into Mom's spare flip-flops.

Her mother called out from the kitchen. "We need to talk. The store —"

Sarah cut off the words by shutting the door behind her.

As she drove, she soaked in the ambiance of her little town. It had this old-fashioned air about it, tucked into the corner of the world, hidden from the effects of passing time. People sitting on their front porches lifted their hands and waved as she passed. Others were already hard at work in their flower beds. Sarah slowed her car for a tractor that was turning off the main road.

A few minutes later, she parked in front of the old store, having her choice of spots in the almost empty lot. She took in the familiar sight of the twin-gabled storefront. Between the gables the red-painted sign read OLD DEPOT GROCERY. Sarah let out a long breath that cleansed her, heart and soul.

She stood from the car and stepped over the dandelions that were sprouting from cracks in the sidewalk. Dandelions weren't pretty things, but they proved more resilient than roses.

The front door burst open, interrupting her musing. Out stumbled a harried man in a suit with a strange little hop in his step. He was followed by Nan, who scowled and jabbed the broom at the fellow, who had already dove into his car and had it cranked and backing out of the lot in no time.

Sarah stifled a laugh at the terror her petite grandmother had incited in the large man fleeing her store.

Nan jabbed the broom toward the retreating car once more for good measure, yelling, "And stay out, you . . . you miscreant! Old Depot Grocery has never been and will never be for sale."

2

June 1965

Glory Ann trudged down the stairs, the morning light filtering through the east-facing windows wrapping her in a soft warm glow. It was a perfect day for the June wedding that would never be.

Her mother stood at the bottom of the stairs, massaging her temple. "Darling, please go change. It's a lovely summer day. That black dress washes all the color out of your face."

The time she'd spent hugging the porcelain commode was the more likely culprit. But Glory Ann would bear any burden for the privilege of carrying Jimmy's child.

"I'm in mourning." Who cared if no one wore mourning clothes anymore? It was her way to make sure no one forgot how much he had meant to her.

Her mother released a sigh that stooped her shoulders. "I know you thought you loved him —"

And there it was — the real reason she didn't like the way Glory Ann had been skulking about for a month in that same dress.

"Mother." Glory Ann hoped her tone was enough of a warning. She couldn't have this conversation again. Not after the fallout around the dinner table when she'd finally confessed to her parents the secret she'd kept for weeks. That at nineteen, she, the minister's daughter, was pregnant.

"Out of wedlock" — the words Momma said would follow her all the days of her life.

She shook her head. The first words out of her father's mouth had been, "What are we going to do now? You can't have a shotgun wedding with a dead man, Glory Ann."

As she stood frozen on the stairs, her father appeared at her mother's side with the newspaper in his hand, his reading glasses perched atop his head. His face was lined and gray. The glory of the morning hadn't lightened the burden her father carried any more than it had Glory Ann's.

Her mother pinched the slim bridge of her nose. "Go change into that nice yellow dress you have. The one with the little white flowers sewn into it. Please."

It seemed her parents not only wanted her along on their visit with old friends today but expected her to play the part of the little ray of sunshine too.

They both looked so weary that she complied. Glory Ann almost always complied. That's why it had been such a shock to her parents — that she and Jimmy, the poster children for good Christian raising, had taken things too far. Just that one time, she'd sworn, but she could tell they doubted.

But it had been just one time. One moment of tears and fear, sorrow and hopes. His name had been called and despite his bravado, Jimmy hadn't made it five minutes over there. She'd known he wouldn't. Those soulful blue eyes of his were made to behold long rows of thriving crops under a southern sun, not the horrors of Vietnam.

In front of the oval mirror, Glory Ann stripped off the black A-line dress and studied the Irish cream figure that was her reflection. Her hand found the slight curve of her lower belly. The place where a little bit of her and a little bit of Jimmy was growing. A seed of love. Perhaps it shouldn't have been planted, but despite the shame she and her family would suffer, she couldn't bring herself to regret it.

After she changed into the cheery dress her mother had requested, Glory Ann tidied her rogue onyx curls and pinched color into her cheeks. She tucked the letter she never sent into her pocket.

If she'd dared to send it, maybe by some postal miracle Jimmy would've received it in time and known he was going to be a father before he died. Maybe it would have made a difference. Somehow.

When she walked out to the car, her father placed a small valise in the trunk. *Mother must be bringing some quilting supplies to the lady of the house.*

"I'm ready."

At the sound of her voice, he lifted his head, his expression startled. "You look lovely."

She fixed the pretty smile that he expected on her face. There had been enough strain and strife lately. It would be best to make this beautiful early summer day a nice time together. She couldn't undo her choices, but she could make today pleasant. She opened the back door of the tan Cadillac.

"Ride up front with me, why don't you?"

"But Momma —"

"Your mother went to bed with a headache." He glanced away. "It'll just be me and you today."

Despite her attempts to stir conversation throughout the drive, her father remained stiff in his seat behind the wheel, offering quiet one-word replies.

Glory Ann gave up and stared out the window at the verdant farmland. It sure hadn't been easy confessing what she and Jimmy had done. It was a secret she'd wanted to take to her grave. But some secrets demanded to be revealed. Some secrets grew with time and had a life and a heartbeat of their own.

What did Daddy think of her now? Did he love her still, or was he more concerned with how their tiny community would react when they realized the minister couldn't even keep his own family on the straight and narrow?

An hour later they pulled into a one-stoplight Tennessee town named Brighton. Her father stopped at what looked to have once been a train depot. The weed-infested tracks were long abandoned by railcars. The sign over the door read OLD DEPOT GROCERY.

Her father killed the ignition and leaned his forehead against the steering wheel.

"Daddy?"

He straightened and offered her a tight-lipped smile. "You ready?"

For what? She'd thought they were going out visiting, not shopping at a small grocery a few towns away.

"Clarence Clearwater is a very nice man. His parents were old family friends of mine. This is his store."

"Okay." She tilted her head. Why should she give a fig about Clarence Clearwater and Old Depot Grocery?

He hesitated, his mouth working as if he intended to say more. "Let's go in and I'll introduce you."

Glory Ann exited the car and watched the people coming and going on the sidewalk. The curious looks she garnered made it clear that new faces were always noticed in a town like this. Some were shabby farmers in threadbare overalls. Others nicely clothed in store-bought dresses in a similar style to her own. Yet all these people seemed to belong here. Like fabric stitched together on a patchwork quilt.

She trailed behind her father. What kind of looks would she receive when her pregnancy became obvious? How would her own little town treat her? Always the little darling everyone admired with her songbird voice, delicate figure, and demure manner. Now a fallen woman.

She squared her shoulders and lengthened her stride. She'd just have to grow thicker skin, keep her chin up, and dare anyone to say a word with fire in her eyes. Her days as a minister's bashful daughter were over.

Once inside, her father approached a man in a green apron. He was probably about ten years her senior. He had narrow, stooped shoulders and a crooked nose that looked like he'd been punched once or twice and never had it set right. But his too-close brown eyes were gentle and kind.

Her father inclined his head toward the man, and they shared a quick, whispered conversation. "Come here, Glory Ann. I'd like to introduce you. This is Clarence Clearwater."

Glory Ann offered her hand. The stranger took it and gave it a soft squeeze. A question in his eyes.

He gave a decisive nod, and his gaze locked with her father's. "Sir, I'd be honored to marry your daughter."

The air became stifling and close. Glory Ann's vision blurred, and the room seemed to tip. Strong arms enveloped her, and her world went as black as the dress she'd donned earlier that morning.

Light filtered back into her view. Glory Ann

was cushioned by something soft and musty. Hushed conversation floated in the air with the dust motes. She struggled to sit and found herself lying on a dingy couch in a cramped office lit by a green desk lamp.

Her father stood from his chair and knelt beside her. "Honey, are you okay?"

He passed her a cup of water, and she took a sip to relieve the cottony feel of her mouth. Her head cleared and Clarence's words the moment before she'd fainted broke through the haze.

She gasped. "I don't know what you think you are doing, but I am not — I will not marry that man. You can't make me do this."

Clarence cleared his throat and rose from where he sat at the desk. He gave an awkward sort of bow. "I'll give you two a minute."

Her father grasped her hands. "Glory Ann, Clarence is a good man. He's respected in the community, a business owner."

"And he wants to be saddled with a pregnant woman who doesn't even want him? What kind of man could he possibly be? The kind no one will have, that's what."

"I've known Clarence and his family for years. I wouldn't be willing to do this if they weren't good people."

"You wouldn't be willing? What about me? I know I made mistakes, but does that mean I should be punished for life?" Her throat tightened, the disbelief taking her normally lilting voice to a rasping screech.

Her father pressed his fingertips to the space between his brows. "I'm not punishing you. I'm trying to help you. Help our family. You've put us in a right tight spot, Glory Ann."

Her mouth fell open. She was the one whose life was about to be turned upside down by a newborn. Whose heart was shattered by loss. She was the one who the town would gossip about and look down on. Was it shame that motivated him to ship her off and tie her to a man she didn't know? "A tight spot?"

"I could lose the church."

A weight sank in her middle.

"The board hasn't been happy. Attendance has been down. And they blame me. Now, with you pregnant and no man in sight to claim the child? I fear it'll be what breaks us." He took her hand, squeezing too tight.

"Don't do it for me. Heaven knows I'd find a way to manage. But your mother? She was raised in that church. Think what it would do to her if we were asked to give up our position."

Mother always seemed to have been made of chipped china, and Glory Ann understood how little it would take to shatter her. She'd spent her life trying to cushion her mother from the harsh edges of life. Turning off the news or hiding a newspaper if the reports were too dark. "I . . ." She pulled her hand out of her father's grip. "So . . . what? Now I'll be banished from home forever?"

"You two will marry as soon as we obtain a license, and you'll go on to have a family. Clarence has agreed to raise the child as his own. This child will be loved and cared for. A part of a solid family. If you don't do this for your mother, then think of the child. Think of how he or she will be treated if you don't go through with this." His eyes were wide, pleading.

Her hands trembled and she clasped them tightly in her lap to make them still. "Can I take some time to think? Get to know Clarence a bit?" The words tasted sour in her mouth.

His gaze went to the floor as he shook his head. "There's no time. Rumors will be bad enough as it is."

Glory Ann's stomach churned, having nothing to do with the little life growing inside. No wonder her mother hadn't wanted her wearing black that morning. She'd dressed her for her wedding and Glory Ann hadn't even known it.

"Momma's not here." She hated the plaintive sound of her voice, but on her wedding day her mother was supposed to be at her side, reveling in all the lacy details.

"She . . . she wanted to be here for you. But she just couldn't bear it. She packed up your hope chest for you."

Her dreams of that someday June wedding had suffered a fatal blow the day she'd heard Jimmy died. This was like heaping dirt on top of a coffin whose occupant was still struggling for breath.

Three days later, in the dim, cramped office, Glory Ann Hawthorne became Mrs. Clarence Clearwater, all to cover up a secret she was not ashamed of.

3

Present Day

Satisfied she'd successfully run off her intruder, Nan lowered her broom, a scowl marring her aged face. She froze and squinted at the sight of Sarah standing on the sidewalk.

"Sarah? Land sakes, is it really you?"

"Glory Nan." Sarah whispered the nickname the four-year-old version of herself had dubbed her grandmother with — a mispronunciation of her given name that stuck for life.

A full smile dissolved the harsh lines that had been etched in Nan's face moments before, and she opened her arms. Sarah hurried to her and sank into her hug — the haven she'd been craving.

After a long moment, Nan pulled back from their embrace and stared into Sarah's eyes like some sort of scanner doing a status check. She released a soft *humph.* "I know it's hard, but you'll pull through. You're a Clearwater girl, and Clearwater girls are made of some pretty stout stuff."

Warmth filled Sarah's middle at her grandmother's misplaced faith, and she was thankful for the absence of the platitudes that had so often been foisted on her over the past few weeks. She could go a hundred years without hearing the words "Everything happens for a reason" or "Time will heal," and it would be too soon.

Nan squeezed Sarah's shoulders as the corners of her eyes crinkled. "I'm so glad you're home."

Sarah sure hoped it could be home again. She picked at a broken thumbnail, suddenly feeling like the empty-handed prodigal. "Any chance you're hiring?" A breathy laugh slipped out of her.

Nan nodded, peering over Sarah's shoulder at the storefront. She focused on Sarah's face with a look in her eyes that Sarah could only describe as fierce understanding. "There's always a place for you here. Always. Let's go inside and see what we can get into." Nan pushed open the front door.

The clank of the miniature cowbells against the glass was a welcome-home chorus. But as Sarah stepped over the threshold, the swell of comfort dissolved.

The bare spaces on the shelves gaped like holes in a once-perfect smile.

Where was the bustle? The hum of gossip and banter that brought the store to life? Sarah walked slowly, the floorboards emitting a plaintive groan beneath her feet. "W-what's going on? Did a delivery get delayed?"

Nan sighed and waved her hand dismissively. "We're going through a bit of a slump. Not to worry. These things happen. When you've been around as long as I have, you'll see. Hard times are just seasons. They come and go. But we stay. Old Depot Grocery always stays."

We stay. Was that an accusation? But no, Nan was looking over the dead quiet store with a determination that stirred something to life in Sarah's chest.

Nan propped her hands on her hips. "Now that you're here, you can help me convince Rosemary that Old Depot isn't going to go down without a fight."

Mom wanted to close the store? Was that what she wanted to talk about this morning? Sarah had figured Mom had been about to give another reminder of how she'd worked that store her whole life to make sure Sarah never had to.

But Mom's claim that she'd never had opportunities beyond Brighton had never held water in Sarah's opinion. Mom's sister, Jessie, was well traveled, educated, and seemed anything but "stuck."

Still. Sarah couldn't deny that both her parents worked hard to make sure she could have any life she wanted. Since graduating high school Sarah had flown far from this little town and seen some of the most stunning views in the world. But there was only one spot on the map she craved, one where she could look into Nan's eyes and absorb her enduring strength and southern sass.

Sarah followed Nan to the stockroom. "All right, honey, if you could organize these dry goods by expiration date, it'll help us know what we ought to put on sale next. We've gotten a little behind." The barrenness in the room felt bigger than a little slump.

"Are you and Mom the only ones working here?"

Nan sighed and spoke over her shoulder as she exited the room. "Yes. We're at this strange place where just the two of us feels like too many working here and not enough all at the same time."

Maybe the three of them was just what they needed.

Nan left Sarah to sort product in the quiet room, and her mind wandered, taking her back to the place she'd fled. To another dimly lit room. This one full of finery instead of dusty canned goods.

Takeout Sarah ordered from the restaurant where she and Aaron had their first date had sat between them. Flickering light from the tapers glinted off the facets in the crystal candelabra. Aaron hadn't taken two bites before the phone rang. The warmth that had been building in her middle shrank away, leaving a chill in its place.

"I'll be there in ten." He stood, wiping his face with his napkin and then offered her a sheepish grin. "It shouldn't take too long. I'll be right back and then we can celebrate our anniversary in style. No more interruptions."

She couldn't force herself to return the smile. "Can't someone else take care of this?"

"Someday I won't have to be so hands-on. We'll make up for every missed moment. I promise."

Sarah shoved the two-week-old memory away and fled the stockroom. Surely a customer had wandered in by now.

She snatched an apron off the hook by the office, slipped it over her head, and tied the waist as she walked.

With the kelly green canvas beneath her

touch a pressure release valve opened, and she took a solid breath.

As promised, Mom arrived just after noon. She stood from her car, chewing her bottom lip and massaging her hands. Sarah watched as her mother blew out a puff of air, then fixed a serene expression on her face as she approached the front door.

Mom waved a greeting on her way in and walked back to the office. Sarah finished totaling Mrs. Warner's order and helped carry her bags out to her car. She watched her drive away with a sigh of relief.

Even here in Brighton, a world so far removed from her life in Kenilworth, a suburb just north of Chicago, there were ripples of concern, or rather pity, for Sarah's situation. But at least here, no one knew Aaron.

How long until she could chat about the weather and the latest town gossip without an "I'm so sorry" tacked on? Words that left her fumbling for a response, forcing her to take yet another swim in her pool of regret.

She returned to her post at the checkout counter and eased onto the stool.

"Sarah, come here, please," her mother called out from the back of the store.

Sarah gave a quick look around. The brief

rush seemed to have ended. She sighed as she walked along the near-empty produce section. She passed a stray shopping cart — a buggy here in the South. Her New England–raised husband had laughed the first time he heard her call it that.

Sarah shook away the thought. The memories weren't supposed to be so fresh and raw in this place she and Aaron never shared other than one brief visit. But they kept creeping in, vivid snapshots of both the good and the ugly.

Her mother stood beside the deli counter at the back of the store and extended a paper plate loaded with a ham sandwich and potato salad toward her. "Here. You look like you could use some lunch. I'll take over up front. Where's your grandmother, anyway?"

Sarah accepted the plate, inwardly shuddering. She normally loved her mother's potato salad, but at the moment the combination of mustard and mayonnaise assaulted her sense of smell. "I don't know. She said something about needing to see a man about a goat."

Mom did a double take. "A what? What is she up to?"

Sarah grinned. "I have no idea." She set her untouched lunch on the counter, dropping the smile from her face. "Mom, why is the store like this? Nan said it was just a little slump, but it's so empty."

Her mother flinched. "The store . . ." She sighed. "Time and life are marching on, and this old place just can't keep up. Your grandmother refuses to see truth. Pray for me, because I'm fixin' to lose my mind with her sneaking around, putting in orders we can't afford, chasing off land developers who actually want this obsolete stretch of land." She lifted her hands and let them fall to her sides. "We need to seize the opportunity to make a profit in selling the store before we miss our chance. If Momma won't say yes, then some other landowner will." Mom locked eyes with Sarah. "Maybe the two of us together can make her see reason."

Sarah's heart seized in her chest. "You can't just let this place go. Old Depot is her life. There's got to be a way to fix this."

Mom stiffened and crimson splotched her face. "We've been struggling awhile now. Which you'd know if you'd visited for more than a red-hot minute once a year." She leveled a look at Sarah that would make a steel beam melt. "Besides, I'm not *letting* our store die. After a while you gotta accept the truth and quit beating an already dead horse."

Panic thrashed in Sarah's chest. "You can't close. You can't. Brighton needs Old Depot Grocery." *I need Old Depot Grocery.*

Her mother wiped her clean hands on her apron. "No it doesn't. Not anymore. Didn't you see the new construction on the way in? A big chain grocery opened two weeks ago. There's no coming back from this. We'll just waste our energy better spent on other things." She let out a long, slow breath. "Just . . . help me convince her, Sarah. She's seventy-five. She'll run herself into the ground trying to make this place survive. She deserves to retire. See a little bit of the world before —"

"I don't need to see the world. This *is* my world."

Sarah and her mother spun to the strident voice at the end of the aisle.

Nan stood, hands on her wide hips. "We can't lay down and let that big box store steal our heritage. I've worked this store for fifty-six years. And I'd work it fifty-six more if the good Lord gave me the wherewithal."

"Momma." The words left Mom's lips as a defeated sigh. "Sarah, tell her. Maybe she'll listen to her granddaughter with the fancy college degree since she finds me to be so woefully inept."

Sarah glanced between the women, both leveling looks that left her feeling like a favorite toy tugged between two warring children.

The cowbells clanked against the glass at the front door. "Oh look, we have a customer." Sarah scurried away, winding through the labyrinth of aisles. Aisles she could navigate blindfolded. Whispered bickering sounded behind her back.

This was not the homecoming she'd been counting on.

4

December 1965

"This baby is getting so big, Jimmy. Must take after you with those long legs kicking around in there." Glory Ann brushed a trickle of sweat from her brow with her shoulder. With a groan, she shifted, cradling her ever-growing abdomen for support. She moved from crouching to sitting at the shelf she restocked with cans of chicken soup.

She looked up into Jimmy's eyes and at his mop of blond curls that had a tendency to resist his attempts to slick it back no matter how strong the hair gel. He leaned against the aisle, smiling that dimpled smile of his. Her heart did a flip, just like it did every time she laid eyes on him.

Then her gaze went to a scar on his index finger, just above the knuckle closest to his hand — a reminder of a childhood farming accident.

The doctors had said it was a miracle they

were able to save that finger. That "miracle" likely signed his death warrant. People were considered unfit for service for a myriad of reasons, surely a missing trigger finger would've sufficed.

Glory Ann pulled her polyester shirt away from where it was plastered to her, trying to get a little airflow across her sticky skin. "I know you said beauty could be found anywhere if you looked hard enough, but you were wrong. Ain't nothing beautiful about a big, round, sweaty pregnant woman stacking cans on this dusty bottom shelf." She huffed.

"Glory Ann? Did someone come in? I didn't hear the bells." Clarence's voice cut into her daydream.

The light in Jimmy's expression faded, replaced by a sadness that twisted Glory Ann's heart. She glanced over her shoulder to the approaching footsteps. "We'll talk again soon."

Jimmy gave a single nod and turned away.

"Glory Ann. Was someone here?"

Clarence stumped toward her in his loud, flat-footed stride. He stopped at her side, arms crossed over his green apron. "Honey, what are you doing on the floor? Mable was supposed to restock. You shouldn't be doing this in your condition."

Her insides squirmed at his use of a pet name. "I'm not an invalid. It needed doing, and Mable had to leave early. The school nurse called and her littlest one is running a fever."

"Come on now, I could've done this if you'd mentioned it." He held out his hand and offered a pained smile. "Let's get you up from there."

She ignored his help and made a less than graceful shift into a crouch and used a shelf to brace herself to standing. She brushed off her hands and straightened her green apron that was twisted across her basketball belly. "No trouble. I was bored out of my mind."

Clarence reached toward her. When she recognized his intention, she stepped back and swiped at the hair stuck to her forehead.

"Are you okay, Glory Ann?"

"Of course." She propped her hands on her hips.

Clarence glanced away, toward the front of the store as if trying to make sure no one approached the entrance. "I . . . I hear you, you know. Talking to him."

Glory Ann clenched her hands so tight her nails bit into her palms. "Talking to who?" Maybe it was hateful, making her husband say the name of the man she loved, but she couldn't help but feel like he'd just tread all over something sacred with his big, clumsy feet.

Clarence stared at the floor, the pause stretching between them. He lifted his gaze and a muscle ticked in his jaw. "Jimmy," he said softly.

Glory Ann blinked back sudden tears, wholly unprepared for the stab she'd taken to her heart when Jimmy's name came off of Clarence's lips.

"I know everyone grieves in their own way, but the way you talk to him, I'm not sure it's healthy." Clarence's brow wrinkled up like a walnut shell and he looked away. "You talk to him like he's right there next to you."

She gazed out the storefront windows. Jimmy *was* right there next to her. Gathering up all the scattered pieces of her heart, holding them tight so she didn't fall apart. Sometimes if she concentrated hard enough, instead of walking these aisles, they walked side by side down the long rows of corn at his grandfather's farm that Jimmy had been so proud of. That was supposed to be her life, and that version was far more real to her than anything in front of her.

Clarence stepped to her and put a hand on her shoulder. She shrank from his tender touch. “I think you need to find someone you can talk to about this, someone real. It’s just . . . you’re about to have a baby. And you’ve already been through so much. It’s like you’re still stuck somewhere else with someone else, not healing at all. I know you don’t see me as a husband, and I don’t pretend that you ever will, but I hope you can at least see me as a friend who cares about you, Glory Ann. I’m worried.”

He gave her shoulder a pat and scooped up the empty cardboard box now delivered of all its cans of soup. She blinked her dry eyes in response to his retreat. Strange how her chest could feel like it had been sliced open in one moment and empty and vacant the next.

Maybe she sounded crazy, carrying on conversations with a dead man. What Clarence didn’t know was that those conversations with Jimmy kept her from losing her grip on the last thread of her sanity. Far easier to think on what her life should have been than to face the reality of what it was. What it would always be.

Forever bound to a man she could not love.

■ ■ ■ ■

Dear Jimmy,
Our baby girl came into the world with a feather dusting of snow on the ground and Christmas music crackling from the radio. Not that anyone could hear it over my screaming and crying.

Don't tell anyone I said so, but she looks like a grumpy old man. Stark bald, wrinkled, and red-faced. I miss her being inside of me. Somehow it made you closer to me.

Over the past few weeks I've caught Clarence looking at me, peering over the store aisles, his brow creased in concern like I'm about to drop off the deep end any minute. Maybe I am.

The nurse keeps asking me if I'd like her to bring my husband to my hospital room. I asked for this pen and paper instead. Is there something wrong with me, that I find more comfort in a memory than a flesh-and-blood person? Maybe, but the fact remains that the one I gave my heart to is too far away to be called. Even by me, it now seems.

It shakes me inside, Jimmy, the way I can't feel your nearness. I've tried to see you here with me, kicked back in the burnt orange chair beside me, proud as a peacock of our baby girl, but it stays empty.

By and by, will I forget the dreamy spark of your eyes? Will the sweet hayfield scent of your hair fade away too? Or will you come back to me? Please, Jimmy. Come back to me just once more so that I can pretend that you and I are together, beholding this child we made.

I wouldn't tell this to anybody else, but I wished for a boy. I would've called him Jimmy, no matter what anyone said. You remember that book of flower meanings you loved? I found a copy of it at the library. I'll find our girl's name in those pages.

No surprise, but Mother didn't come. I know I shouldn't have hoped. She hasn't visited once since I moved here. Not even for the baby shower the church in Brighton hosted for me. I gave birth to our baby all alone in a stark white room with a nurse holding my hand.

I can't send letters to heaven, I know that. And I know the images of you were only makings of my lonely heart. But if somehow you can hear from heaven, I want you to know that I'll be all right. I don't love Clarence. But he is kind. And he doesn't expect much. I guess its gratitude, this feeling I have for him.

Your daughter will grow up taken care of, Jimmy. And I'll find a way to be okay. To find the beauty you always saw in this drab world.

Always Yours,
Glory Ann

5

Present Day

Summoned by the clank of bells, Sarah hurried to the front of the store. Mom and Nan's hushed bickering provided the ambiance of the empty grocery. Their fussing had been her constant companion for the past week.

A tall, lanky man stood by the register with his back to her in worn-in jeans and work boots. The battered cowboy hat he absently tapped against his leg looked like it had been a casualty of a cattle stampede. A crate of vegetables sat at his feet.

"Welcome to Old Depot Grocery. Is there something I can help you with?" she asked.

He turned. His blue-green eyes a shock against his suntanned skin.

"Afternoon, ma'am."

She soaked in the comfort she found in his slow, easy southern drawl.

"I know your manager said the other day

she didn't need any further orders, but I had a little bit left over from my stand today. Thought y'all could sell 'em. No charge or anything."

"My . . . manager?" Sarah blinked, trying to follow the conversation.

"Ms. Rosemary?"

A snort slipped out of her. Manager might be one way to describe her relationship with her mother.

A question formed in his eyes.

"Rosemary is my mother. I'm her daughter, Sarah."

A friendly smile took over his face. "Hello, Sarah. I'm Clay. Here for a visit?"

Sarah shrugged and smiled. "I'm here for . . . for . . . well, I'm here for now."

He glanced at her apron. "They didn't waste any time putting you to work, I see."

"Nan always said that idle hands were the devil's playthings."

Clay gave a nod, but something guarded flickered over his expression. "Wise woman."

"That she is."

He lifted the crate of vegetables and stepped toward the produce section. The volume of Nan and Mom's voices escalated.

Sarah winced. "Just leave them there on the counter, if you don't mind. I'll see to them." She offered a sheepish smile. "Please. I need any excuse I can get to look busy and stay out of their henpecking."

A corner of his mouth twitched, and he placed the crate on the edge of the checkout counter. He set his battered hat atop his head. "Have a good day, Sarah." He raised his gaze toward the back of the store where her mother's and grandmother's bickering sounded. "Give Ms. Rosemary and Ms. Glory Ann my best."

The man tipped his hat and exited the store.

Sarah reined in her grin at his gesture. Tipped hats and ma'ams and misses. She was definitely back in the south again.

She hefted the heaping crate of vegetables he'd left behind and stocked the bare places. When the task was complete, she admired the contrast between the vine-ripened tomatoes, zucchini, and crookneck squash.

Old Depot Grocery no longer looked so forlorn and forsaken with fresh produce filling the shelves. As long as she ignored the other sparse aisles at her back.

Her mother and grandmother strode toward her, still carrying on about spreadsheets and orders and the fate of the town.

Her mother stopped short with a sharp gesture directed toward the produce display.

"What's this? Momma, I told you we weren't taking any more produce orders. I had to throw half the last one out."

Nan propped her hands on her hips. "I didn't. I left that to you, which was obviously a huge mistake."

Sarah cleared her throat. "A man named Clay dropped them off. He said it was leftovers."

Nan's face softened. "You met Clay? He's a fine young man."

Mom rolled her eyes skyward. "A little soft in the head, if you ask me. Giving us his vegetables to sell for free. Those don't look like leftovers to me."

"Don't mind your momma, Sarah. She's in one of her moods. Clay's just being kind." Nan wriggled her eyebrows. "He's a looker, ain't he?"

Sarah grinned. Was that a faint blush coloring her grandmother's cheeks? "Sounds like somebody's got a crush."

Nan wagged her finger playfully. "I'm far too old for such foolishness. But I can't help it if he's a little sweet on *me.*"

Sarah laughed at Nan's teasing words.

Nan tilted her head. "You oughta get to know him, Sarah. You'd like him."

"For heaven's sake, Momma. Her husband's not even cold in the grave. She's grieving, not looking to make eyes at Clay Watson."

Nan huffed. "That's not what I meant —"

Sarah's ears began to buzz, and her chest grew tight.

Grieve. A good wife would grieve. But she just wanted to forget. Her stomach churned. Sarah clapped her hand over her mouth and rushed to the back door lest she empty her stomach on the waxed wood aisles.

Rosemary walked down the sidewalk in the town square, rubbing a hand over her face. As if it could scrub out the horrified way Sarah and Momma looked at her whenever she mentioned that the store needed to close. Like she held a dripping knife, fresh from stabbing them both in the back.

Momma she understood.

But Sarah? Her daughter hadn't batted an eye at that store since she'd moved out twelve years ago.

She huffed. She'd spent her life fighting for that store. Did Sarah and Momma truly have no idea how hard she'd worked through recessions? The many times the store had been on the brink of failing and she'd worked herself to the bone to pull it back from the edge. The never-ending tension between the cost of doing business and the needs of the community.

"Hey there, Rosemary."

Rosemary raised a hand and waved to Karl across the street. He was locking up at the hardware store that had been the centerpiece of the town square for years. A yellow closeout banner spanned the front window. Old Man Benton had spent his last days trying to keep his store going. Working up until the day he died. She wouldn't let that happen to her mother.

If they went ahead and sold the store to the development company while they were eager to make a deal, they would both be able to tuck away a tidy sum. At least enough to make sure Momma was well cared for and create a savings account to help with her own uncertain future. She loosened and tightened her hands, trying to fend off the tingling in her fingertips.

Rosemary had taken it upon her shoulders at the tender age of seventeen to make sure her mother was provided for. If the store sold, she could finally count her mission as complete.

She slipped into the travel agency in a little historic home on the outskirts of the main square and plopped onto the couch with a groan, freeing her swollen feet from her Keds.

High heels clicked on the hardwood. "Girl, just wait until you see the cruise package I've got picked out. Even your stick-in-the-mud husband is gonna love it." Cathy, her lifelong friend, stepped out of her office with a file as thick as her tiny waist. A file full of dreams the two of them had been working on for over a year. Ever since Rosemary had gotten wind of the big grocery chain coming to town. Dreams that had become further expedited after her diagnosis. With her cut from the store's sale, she'd make one little splurge for her and Bo to make up for all the trips they'd never taken. And then the rest would go into a health savings account.

Rosemary held up a hand. "Might as well stuff it away in the back of your filing cabinet. Momma's gonna keep at that floundering store until she's racked up enough debt to drain every bit of equity out of it."

Cathy perched her birdlike frame on the edge of the couch and put a hand on Rosemary's shoulder.

"Besides," Rosemary said, "you and I both know Bo was never going to agree to this trip. He calls himself a fisherman, but he's scared to death of being on the water."

"We could always make it a girls' trip. Me

and you, some yellow polka-dot bikinis." Cathy bumped shoulders with her.

Rosemary choked back a laugh at the mental image. Cathy could probably get away with such a thing, even at their age. But Rosemary had more curves than any bikini could contain with any amount of decency. She shook her head. "Momma's not going to sell. And if we don't, I don't know how we'll manage the bills, much less a dream vacation."

"It's all gonna work out. You'll see."

Rosemary stood and paced the narrow foyer. "You haven't seen the way Momma and Sarah look at me. Like I'm 'bout to head out back and shoot Old Yeller."

"I'm so glad Sarah came home. I know she said she didn't want to trouble you with driving all that way to go to the funeral, but a girl needs her mother in times like these."

Rosemary sat back down. Didn't want to trouble her? More like Sarah didn't want to be embarrassed, *again,* by her hillbilly relations. Rosemary knew that she and Bo had stuck out like a couple of sore thumbs at Sarah's elegant wedding. "She's here for a quick visit. Can you believe my mother was trying to rope Sarah over to her side? Sarah's not the one trying to eke out a living here. Sure, she is sentimental about the place, but Momma and I can't afford sentimentality."

Cathy plopped the file onto the couch next to Rosemary. "Trust me, Glory Ann is going to see reason and you are going to get the chance to take that dream trip and all the other things you've been putting on hold for all these years." Her hands flicked and fluttered while she spoke.

Rosemary grinned. The woman wouldn't be able to speak if she was forced to sit on her hands.

"What I don't understand is why you don't just tell them the truth." One hand on her hip, Cathy shook a finger in Rosemary's direction. "If they knew the real reason you're so eager to sell, they'd change their tune. Take a page out of your sister's book and take care of yourself for once."

Rosemary sighed. It was so much more complicated than that. She'd tell Sarah about her health problems, but not until Sarah got herself resettled and moved forward with her own life. After all Rosemary had done to make sure her daughter never made life choices based on obligation, she couldn't fail now.

Rosemary forced a smile and grabbed the bulging folder next to her. "You're right. It'll work out. One way or another. Might as well dream a few minutes longer."

Cathy passed her a tin from the side table. "I made some chocolate-covered pretzels last night. Your favorite."

"Well fork those over, sister. I sure as shootin' need some chocolate therapy this afternoon."

6

March 1967

Glory Ann scooped her daughter from the back seat, relishing the sweet pudge still lingering on the fifteen-month-old's lengthening legs. The curly-haired tot pushed back from her mother's embrace and bore her blue-eyed gaze into Glory Ann's. "Down! Me do it."

Glory Ann swiped a thumb across the child's sticky cheek. "Okay, but stay close and no running. It's Gramma Hawthorne's birthday." Her chest tightened. "And we must be on our very, very *best* behavior."

Glory Ann put her daughter down and straightened the crumpled flounces of the tiny pink dress. She then smoothed the front of her own orange shift. "Now, hold my hand."

It had been months since she'd been home to see her parents, and though her mother promised she'd come to Brighton, she had never made the one-hour drive. Not in the many months her little one grew in her middle. Not when she'd labored in the sterile hospital, longing for her mother's hand to hold. Nor any other time during the fifteen months of her daughter's life.

She took a shaking breath and found an anchor in her child's tight grip on her thumb. It had seemed a fun idea to surprise Mother on her birthday, but with all the cars filling the driveway, it appeared she was a gate crasher, not even an invited guest to the only place that felt like home.

"Come along, love." Glory Ann steadied her daughter as she toddled up the porch stairs. She didn't bother knocking, the buzz of conversation inside pulling her onward. All went quiet before a chorus of "Happy Birthday" rose.

Glory Ann scooped up her daughter and together they entered the dimmed room but stayed outside the circle of familiar faces gathered around the kitchen table. The glow of birthday candles softened the lines on her mother's face, making her appear years younger than Glory Ann ever remembered. Something in her middle twisted, and she fought back swelling emotion she couldn't name.

The song ended and the room silenced as

the company waited for her mother to blow out her candles. In the silence, the tiny girl in Glory Ann's arms burst forth an exuberant "Happy birday, Gamma!"

Collectively the room shifted in their direction, and Glory Ann shrank back.

A gasp sounded to her left. Jimmy's mother stood with her hand pressed against her chest, staring at the child. Glory Ann swallowed. *Jimmy's daughter. Surely Mrs. Woodston didn't recognize . . .*

Her father appeared at her elbow and steered her from the room just as her mother blew out the candles. He spoke over the applause, forced cheer straining his voice. "So glad you could make it, darling. Come, we have a room set up where the children can play and give the grown-ups their space."

Glory Ann clutched her squirming child close and quickened her pace to match her father's hurried climb up the steps. He pushed open the door to Glory Ann's old room.

"Here, this will be a nice place for our little moppet to play." His voice was light, but there was a tension around his eyes that made Glory Ann's stomach knot up.

Glory Ann surveyed the room, clear of all of her personal artifacts and now sporting only a dresser and her old iron bed, covered with a patchwork quilt. "Where are the other children?"

"Oh, um, it's just her." He nodded to the toddler who now sat on the braided rug, running her fingers over the ridges, babbling quietly to herself.

Momma appeared in the doorway a tad breathless.

Daddy grimaced. "I'll make sure all our guests are comfortable while you two chat." He made his escape.

"My, my that sure was a . . . a *nice* surprise. You two showin' up." Momma folded her hands in front of her, spine ramrod straight.

Glory Ann knelt close to her child. "I'm sorry. I didn't know you had company." She tore her gaze away and stared at the filmy curtains where late afternoon sun made them appear ablaze. "You didn't mention anything about a birthday party when I called last week."

Momma crossed the room and sat on the quilt, then started toying with a frayed seam. "Honey, I love you and my sweet granddaughter. You know that." She cleared her throat and lifted her chin. "But . . . but I think it would be best if you didn't come to Humboldt for visits anymore. Let us come to you. Now that you have a little one, it's too much hassle for you to make the trip."

"I don't mind it. It's nice to be home."

"Glory Ann, honey . . . I'm trying to be gentle about this. Visit if you want, but don't bring the child back here. She's . . . she's like a facsimile. Those eyes. That fair hair. The older she gets, the less it can be denied. Jimmy's mother about had the vapors after you left the room."

Surely Momma was just being paranoid. Glory Ann's pulse pounded in her ears, and her chest grew tight. "It's wrong, what we've done. Keeping her from them. They lost their son. They shouldn't lose the chance to know their only grandchild too." She pulled her little girl into her arms and inhaled the comforting scent of her hair before the child squirmed away, entranced by a hatbox beneath the bed. She pulled it onto the rug and opened and closed the box full of Glory Ann's keepsakes, whispering "peekaboo" over and over again.

"We should tell them the truth."

Momma knelt in front of Glory Ann and gripped her arm. Her complexion, warm and rosy in the light of the birthday candles, had gone anemic. "You . . . you can't. You'll ruin *every*thing."

Her mother's long manicured nails bit into her arm, eyes over-bright.

Glory Ann shivered. "We could ask them not to tell. To keep it a secret."

"It's not just our family's reputation anymore. What would it do to Clarence if people found out the child he totes around isn't his? They'd call him a liar. It would bring shame on him and his family." Momma shook her head. "The Woodstons can't know about their grandchild. *Ever.* Who's to say they would even accept it as the truth? They could see it as an attack on their deceased son's character. Clarence is the one who has been by your side through all this. You don't owe anything to the Woodstons."

Who was this woman in front of her?

"It will be all right," Momma said. "You'll see. I'll visit."

Numb, Glory Ann collected her daughter and the hatbox. "We'll go then, Mother. It's clear we were never welcome here in the first place. Tell Father I said goodbye."

As her car rolled down the lane, Glory Ann spared a final glance in her rearview at the home she was raised in. At the second-story window, where a naive girl once stood daydreaming about the grand possibilities the future held, a woman's rigid form took her place. She pulled the curtains closed, disappearing from view.

On the drive back to Brighton, each mile stretched like a thousand, expanding between her and the people who raised her. Glory Ann wasn't a fool. Her parents would never come to Brighton.

And Glory Ann would not return where her daughter wasn't welcomed.

She parked behind Old Depot and swiped at her swollen eyes.

"Ma-ma, what wrong?"

Glory Ann raised her gaze to the rearview mirror, soaking in the sight of her sleepy-eyed cherub. "Nothin', baby. Let's get you out of the car."

Free from her confines, the little girl scampered through the back door and down the aisles while Glory Ann trudged in her wake. In the canned goods section, old Miss Lettie knelt and brushed a stray curl from the child's cheeks. "Hello, little doll! Helping your mother today?"

The little girl twirled and grinned. "Yes. I help."

While the sweet woman chatted, loving the child in a way her own grandmother wouldn't, Glory Ann slipped around the corner. The boards squeaked beneath her feet, and for the first time, they whispered a new sound. Before, they had been boards that just needed nailing down after time and wear. Now they were a welcome-home song.

Because it was here she was loved. Accepted. And no, the town didn't know the truth. But Clarence did. Though he'd promised her this marriage could remain in name only, she knew enough from the tender way he looked at her that he wanted more.

Clarence stood at the door of the storeroom. His little girl ran past and dove into his arms. "Daddy, Daddy, Daddy!"

He swept her skyward and spun her in a circle.

And something new sprang to life in Glory Ann's chest, wriggling up between the cracks. It wasn't the heady rush she felt every time she had looked at Jimmy, but the way Clarence showed her child love, accepting her as his own, soothed the aching places others left behind.

Maybe she would never love Clarence like she had Jimmy, but Clarence was a good man. From her purse she removed the tattered envelope that traveled everywhere she went. The letter she'd been too late to send. In the back corner of the store, she lifted the loose board she'd been meaning to fix, and slipped the envelope beneath, entombing it with the plank.

When Clarence set the toddler down, Glory Ann approached him. She wrapped her arms around him, and his body went rigid. Glory Ann tilted her head back, reading the questions in his brown eyes. Nearly two years together and they'd been little more than roommates and business partners. She'd never touched him like this. With intention. She leaned up on her tiptoes and brushed a kiss to his lips.

No zing of fireworks shot through her. Both her feet remained planted firmly on the floorboards. Nothing like the kisses with Jimmy that had left her floating heady in the places where dreams lived. But Jimmy was gone. And no matter how much she wished it every time she looked at her daughter, he was not coming back.

Clarence's return kiss was sure and sweet, and that was exactly what her new life needed. Something sure and sweet.

7

Present Day

Sarah perched on the stool across from her grandmother's desk in the back room. Nan hunched over the ledger. The light of the green-shaded banker's lamp threw her wrinkles into stark relief.

"Don't you do all this on the computer, Nan?"

"Bah." Nan flicked her wrist. "Your *mother* does. I keep my own records. Never trust a machine, Sarah."

Sarah reached for her smartphone to run a quick calculation and cringed at the multiple missed call notifications. Two from her realtor and another from Aaron's lawyer. Responsibilities she couldn't bring herself to face. Not yet. She tucked her phone back into her purse. "Of course. Never trust a machine. I learned that from *The Terminator.*"

"What?"

"Never mind." Sarah hid her grin behind the saltine she nibbled. "So, what do the books say? What do we need to do to keep the store kickin'?"

Her grandmother released a long sigh. "We just gotta keep on keepin' on, my dear. It's not about chasing what's bigger or better. It's about who can stick it out when all seems lost." She tapped her pencil against the ledger. "Sure, everybody's all wound up about that big, shiny new store where people don't even have to go inside to get their groceries if they don't want to. They've got people who'll deliver them right to the car. It won't last. Just another passing fad."

Sarah worried her bottom lip between her teeth. "I don't know. It's the way things are most places now. People want convenience. Variety. Quickness. We'll just have to come up with some way to compete. We could try out our own order-ahead system."

Nan shook her head, grimacing. "No, no, no. Don't you see? We don't need to become like *them.* People *want* convenience. But that's not what they *need.* What they need is what Old Depot Grocery already offers."

"Which is . . . ?"

"Child, child." Nan's dark brown eyes went razor-sharp and bright. "Why are you here right now?"

Because she was a coward. Because she was lost and alone and afraid. Because she didn't know where else to go. "Because I missed you."

Nan raised her eyebrows. "Took you long enough."

A knife twisted in Sarah's chest. If she'd said no to Aaron the summer after her freshman year, when he and his family invited her to travel Europe with them, her whole life could've taken a different course. Even with the promise of seeing the world, going home to Brighton pulled harder. Until Mom told her it was an opportunity of a lifetime and that she wasn't *needed* at home. Mom meant well, but those words had stung. Hard. So she went with Aaron that summer and every summer after. Every year growing more and more distant from the small-town dreams that had once filled her heart. "Nan, I'm so sorry, I . . ." But what could she say? There was no excuse.

Nan made a shoo-fly motion at her. "I'm not guilting you. I just think that answer you gave is a bunch of baloney. Anyhoo, you and everyone else comes through these doors comes here because this place doesn't change with every blowing of the wind. We're stable. We're steady. We're dependable. Or at least we were until that mother of yours stopped produce orders." She grumbled on under her breath.

Sarah picked salt crystals from her cracker and sucked them off the end of her finger. "But what do the books say? Do the spreadsheets match what you're saying, that we can pull through this?"

Nan smacked the ledger closed and braced herself to stand with the edge of the desk. "Never mind the books. Never mind the numbers. Old Depot has never been about the numbers."

"Yes. But —"

"But nothing. I thought you were on my side."

"I am. I just need to know where we are to know how to help."

"We're hanging on. We're fighting. That's where we are. That's all that matters. Will you fight with me?"

Sarah stood from the stool. "Of course."

Nan rounded the desk and embraced her. "We can't let this store fail, Sarah. If the store closes, I don't know . . ." Nan pulled back, clutching at the neckline of her shirt. Her chin trembled.

Sarah placed her hands on her grandmother's shoulders. "We won't let that happen, Nan. We'll find a way." Because the only other alternative was to go back to

Chicago. To the house of marble and glass. "I'm going to run home in a minute and help Mom with dinner. Are you coming over tonight?"

"Not tonight. I've got poker night with the girls."

Sarah did a double take. "Poker night?"

Nan flicked her hand. "That's what that scamp Paulette named our sewing group, the Poker Night Prayer and Sewing Circle. Me and her and Mable get together to sew and pray through the church's prayer list." Nan sighed and rolled her eyes. "Paulette's contribution is the town gossip. I try to straighten her out, but I haven't had much luck yet."

Sarah grinned. "I'll talk to Mom over dinner, see if she has any thoughts on how to get more business to the store, and let you know what we come up with."

"Bah. She's already raised a white flag over this place." Nan shook her head. "I never imagined she'd give up on her daddy's legacy like this."

Sarah straightened. Momma never talked about Granddad. "Maybe all her memories here aren't as happy as ours are."

Nan scoffed. "I'll tell you this. Her father and I gave everything to make sure her life was the best it could possibly be. And for her to want to sell out? It boggles my mind."

Sarah parked in front of the little blue house she was raised in. Her heart leapt at the sight of her dad's pickup in the drive. He was a day earlier than she expected. Purse over her shoulder, she mounted the steps and flung open the door. "Daddy?"

Her father looked up from where he sat in his favorite recliner, reading glasses perched on his nose. He stood and wrapped her in a hug. "Good to have you home, sweet pea." He smacked a kissed on top of her head. "I've been praying for you nonstop. How are you hol—"

"Can we *please* not do this, Dad?"

"Fair enough."

She sank into the embrace, enveloped in flannel and Old Spice. "Where's Mom? I thought she'd be home by now."

He shrugged as he returned to his seat and glanced at the quirky clock on the wall. A blue hen whose legs functioned as the minute and hour hands. "She'll probably be home in a minute or two. When I called, she'd stopped off in town to visit with Cathy."

Sarah stepped forward and then stifled a shriek when she almost tripped over a great black lump on the floor. The great black lump lifted its head, and a lazy pink tongue lolled out.

"Meet Huck. Terrible duck dog and a worse guard dog. As you can see." Dad scrubbed a hand over his graying five o'clock shadow and propped his ankle on his knee.

She sidestepped the Labrador and sat on the sofa opposite her dad, tucking a knee up under her chin like she used to when she was a little girl. The dog uncurled and stretched out with a grunt and yawn and rested his head on her dad's slipper. She nodded to the duck hunting magazine he'd been reading. "New hobby?"

He wagged his head. "Well, I tried. But come to find out the stinkin' dog is scared of water *and* gun-shy. We go out, but we're more cut out to be hikers than duck hunters, it seems."

Sarah laughed. "What I can't believe is that Mom is letting you keep a dog inside."

"Small miracle, huh? She doesn't mind as long as Huck minds his manners. And he travels with me, so she doesn't have to put up with either one of our snoring too much."

"Still thinking about retiring?"

He sat forward, bracing his hands on his knees. "Part of me wants to. I'm not sure it's the right time. Thought I'd try to find some local routes instead of doing the long hauls. Although, I don't know how your momma will feel about me being home all the time."

It would be an adjustment for them. Her dad's life had been a series of comings and goings, but that was the life of a trucker. Over the years, her independent mother had never seemed too bothered by Dad's long stretches out on the road. She said she missed him, but she always seemed to cope just fine whether he was there or not.

But for Sarah, his absence had been deeply felt, especially in her teen years. Daddy's calm demeanor had always been the perfect buffer between her and Momma's higher-strung personalities.

"What do you think she'll do if Old Depot goes under?" Would she retire? Find something new to pursue? Sarah couldn't picture her mother anywhere else besides the aisles of the store or the kitchen of the small country home overrun with her collection of chicken figurines.

"I know Cathy's been talking about them becoming partners at the travel agency for a while now." His eyes crinkled, and a muscle in his cheek jerked. "Although, I was kinda hopin' she'd take up duck hunting. If anybody could order old Huck here into submission, she could."

The screened back door slapped in its frame, followed by a rustle of paper bags. "I heard that, Bo Anderson. Not my fault you paid an arm and a leg for a dog who won't hunt."

Huck lifted his head at her entrance. Looking properly penitent for his deficiencies as a duck hunter, he whined and rested his head between his front paws.

Mom set the brown paper bags on the coffee table. "Picked up some food from down at the diner. Overstayed at Cathy's and wasn't in the mood to cook." She shrugged and fixed a glare on both Sarah and her father as if daring them to make a comment.

Sarah glanced at her father. He gave the paper bags a baleful look but didn't say a word. Mom's home cooking was probably one of the highlights of being home.

She glanced at Sarah's purse on the floor. "Put your things away and go wash up for dinner."

And just like that Sarah was twelve years old again.

8

December 1967

Glory Ann was elbow-deep in suds, her shirtfront soaked, scrubbing dinner dishes. No matter how careful she was, her great big belly always ended up dripped upon. From the sound of things, the bedtime routine was not going to plan. She could hear the fluctuating tones of Clarence's voice, apparently on a repeat request of reading *Little Red Riding Hood* with all the voices. The big softie. He'd probably read it a third and fourth time too. He had the hardest time telling that little sprite no.

She hummed along with the radio. The child inside her rolled and kicked. In a few weeks they'd move from being a family of three to a family of four. It was so different this time, being pregnant. Motherhood was not as much of a mystery, and she didn't feel so alone. This time she let Clarence love her.

As sweet as the past nine months had been — since she'd started seeing Clarence as more than a stand-in father and began seeing him as the husband he'd always longed to be — she couldn't help but dread the inevitable change barreling their way.

Clarence entered the kitchen. "I finally escaped. She's sleeping like a little angel." He scuffed across the floor in his house shoes, picked up a dish towel, and began drying plates and putting them away.

"She loves you, you know."

He smiled softly. "And I'm pretty sure she hung the moon." He studied her, and she pulled her eyes away, uncertain of how to voice the things that kept her up at night.

Clarence stepped behind Glory Ann and turned her from the sink. He dried her hands with the towel in his own. "What's troubling you, my sweet Glory Ann?"

Most wouldn't consider him classically handsome, but she had witnessed firsthand the selfless way he loved, and he'd become so incredibly beautiful to her. "I —" She cut away her words. She couldn't say it.

He tipped his head. "Do you love me? Really love me?"

"Of course," she breathed.

"And do you believe me when I say that I love you?"

She nodded.

"Then what do we have to fear? Tell me what troubles you. It's the things we don't say that have the power to rule our lives without our permission."

Glory Ann placed her hands on her round middle. "I'm afraid of the way this might change things."

He placed his hands atop hers. "Just more to love. What's so scary 'bout that?"

She shook her head. "This child is yours. All yours. Not just in name. There will be no pretending this time. How . . . how could you possibly feel the same about this one?"

He smiled, his eyes so tender. "I chose that little girl snuggled down in her blankets fighting sleep. She might not share my DNA, but I love her because of who she is and whose she is. That little girl is mine. And I am hers." He squeezed her hands. "And you are mine, and I am yours. I've not once pretended anything."

Clarence raised the volume of the love song crackling through the radio. Dancing a slow sway, they circled in the little kitchen with her round belly brushing his flat front.

He turned her in a half spin and pulled her tight against his chest and kept swaying.

She rested her head back against him and closed her eyes. No matter what Clarence said, things would change. But right now, in this quiet moment, she'd let herself believe that he'd be able to love both her children the same.

When the song ended, she faced him. "Why'd you do it?"

His forehead creased. "Do what?"

"Say yes when my daddy asked you to marry me. Cover everything up."

Clarence had integrity that even had a greater strength and conviction than her minister father, but he'd so willingly played the part in this deception. Explaining away her short pregnancy by telling everyone he'd married a family friend months prior, but had refused to bring her to Brighton until he'd purchased a house for his bride. That using Old Depot's office as an apartment was just fine for him but not the woman he loved. He looked at her with such tenderness when he'd said it, no one ever questioned him.

His eyes went wide. "My gosh, woman. I had one chance to marry a girl as beautiful as you. I might not be much to look at, but I'm not dumb."

She playfully smacked his shoulder. "Stop. I'm being serious. I want to know."

He released a heavy breath. "When you walked in my store, you gave my life a purpose I'd never known before."

Glory Ann pursed her lips. "What? Taking care of problems that don't belong to you?"

"You've had a long day. Let's get you off your feet for a bit and we'll talk." He pulled out a chair for her and when she sat, he slipped another one beneath her feet.

He went to the stove and put the kettle on. He pulled out the tin of the herbal blend she loved drinking at night. All the while she watched him, suddenly quiet and pensive in everything he did.

After he prepared her tea, he brought another chair around and sat at her side. A determined set to his jaw. "The family I come from, they don't have a lot of money, but they have something more powerful. Influence."

Glory Ann nodded. Her father had said as much.

"When names began getting called for service, they told me they would make sure I didn't have to go."

Glory Ann's heart twisted in her chest. If only someone had been able to do that for Jimmy.

"I refused their help. It wasn't fair that my dirt-poor friend from high school had to go and I didn't just because my family had friends in high places. So I left my job at the bank Dad ran and came to Brighton."

He looked at the ground. "Despite my rebellion and taking what I believed to be the moral high ground, I was deemed unfit for service anyway."

Glory Ann tipped her head. "Your asthma?"

"Yes. After that, I bought the abandoned train depot for a song. But I was miserable. Even though I didn't totally understand that war — who we were fighting or why, my friends were there, risking their lives while I was home sweeping floors." He stared at the space between his feet.

She couldn't blame him for feeling that way. It was one reason it had been so, so easy to stay angry at him even though he'd been so breathtakingly kind. Because Jimmy had to go, and Clarence had stayed.

"So, my dear, when your father contacted me, it gave me hope. A ray of light in my world. No longer was I useless." Clarence wrapped his hands around his mug.

"Because there was someone who needed you?"

He took a long sip of his tea. "I couldn't go to war and fight. Because your fiancé had, he couldn't be there for you in the way you needed. So I married you, not because I was desperate or lonely, or as an act of charity. I married you in Jimmy's honor. I didn't know him. But I saw the hurt and the loss in your eyes when you walked in my store that day. And though I couldn't take his place in your heart, I could give you a few things. A home to rest your head. A store where your hands had something to do while your heart healed. And my last name as a shelter from a world that is not always kind."

He took her hand. "When I married you and had the privilege of loving our little girl, suddenly Old Depot wasn't just a store to me anymore. I was serving my country by offering stability and love where it was needed. And I did, you know, love you from the start. Maybe not as a husband, but as someone who knew what it was to be alone, who wanted to be a friend."

He put a hand on her round belly, the place where their child grew. "I could never take Jimmy's place. But I am so thankful that we've found our own way forward, together, in this world that is rarely gentle and fair."

She lifted his hands and kissed his calloused knuckles. "I love you, Clarence Clearwater. I really do."

9

Present Day

Sarah wandered into the kitchen, rubbing sleep from her eyes. Her body heavy and stride sluggish. Her mother stood in front of the stove. The bacon and sausage popping in the skillet scented the air.

Her dad put down his duck hunting magazine when Sarah entered the room. "Mornin', sweet pea. Sleep good?" His eyes flicked upward, and laughter creased his eyes.

She swiped at her sleep-tangled hair. "Yeah, I really did." Better than she had in weeks. But somehow she still felt like she'd been thrown in a washing machine during the spin cycle. "What time is it, anyway?"

Her mother turned from the stove. "Almost nine. I have to be at the store in half an hour. Mom opened up this morning." She plopped down a big plate of biscuits and a bowl of redeye gravy on the table next to the eggs and grits. "I made all your favorites. Except for the gravy. That was your daddy's request."

Her dad took a long drink of coffee with a faraway look in his eyes. "When you were a little girl, you used to wander in here just like that. Your hair like a tangled golden crown on top of your head. Your mother always fussed and fussed about how long it took to detangle it all."

Mom, still placing heaping plates on the small round table, chimed in. "It was like trying to untangle a spider's web. I always thanked God that I only had one child's head to untangle."

Sarah chuckled under her breath at her reminiscing father and her practical mother.

All seated around the table, they held hands while her father prayed a blessing over the food. It had been a long time since Sarah had paused to thank God, before a meal or any other time. It had been such an ordinary part of her life when she lived at home. But when she'd left and entered an entirely new world, those things that had been etched in her upbringing faded more easily than she'd like to admit.

She needed this. This returning to her roots — mentally, emotionally, physically. Spiritually. If she watered what was left of these roots, would something still grow?

Her parents began loading their plates with food. Sarah selected a biscuit and picked at its soft middle, hoping it would settle her uneasy stomach.

"I've been cooking for an hour and all you want is a biscuit? You've spent too much time up north. I bet you'd rather have a bagel and coffee than this spread."

The past week the only thing remotely appetizing was saltine crackers. But Sarah had learned from experience that avoiding food altogether only made the nausea worse. "Illinois isn't 'up north,' Momma. It's the Midwest."

"If there's no sweet tea on the menu, then it's up north to me."

Mom's continued discourse on the geographic availability of sweet tea faded from Sarah's ears as a buried memory rose to the surface. Their first breakfast at home after their honeymoon. Her Connecticut-born husband going green when she announced with pride that she'd succeeded in making her mom's recipe for biscuits and chocolate gravy. Laughter and teasing filled the kitchen when she explained that it wasn't *gravy* in a literal sense, but a sweet chocolate sauce.

A knot formed in her throat. At one point

there had been laughter in that Chicago house. Stolen moments before Aaron's falling out with his father took over so much of his life. Before their time together was replaced with IOUs and promises of "someday."

"Sarah?" Mom's voice called her back to the present.

She blinked to force back the moisture gathering behind her eyes and focused on her mother. "I'm sorry. Your food is delicious. I'm just feeling a little off this morning."

Mom paused, fork loaded with a bite of sausage and scrambled eggs. Sarah swallowed hard, trying not to think about the greasy meat or the texture of the eggs wobbling on the fork.

"Honey, if you keep holding everything inside, you're going to make yourself sick." Mom reached across the table and squeezed her hand.

"I just haven't had much of an appetite lately. And right now, the last thing I feel like doing is discussing my husband's death over breakfast."

Her father lifted his eyes from his magazine, peering over his reading glasses at Sarah. "Of course you don't have to talk about it." He traded the magazine for the morning paper. He shook the crease from the newspaper and leveled a look at his wife. "Does she, Rosemary?"

Mom pursed her lips and went to the refrigerator. She removed a pitcher of orange juice. "Well, no. But it's not good to bottle everything up."

She was one to talk. Sarah couldn't recall a single moment her mother blathered on about her own hurts and loss. Besides, this wasn't the normal grief of a wife aching for her husband. Mom and Nan couldn't possibly understand the toll a lonely marriage could take.

Mom poured Sarah some orange juice.

Sarah brought the cool rim of the glass to her lips and pretended to take a drink. "So, what do you think we need to do to get traffic back up at the store?"

Dad lifted his newspaper higher and disappeared behind it.

"Sarah . . ." Mom set down the pitcher. "The store has had its day. Surely you can see that. Don't tell your grandmother, but I actually have a potential buyer coming in today to take a look at the property. Thankfully he's still interested after your grandmother's less than welcoming reception the last time he stopped in to inquire."

"A what?" Sarah's voice went shrill.

"They've already been throwing out numbers. They aren't playing around. If we sell now, both your grandmother and I could walk away with a good sum. I've tried to tell her that this is the wisest direction to take. She could be well provided for, for the rest of her life."

"What would they want with Old Depot? You said it is failing. Unsustainable. If they are already asking before it's on the market, then they must think the store isn't a loss."

Her father's hand snaked around the newspaper and grabbed his cup of coffee, bringing it into his hideaway.

Mom let out a puff of air. "Well . . . it's not the business . . . or . . . or the building they're interested in."

Sarah clenched her hands in her lap.

Her mother shrugged. "It's more the land underneath the building."

Sarah stared, envisioning a wrecking ball hurtling toward her safe haven.

Mom took a long drink of juice. "I don't pretend to understand all the ins and outs, but this big online distribution company needs warehouses to store goods. Brighton's location makes it an ideal bridge between larger cities in this region. We need to jump on this before they move on to someone else." Mom cleared her throat. "The new warehouses could be an amazing opportunity for your father to switch from cross-country routes to more local opportunities."

Dad choked behind his paper. He lowered it. Red-faced, he said, "Rosemary, honey, please don't bring me into —"

"You want to bulldoze Old Depot Grocery for a warehouse?" Sarah pushed back from the table. "Mom, you've got to be kidding me. Forget the fact that you want to sell out and demolish the place of my happiest childhood memories. Eighteen-wheeler traffic will exponentially increase. With that big chain grocery coming into town and now this? Brighton will change forever."

Mom lifted her hands and let them fall. "It already has, Sarah. If we don't sell, they'll buy from someone else. They've already gotten an agreement from the vacant parcel right next to us, contingent on them being able to secure an adjacent piece of land. Brighton's not land-poor. If they don't purchase from us, they'll just go after another tract of land. If we don't take this opportunity, we all lose. Your father. Me and your grandmother."

"Please don't do this. Old Depot can't close." Sarah hated the plaintive way the words sounded in her ears, but all she had left was a desperate grab at her daydreamed future.

Her mother stood and started raking leftovers into repurposed margarine containers. She shook her head. "You left home twelve years ago and haven't looked back. Your life isn't here. Old Depot is a business, not a scrapbook."

"I'll stay here. I'll take on responsibilities at the store." Sarah stood and paced the kitchen. "I'll put my dormant business degree to work and we'll make this happen. The store is good for Nan. It keeps her active. We can do this. Together."

Her mother stepped closer, a serving spoon clenched in her hand. "You *cannot* move back here for that store."

"There's nothing left for me in Kenilworth."

"I'll tell you exactly what'll happen. You'll stay here for a week or two, max, and then you'll be bored out of your mind. Then you'll go back to your real life. And Nan and I will still be here trying to make a living on nothin'."

"Leaving here was a mistake. A mistake I want to make up for."

Mom shook her head. "How could you say that? I know the pain from losing Aaron is unbearable. But getting out of this town was exactly the right decision for you. You think holing up here, hiding from the world can spare you hurt, but it won't." For the briefest moment, the fire left her mother's eyes and something raw flickered there.

The grief *should* be unbearable. It should leave Sarah curled in a ball, aching for the man she promised her life to. Instead, she felt empty inside. Except when she crossed the worn wood floors and breathed in the homely scents of that old store. "You should be thinking of Nan, not dollar signs. Seeing the store bulldozed to the ground will kill her."

Mom stiffened and turned from the counter, wooden spoon still gripped in her hand.

"Don't you take that tone with me, young lady. You have no idea what you're talkin' about." She propped one hand on her hip and leveled the spoon at Sarah. "Nan and your father and I, we're not getting any younger. We've got to make plans for the future while we're all still healthy enough to have some choice in the matter."

"Sarah. Rosemary. Please." Her father stood from the table. "Let's calm down."

Sarah ground her teeth. Mom acted like she and Daddy were about two steps from their grave when they weren't even retirement age yet. Nan was in great health and had more energy than most people half her age. None of this was as urgent as Mom made it. Why was she doing this?

Huck trotted into the kitchen and let out a whine. Sarah grabbed his leash from a hook by the back door. "I'll take Huck for his walk." Her stomach roiled. Anything to get out of there. It was like she was seventeen again. Mom pushing her to get out of Brighton. To do something that mattered. Why couldn't she understand that was what she was trying to do?

When the screen door smacked into its frame, Rosemary sank back into her dining chair with a groan.

Bo stood and brushed a crumb off his cheek with his napkin. "Breakfast was delicious, honey. Want me to help you put some of this away before I head out to the pond?"

Rosemary looked up at him. "Won't you wait until Sarah comes back? Maybe she'll listen to you."

He held up his hands in front of him. "Oh, no. No, thank you. I'm not getting in the middle of this."

"Surely you see my side. Think how good it would be for you to be able to have a local route. Between the new warehouse and the new grocery store you'd have tons of opportunities."

"Our daughter is hurting right now. She's more interested in talking about saving the store than the death of her husband. I think she's in a really fragile place. It's like losing Aaron stole Sarah's future and now it feels like her past is fading too."

A weight dropped in Rosemary's middle. "You want me to miss out on this opportunity to provide for all of us because Sarah is feeling sentimental about her childhood?"

"I didn't say that. And yes, I'll try to talk to her. But not about the store, or even her husband, or what's next in her life. I'm not going to be here long before I have to go out on the road again, and my job is just to let her know I am here for her. Not to try and sway her."

Rosemary crossed her arms over her chest and stared at the gingham tablecloth. Keeping Sarah from hiding away in Brighton was the best way she knew to love her daughter at a time like this. "You think I'm a monster too. Don't you?"

He stepped to Rosemary and placed his hands on her shoulders. "No, I don't. But I also don't believe the store selling or not selling is going to make or break the course of the rest of our lives. That's in God's hands. Just take a breath and see how it all comes together."

Easy for him to say. He hadn't seen the financials. Bo didn't worry every single day about how they were going to take care of her mother in her last years. He didn't seem to worry enough about anything. "Deep down, I know you're right, Bo. But I just can't stop thinking about —"

"I know." He pulled her against his chest and rubbed circles on her back. "You don't have to explain."

She laid her cheek against his shirtfront and inhaled the scent of him, easing the tension in her chest. That man's constant calmness might drive her batty most days, but their differences always had a way of balancing each other out.

He grabbed a dishrag. "How about I clean up in here, and you get ready. What time did you say the buyer was coming by? If he gets there before you can intercept him, your mother will have him flying out of there faster than a scalded haint."

Rosemary glanced at her watch and groaned. "Momma's going to kill him and me both."

It really wasn't fair that her sister had so completely escaped this small town and all the responsibilities that went with it.

10

April 1972

“Ready or not, here I come!” Rosemary caught a glimpse of her sister, Jessamine, in the convex mirror that rested above the tall shelves of canned goods in the back of the store. In the reflection there was a flash of Elmo’s red face on the white knitted vest that exactly matched the one on Rosemary’s chest. She followed the slap of Jessamine’s feet against the floor. “I’m going to catch you this time, Jessie.”

Her sister always won at hide-and-seek. Mostly because she cheated. Jessamine cheated at everything. Rosemary tiptoed, skipping all the boards that creaked like she was doing a dance. If she snuck up on her, instead of trying to chase her, she might win this time. Plus, Mommy might not mind so much if they played the game quietly without yelling and running the aisles.

Before rounding the corner, Rosemary gave a long look back at the office door. The place she'd been told to stay. On the rug, a stack of library books waited. She was supposed to be reading to her sister. But Jessamine had whined and wheedled and fidgeted until Rosemary couldn't take it anymore. Her sister took all the fun out of reading. And reading was one thing she was good at. Her teacher, Mrs. Franks, said she was best in the class.

Rosemary sneaked down the side aisle, ears tuned for the sound of quick, light footsteps. Sounds easily lost in the hum of grownup conversation. She leaned around one of the aisles, and then leaned away, back pressed close to the shelf. Miss Susan and Miss Carla, two old bachelor sisters who lived together, shopped the baking aisle.

If Rosemary had any chance of catching Jessamine, she'd have to get past those two. They'd give her away in a heartbeat, with their "Hey there, Rosemary. Darling, you've just got to come over and see the new litter of kittens Sadie-cat had." Not that she would turn her nose up at the chance of kittens. She'd even endure the old ladies' mothball-laced hugs, but right now she was on a mission.

On Rosemary crept, navigating squeaky

boards and conversational store patrons. Peering in corners looking for any sign of her sister.

Jessamine wasn't in any of her normal hiding spots. Rosemary peered through the distorted curved glass of the deli counter, past the huge blocks of deli meat ready for slicing on the sliding guillotine her father worked with a speed and accuracy that left her entranced. No Jessamine tucked in the corners or under the chairs.

Grady Harrison stood in his holey overalls making an order. Daddy opened the giant jar of pink eggs. He caught Rosemary's eye and grinned at her grimace. Really, though, how could anybody eat those pickled eggs? She put a finger over her lips. Daddy offered a conspiratorial wink and nod in response.

Warmth filled her chest. Her knight in shining armor. He'd stop everything and help her find Jessamine. She was sure of it, if only Mommy let him. She could tell by the way his eyes twinkled.

Rosemary braved the storeroom with its tall shelves and long shadows, even though she knew her sister was even more scared of that cavernous space than she was, with its vaultlike door that was too heavy to budge if it slid shut. Still no Jessie.

She stuffed her hands into the pockets of her stiff Toughskin pants. Matching pants. Matching Elmo sweater vests. Were these matching clothes they always wore Mommy's attempt to make them the same? To make her more like Jessie? Jessie who never seemed to get into trouble, even though Rosemary was the one who tried so hard to follow the rules.

Growing bored with the game she couldn't seem to win, Rosemary wandered to the front of the store. Mommy was busy smiling and talking to a gray-haired farmer named Bert, who brought in weekly trucks of produce. Those pinched places around Mommy's eyes that so often marred her pretty face had relaxed. She smiled and laughed at something he said.

Drawn by the sweet sound, Rosemary edged closer. It was then she saw her — Jessamine — tucked behind the register at Mommy's feet, playing with a Matchbox car some little boy had left behind. Her sister looked up and grinned at her like that awful Cheshire cat from *Alice in Wonderland.*

So, Jessie thought she was safe, hidden behind Mommy's legs? She'd show her. Today was Rosemary's day to win. Rosemary crept closer, making sure her mother's attention was still on the people coming through the line to ring up their purchases.

Jessamine wriggled backward, pushed as tight as she could against the shelves beneath the checkout counter. Her mischievous grin faltered.

Nowhere to run this time.

When Rosemary was almost to Jessamine, her mother stepped outside of the counter and embraced a young woman whose eyes were sad.

Jessamine eyed the new opening for her escape and darted forward.

Rosemary lunged to tag her. Her fingers tangled in Jessamine's purple streamer barrettes.

Jessamine shrieked. "Ow! Rosemary pulled my hair!"

Rosemary rolled her eyes at the piercing sounds of her sister's exaggerated agony and freed her fingers from the dangling ribbon. "You're just mad I won."

A vise grip clamped down on her shoulder. Rosemary looked up into her mother's stormy expression.

"Rosemary Jimson Clearwater."

She shrank. Now the whole store knew her hideous middle name. A name she shared with a poisonous weed.

"I told you to stay in the office. Not run around the store like a hooligan, disturbing the customers. Yesterday you almost knocked over old Mrs. Steventon. Today, I gave you explicit instructions to stay in the office and out of the way."

"But Jessie —"

"Jessie was playing quietly by my feet until you came along and picked a fight."

"I wasn't —"

Her mother held up her hand. "Enough. Go back to the office and read. Or ask your father if he needs any help in the back."

Rosemary looked to the grown-ups around her. Five pairs of eyes were on her. Lips pursed. Didn't anyone else see how unfair Mommy was? But all they heard was Jessamine's wailing. And all they saw was Rosemary's fingers tangled in her sister's hair.

A hot knot formed in her throat and Rosemary scurried away before she cried in front of all those prying eyes. She curled into a vacant shelf in the back corner of the store. Tears she'd held so tight leaked free.

Mommy always favored Jessamine. If they fought, it was Rosemary's fault. If her sister fell and scraped her knee, she was supposed to have been watching her more carefully. No matter how hard Rosemary tried to be good, Jessamine was better.

Her sister's middle name was Hope. The

old-timers around here had another name for Jimson weed. Devil's Snare.

The way she saw it, Jessamine ought to have borne that ugly middle name. Her sister probably planned the whole thing. Talking Rosemary into disobeying Mommy's instructions to stay in the office, knowing the whole time that Rosemary would end up getting in trouble and she wouldn't. Why did Mommy love Jessamine more?

Rosemary surrendered to the silent sobs shaking her shoulders. She spilled out the hurt and prayed, asking God to help her be a better girl. One Mommy would love as much as she loved Jessie. Rosemary cried until her body grew heavy and her eyes became raw from tears.

"Rosemary, sweet pea. Wake up."

Rosemary opened her eyes at the sound of her father's gravelly voice. His hulking figure squatted beside her hideaway. He opened his arms and Rosemary scurried from beneath the shelf and wriggled against his chest. He nuzzled her curls, hugging her tight.

"Whatcha doin' in this back corner, huh?" His voice was like a towel warm from the dryer wrapping around her.

She blinked up at Daddy's kind eyes.

"Why does Mommy love Jessie more?"

He squeezed her tight. "Oh, honey. That's not true. I know it might feel like that sometimes. She expects a lot because you're older. But it doesn't mean she doesn't love you. I promise."

She wanted to believe him. But there was always love and light in Mommy's eyes when she looked at Jessamine.

"I make Mommy sad. I try so hard to make her happy, but sometimes when she looks at me, she just looks upset. And then when I ask her what I did wrong, she gets all . . . all . . . all prickly."

Her father's chest rose and fell. In the silence the thumping of his heart filled her ears.

"No, baby. *You* don't make her sad. I think sometimes she just *is* sad."

"Why?"

He rubbed a hand over his face. "I reckon everybody feels sad sometimes."

"Even you?" Her gentle father who always had a smile and ready laugh? Surely not.

He stood, hoisting her on his hip, even though she was a big girl now and too old to be carried. He walked the quiet aisles with her. The world beyond the front windows was pitch-black.

"Sometimes, I get sad, I guess. But the

Lord has blessed me with so many reasons to feel joy that the sadness, well, it seems pretty small when you stack it next to all the wonderful things I have." He squeezed her tight. "The love in my life is so, so much bigger." He planted a loud smacking kiss on her cheek and she giggled.

She wiggled until she tucked her head in that warm place beneath his chin and listened to the loud thump of his heart.

"Mommy is going on a little trip to see some friends of hers tomorrow. She wants you to come with her. Just you and her."

A couple of times a year, the two of them would take a trip to a little town called Humboldt. Always on a Thursday at exactly one in the afternoon. Always to the same little white house. Mommy's friends were older than she was. Sometimes when the older couple looked at her, they looked sad too. But whenever Rosemary sang or read them a story or told them about helping at the store, that sadness would turn into happiness.

Watching their faces change was the warmest feeling in the whole wide world.

But when the little cuckoo bird popped out of the wall clock and cuckooed three times, Mommy would hurry out the door, tugging Rosemary out with promises to return soon, even if Rosemary wasn't finished eating the apple pie the woman always made for her.

The older couple would smile and wave as Mommy backed their car out the drive.

But it was always the same when Rosemary stole a glance back. The lady would bury her face in the man's chest. And he would wrap his arms around her, both of their shoulders shaking.

11

Present Day

When Sarah walked into Old Depot, all was quiet. She approached the office. Muffled voices filtered through the door in front of her. She crept forward and listened. "I can't believe that man," she heard Nan saying. "Walking onto my property again, acting like he already owned the place. I done told him that he'd better hightail it out of Brighton and not come back." Sarah stifled a snicker. When Nan was mad, her accent went from sweetly southern to straight-up country in a half second.

"Mother, please. Right now would be a good time to sell. When they are coming to us. Have you not noticed all the commercial property sitting around with for sale signs? Nobody is buying."

"Don't you start that with me, Rosemary. Don't you dare start. You've said your piece about selling the store, and you know how I feel about it."

"There's something you need to know. Momma, wait."

Footsteps approached and Sarah backed away and skirted down the nearest aisle before she was caught eavesdropping.

Nan rounded the corner, muttering. She started at Sarah's presence. "Hello there, dear."

"Hi, Nan. Rough day?"

Nan growled under her breath. "A bunch of circling vultures, these people. Just waiting to swoop in."

Her mother followed out in Nan's wake. Tight-lipped, she made eye contact with Sarah from behind Nan's back. She gave a slight headshake with pleading eyes. So, Nan didn't know it was Mom who invited the potential buyer.

Nan eyed her daughter. "If you are so ready to be done with the store, sell your part to Sarah. She wants to be here, don't you, hun?"

Sarah opened her mouth. "I —" She did want to be a part of the store, of this legacy. But not like this.

"Sarah does not want to squander her money on half-ownership of a sinking ship."

"Actually, I —"

"No, Sarah. Just no." Mom lifted a palm

toward Sarah, silencing her, and directed her attention back on Nan. "You've got to face reality." Mom shouldered around Sarah and Nan and went to the front.

The empty store was far too small for three generations of mule-stubborn southern women.

"I need some air." Again. Here in Brighton, Sarah was supposed to be able to breathe easier.

She hopped into her car and drove. Passing small family-owned businesses that once were thriving, now many of them abandoned and boarded up. For sale signs posted in the knee-high grass had been there so long they'd faded. She released a sigh. There had to be something she could do to help Old Depot avoid that fate. But her view as she drove only confirmed how right Mom was.

Sarah parked in the lot of the tiny public library and walked through the doors, inhaling the musty scent of old books. It was cool and quiet, soothing the heat inside of her. She wandered through the stacks, running her fingers across the worn spines, scanning for biographies. There was something about knowing people's stories that always attracted her. Listening to their strength in adversity had a way of bolstering her own wavering strength. Even though she'd read it dozens of times, she selected *The Story of My Life* by Helen Keller and walked to the front.

Mrs. Parsons, who'd been the librarian there since Sarah was in grade school, smiled as she approached. "Well, hello there, dear. So nice to see you." Mrs. Parsons spoke in her customary quiet but warm voice. Had she always been so soft-spoken or was it her years in the library that had shaped her tone?

"It's nice to see you too. How've you been?"

"Oh, you know me. I stay busier than a one-legged cat in a litter box."

Sarah laughed softly at the woman's signature reply. "I don't have a library card anymore, but I was hoping to check this out." She slid the biography across the counter.

Mrs. Parsons took the book and scanned it. "You're probably still in the system. It shouldn't be a problem as long as you don't have any unpaid fines."

Sarah gulped as she remembered a Marie Curie biography that accidentally made the trip to her college dorm and never returned. "Yikes. That might be a problem."

Mrs. Parsons chuckled. "No need to duck

and run. I was just teasing you. I don't think there is a soul in Brighton who knows how to turn their books back in on time." She tucked a return slip into the book and slid it across the counter.

The corners of her mouth tugged down and she reached for Sarah's hand, giving it a squeeze. "I was so sorry to hear about your husband's passing. I'm praying for you."

Sarah fixed her sad smile in place — offering the only response that she could muster. "I appreciate it." She picked the book up from the counter and lifted her hand in an awkward wave on her way out.

When she returned to the store, Nan offered Sarah her favorite post, the checkout counter. But after the store stayed quiet for a good fifteen minutes, she considered joining Nan in the stockroom.

The bells jangled and Clay walked in. "Afternoon, Sarah. Have things calmed down since the last time I stopped by?"

Sarah propped her hands on her hips. "For the moment, at least. Nan's sorting in the stockroom and Mom is holed up in the office. There's usually a spurt or two of fireworks every day until they burn up whatever's gotten them riled."

Clay grinned. "They are some pretty feisty

ladies. I don't know how one corner grocery store contains 'em."

Sarah set her book on the register line, facedown with the pages splayed open, so she didn't lose her place. "I'm not sure either. This place should've rocketed off to the moon by now."

"Don't let me interrupt your reading. I've got a little shopping to do and a few questions for your grandmother." He tipped his beat-up hat and grabbed a buggy.

A little while later, she heard Clay's deep tones mingling with her grandmother's voice. Something about this year's *Farmers' Almanac.* Sarah smiled, listening to the amiable chat. Now that was a story she'd like to know more about. How her aged grandmother became best friends with the thirty-something newcomer to town.

Glory Ann walked through the door that evening, heart weary. Passing a picture of Clarence on the wall, she ran her finger along the bottom of the slim gold frame. "What am I going to do, Clarence? I can't just give in. If you were here, you wouldn't. You never gave in, and you never gave up. Not on me. Not on Old Depot. But I'm not sure I can fight this fight without you."

She looked at the pictures on the wall on

the way to the kitchen, the hallways covered in snapshots from her life. Despite the fact that her nineteen-year-old self had given up on happiness the day she'd said "I do," it had found Glory Ann just the same.

She picked up the handmade kaleidoscope from the hall table. She peered through the eyepiece and spun the little wheel covered in fractured bits of colorful glass. One of Clarence's last gifts to her. All those broken pieces making something new and beautiful every time she turned the wheel.

Was she making the wrong decision? Pushing so hard to hang on to what once was? She might believe it if she hadn't seen the ache in Sarah's eyes. That girl still needed Old Depot in the same way Glory Ann had so, so many years ago. It was worth risking financial ruin if that old store could be refuge for one more aching heart who needed to keep their hands occupied while they muddled through their grief.

The phone rang, breaking through her thoughts. "Hello?"

"I'm calling an emergency meeting of the Poker Night Prayer and Sewing Circle. Mable's on the line too. Say hi, Mable."

"Hey, Glory Ann." Mable sounded as weary as Glory Ann felt. Or maybe she was just annoyed by whatever scheme Paulette had dragged her into.

Glory Ann shook her head. "What's this about, Paulette?" It could be anything from spilling the juicy details of her neighbor's latest tiff to a sale at Cato's.

"Surely you know. The whole church knows. Lissie Baker sitting by Clay, making eyes at him when she was supposed to be listening to the preacher. I'll tell you, she's set her sights on that boy. We've got to do something."

Glory Ann almost said that if Paulette was listening to the preacher herself, she wouldn't have paid half a mind to what Lissie Baker was up to, but she bit her tongue. "Lissie is a fine young lady. I wish them the best."

Paulette harrumphed. "How can you say that? We all know Sarah would be perfect for him. You think she'd consider moving back here?"

Mable piped up in her whispery voice. "Paulette! Shame on you. Sarah is a married woman."

A weight sank in Glory Ann's middle as the line went silent. This wasn't the first memory slip Mable had had lately. "Sarah's husband passed, Mable. But you're right about one thing for sure. We definitely don't need to be meddling in this delicate situation."

Glory Ann's cell phone on the side table lit up and began chirping. "Girls, it's time for Jessamine's weekly call. I can't keep gabbing on about poor Lissie Baker and her romantic hopes. Have a good one, y'all." She hung up her house phone and answered the cell phone Jessamine had bought her for her birthday last year.

"Mom? It's Jessie."

"My, my. What have you been up to, my sweet girl?" Jessie had turned fifty-three that year, but she'd always be a bright-eyed daydreaming girl to her mother.

Glory Ann relaxed into her rocking recliner as she listened to Jessie's latest exploits. Always something. Conquering new feats at that tech company she ran or climbing mountains or learning to surf. How different Jessie was from the rest of them. Glory Ann couldn't pretend to understand the life Jessie chose, but she sure seemed happy. If only Rosemary seemed as at peace as her sister.

Words burst from Glory Ann's lips, puncturing Jessie's retelling of her week. "Rosemary wants to sell the store."

The line went silent for a moment. "Are you serious?"

Rosemary had been hinting around about it for the past year, but recently something had shifted. "I wish I wasn't. I don't understand her. I always thought she loved the store. She's been so dedicated. Her whole life, wrapped up in that place, like mine."

"I always kind of thought she stuck around there because she felt guilty about Dad."

Glory Ann clutched at the neckline of her blouse as words that had haunted her for decades played in her mind. Words spoken through blinding pain to her eldest daughter. How different things might be if she could go back in time to unsay them.

"Did you leave because it was too hard being here after he was gone?" Glory Ann worried her bottom lip between her teeth. She'd done her best to fill the place her husband had left behind. But he was the one who'd always been their glue, not her.

A sigh came through the line. "Brighton was never home for me like it was for you and Rosemary. There was a whole world I wanted to see."

"I just wish I knew what has gotten into her."

"Maybe she's finally figured out that you can't outwork your guilt."

Rosemary certainly hadn't stayed and worked all these years at the store out of some sort of dedication to Glory Ann. While they'd remained physically close, they somehow managed to remain miles apart, even on the best days.

Rosemary always insisted everything was fine between them. But after Clarence passed away, some unspoken thing happened that altered their already tenuous bond. How could you fix something when the other person wouldn't voice what had been broken?

12

March 1973

Clipboard in hand, Glory Ann crossed the dimly lit stockroom. The sounds of Jessamine and Rosemary's feet running up and down the vacant aisles punctuated the air. The girls had been so cagey today. It was a relief for all of them when she'd been able to flip over the closed sign and let the girls have free run of the place.

When she finished with inventory, she went to the front of the store and picked up the paper she hadn't had time to read in the early morning rush. But all day her heart ached, the headline echoing in her mind from the moment the paperboy dropped off today's stack — that story about the POWs finally coming back home. That ache she carried had a name. Grief.

All this time had she been subconsciously holding on to this idea that there had been some mistake? In some fantasy she wouldn't even admit to herself, did she long for an alternate universe where, out of the blue, Jimmy would come back home, looking just like he did the day he left? Another version of life in which she still waited for him?

She shook her head. And what if this fantasy scenario somehow played out? She was a happily married woman with two daughters. It was a double-edged sword, this life of hers. Loving the blessings she had, sometimes still aching for what couldn't be.

The bell chimed and Clarence walked through the front door. He smiled and that vise around her heart loosened a fraction.

He cupped his hands around his mouth and bellowed. "Hark, princesses of Old Depot Grocery, come forth!"

Squeals, laughter, and the patter of feet rose as the girls emerged from whatever nook they had been playing house in. Rosemary had the lead. Running as hard as she could, always trying to be the one who reached her father first. Daddy's girl, through and through.

Even though her daughters were seven and five, her giant tree of a husband scooped one girl into each arm like they weighed little more than loaves of bread. One with unruly blonde curls and blue eyes. The other — the spitting image of Glory Ann at that age.

"Are we all ready to head home? I'm fixin' to starve to death if I don't get some of that soup your mother made yesterday."

He set the girls down and together they turned out the store lights and double-checked that all the doors were locked. On the way to the car, his large hand scooped up Glory Ann's. While the girls scrabbled into the car, squabbling over their seats, Clarence tugged her to a stop. His expression so serious it made her heart stutter step in her chest. "Are you okay, Glory Ann?"

She pushed her lips into a smile. "Why would you think I'm not?"

He tilted his head. "I saw the newspaper too, you know."

She was the cause of the little bit of sadness turning down his eyes. A little piece of her would always love Jimmy, and he knew it. But a great big part of her had come to love Clarence — a big sweeping love that brought comfort and joy.

Glory Ann heaved a sigh. Might as well be honest with him. It was one thing they'd both been good at. Even when it hurt. "It was hard to see. I'm so happy to hear about people coming home. And . . . it's wrong, but I feel a little jealous, I guess . . . like I was cheated out of something that should have been mine."

Clarence flinched. A micro-movement in his jaw, but she saw it nonetheless.

Glory Ann looked away. "I'm sorry. I shouldn't say things like that to you. It just comes out sometimes, because you're the only one I can speak his name to."

"Really, it is okay."

She shook her head, tears welling up from that tamped down tight place. "It's not. Those feelings for Jimmy, they're just feelings. Feelings based on a long-ago dream. What you and I have is real. It's every day. It's honest. It's kind. It's home. This war cheated us both. I lost a boy I dearly loved. And you . . . you ended up with damaged goods."

He thumbed a tear from her cheek. "You're Glory Ann, and I'm Clarence." He pointed to the two girls playing in the back seat of their sedan. "And those are our precious girls. I'd say, broken pieces and all, we have a pretty beautiful life." He tucked her hand in the crook of his arm. They walked slow. Lingering in their quiet moment a few seconds more.

"I just wish you could have had a version of me that wasn't so lost and confused. You deserve someone whole."

He shrugged. "Glory Ann, answer me

honestly, would you have even seen me if life hadn't broken you?"

"I . . ." She clamped her mouth shut, knowing he was right, and hating herself all the more for it.

He shook his head. "Sometimes looking through a broken lens lets us see something wonderful and unexpected."

He opened her car door and kissed her cheek. "I love you, Glory Ann."

"I love you too." And she did. She really, really did.

On her way home, listening to Clarence's out-of-key baritone singing along with the radio and Rosemary and Jessamine's imaginary game in the back seat, Glory Ann offered up a prayer, letting go of her hurt just a little more.

When they walked up the steps of their little blue ranch-style home, there was a package on the porch. Glory Ann lifted it.

"What is that?" Clarence stood behind her shoulder.

She stepped to him and lowered her voice to a whisper. "A gift from the Woodstons."

It was so hard when the older couple had moved to the West Coast. Like losing Jimmy all over again in a different way. They said living in Humboldt, in that house, was just too painful. And they had extended family that lived in the Pacific Northwest. But they sometimes still sent little gifts, sweetly including things for both of Glory Ann's daughters. Their love was so constant in comparison to Glory Ann's parents, who had so easily faded from the grandparent role.

She brought the package inside and went to the stove to heat up leftover stew.

Clarence and the girls played in the living room. He growled like some hulking beast. The girls giggled and shrieked.

Glory Ann slipped a knife from the drawer and slit open the packing tape. A note sat on top.

> Dear Glory Ann Clearwater,
> I am so sorry to inform you of the sudden and unexpected passing of James and Aurilee Woodston. While going through their things, we found this little porcelain dog set aside in a box with your name on it. We thought you must be a friend from back home and wanted to get this to you.

Glory Ann gripped the paper in her hands. Clarence came into the kitchen. "I sent the girls to wash up for dinner." He reached into the cabinet and brought down a stack of four bowls. "Glory Ann, what's wrong?"

She unfroze, his gentle tones softening her shock. "That package on the porch. It had a note. Jimmy's parents . . . they passed away."

"Oh, I'm so sorry." He pulled her into his arms.

Her two daughters bounded into the room. One of them, the last bit of Jimmy she had left on this earth.

Later, after everyone in the house was asleep, she crept back to the kitchen. She lifted the carefully wrapped object from the box. Layer upon layer of packing material. Inside was a little dog figurine. It had great big blue eyes and hang-down ears. It looked just like the ugly stray hound that used to follow Jimmy around.

She buried her face in a dish towel to muffle her sobs. The figurine had been a gift left at Jimmy's memorial service. One of the few things that made her smile that dark day — a little ugly dog sitting there amongst all the pretty flower arrangements. Just the sort of thing Jimmy would've appreciated.

Glory Ann sat on the kitchen chair, the smooth porcelain cool in her hands, and cried for the family she'd been losing by degrees since Jimmy's death. Now all that remained of it was her daughter.

13

Present Day

Early Wednesday morning, Sarah donned her green apron, flipped the welcome sign, and unlocked the front door. She tuned the large knob on the vintage Roberts radio to an oldies rock station and cranked the volume.

Mom and Nan had insisted they could come help, but she'd finally convinced them they both deserved to take a morning off for once. Thank goodness, because she couldn't take one more moment of their arguing.

She perched on the stool, surveying the now-full shelves. Nan had made an executive decision and took over the responsibility of purchasing, and then Sarah and Nan had spent late into the evening restocking and getting everything ready for today. Now if only customers would come.

As much as she wanted to side with Nan,

they couldn't keep doing the same things and expect a different result. She wanted with everything in her to believe that the store's demise wasn't inevitable, but no solution presented itself.

She lifted her latest pick from the library, *I Know Why the Caged Bird Sings.* The ache and hope and strength found in Maya Angelou's words reached up from the page, swirled around Sarah's own hurts, and comforted her.

She jolted at the clank of the bells on the front door. An elderly woman, probably a little senior to Nan, tottered inside with a curved spine and a shopping bag hanging from her arm. Ms. Mable Lee made up one third of Nan's group of friends that was one part sewing circle, one part prayer group, and one part gossip ring, although Nan had tried to reform them without success on that last point.

Ms. Mable looked up when she entered. "Sarah Anderson? Is that you?"

Sarah's ready smile faltered at the sound of her maiden name. "Yes, ma'am. It's so good to see you. My goodness, you look even younger than when I saw you last. What's your secret?" She came out from behind the checkout counter and gave the elderly lady a conspiratorial wink and a hug.

"Oh, hush. You know better than to go around spouting lies, young lady." Ms. Mable swatted playfully at Sarah's arm, but a grin curved her mouth.

Sarah walked the aisles with her, stooping to gather things from the bottom shelf or reach where Mable couldn't. Sarah then went to the deli counter in the back and sliced her half a pound of smoked turkey and some sharp cheddar to go with it. All the while, she listened to Mable's stream of conversation about her children, grandchildren, and the brand-new great-grandchildren.

"Things are pretty slow around here. Especially now that Shop n' Go has opened," Sarah said while escorting her to the front of Old Depot with her loaded shopping bags. "You live closer to the new store, don't you? Why haven't you made the switch?"

"Ah, I've been around long enough to not put much stock in shiny new things." She grinned up at Sarah. "Although shiny things are nice sometimes, I come here for the people."

The longing in Mable's voice gave a hard tug at Sarah's heartstrings.

She stepped behind the counter. One by one, she lifted the canned goods, found the neon orange price sticker, and typed in the prices on the curved cash register that had to be at least circa 1950s. How she loved the heavy mechanical feel of the keys. Something solid and tactile.

"Ms. Mable, how do you think we can get people coming back to the store?"

Sarah tucked the groceries into the large burlap tote the older lady had brought.

Her shaky, liver-spotted hands reached for a box of crackers to help. "It's hard to get people to slow down if they don't have to. Especially when more, bigger, faster is the motto of the day."

Together they walked to Mable's car, Sarah carrying her bag. She gently placed the load in the back seat. Before opening her driver door, Mable wrapped Sarah in another hug. "I hope you stay for a little while. You know, Brighton would be a nice, quiet place to raise a family."

"Uh . . ." Sarah stammered. Had she somehow not heard the news? There would be no family. And even if there had been, Aaron would never have wanted them raised here. He'd want them at the most prestigious private schools. He'd want them a part of club swim teams. Tennis teams. Not to mention that there was no place for his business endeavors here. Brighton could have never been the place to raise her family. That was a different life. Not a better or worse one. Just different. Incompatible.

As Mable pulled away, Nan arrived and came to stand beside Sarah, lifting her hand in a wave to her departing friend. "I hate that I missed Mable. She was earlier than usual today." Nan placed a hand on Sarah's shoulder. "If she said anything strange, give her a little grace. I've noticed she's starting to forget things sometimes." Nan drew a shaky breath. "Maybe that's why I'm so determined to keep this place going. I think that if I show up every day and put that apron on, all the little details of my life won't be allowed to slip out the door of my mind." She smiled up at Sarah, sadness creasing her face, then went inside.

A few more cars pulled into the lot, and Sarah followed Nan inside to get ready for the next small stream of customers.

"When are you going to tell her, Rosemary? When are you going to tell both of them the truth?"

Rosemary's spine stiffened and she turned to Bo, dish towel in one hand, dripping plate in the other. "Not now. Sarah'll stay. And she can't stay. And Momma . . ." She wasn't quite sure why she hadn't told her mother about her diagnosis. Maybe if she didn't speak it out loud things wouldn't progress beyond the occasional tingling and numbness in her hands or the stiffness in her legs.

Bo stood and took the dish and towel from her, setting both on the counter before taking her hands. Her reflex was to harden so that she didn't crumble. But today Bo was here. There would be plenty of days ahead she'd have to be strong, to steel herself against the despair that tried to wriggle in. She leaned into his embrace, pretending for the moment that his steady arms could actually shield her from late-onset multiple sclerosis.

Cheek resting against the flannel, slowing her breaths to match his steady inhale and exhale, she asked the question that repeated like a refrain inside her head from sunup to sundown. "Am I being selfish?"

Bo pulled back from the embrace, cupping her cheeks with his large, work-roughened hands. His gaze, gentle and kind, bore into hers. "You are doing what you always do. Trying to make sure everyone is taken care of. But they don't know that, because you haven't given them the full story."

Rosemary stepped back and paced the small kitchen. "It doesn't matter what they think of me, as long as what needs to happen happens."

He crossed his arms over his chest and leaned against the counter. "I think you do care."

Rosemary heaved a sigh. "I just need to get Sarah back to Illinois and refocused on living the life she's supposed to have. She's got connections there, maybe she could get a business administrative job at the hospital where she was a board member. Or do something in finance. Aaron knew a lot of powerful people." She wrung her hands, still damp from the breakfast dishes. "I don't want her giving up the life she built because of me."

Bo put away a big stack of plates. "First of all, I don't know all the details, but I don't think Aaron left her in dire financial straits. I'm pretty sure she's got some wiggle room to figure out her next steps. Second, and more importantly, what if being here for you is what she wants?"

She shook her head. "She might think so now, in this fleeting moment when everything is falling apart, but Sarah is meant for bigger and better things than Brighton can offer."

Bo stilled, one hand lingering inside the cabinet. "If you had to do it all over, would you settle down here? Do it all the same?"

"What does it matter? We don't get do-overs." Pain throbbed in her chest. "I can't undo the one choice I regret more than anything. And because I can't, then the rest is irrelevant. I had to take care of the store. Of Mom." She looked into his gray eyes and squeezed his hand. "Besides, I'd never undo us." Her throat contracted, making her voice quiet and raspy. "I just don't want to be the reason Sarah thinks she has to stay."

He placed his hands on her shoulders. "I'm working hard to find a way to be home more. I am going to be there for you. And you will pull through this health stuff. What's that your mom always says?" He tapped his index finger against his chin. "You're a Clearwater girl. And Clearwater girls are made of some pretty stout stuff."

He leaned his forehead against hers. "It's going to work out one way or another."

14

July 1975

Fried chicken and mashed potatoes. There was nothing better than Sunday night dinner — sitting at the kitchen table while Momma cooked and gospel radio played.

Rosemary sat with her sketchbook and a little porcelain dog. A gift to Momma from some friends of hers. Rosemary tried and tried to portray the sadness of the little hound in her sketches, but no matter how she drew and redrew those droopy eyes, they didn't quite match the original.

"Would you like to have it?"

Rosemary lifted her head.

Momma looked at her, spatula in hand, hair tied back in a red handkerchief with white polka dots. "The little dog. Would you like to have it?"

Something warm filled Rosemary's chest. "Me?"

Momma smiled and nodded, but her eyes

were pained. “You seem to like it so much. You should have it.”

“I’ll be so careful with it.” Rosemary jumped up and wrapped her arms around her mother’s soft middle.

“Oh, get on with you. My chicken is going to burn if I don’t mind it.”

Momma sounded gruff, but she didn’t mean anything by it. Daddy said it was just her way. Besides, she’d given Rosemary something precious when it wasn’t her birthday, and she hadn’t even said Rosemary had to share with Jessamine.

Rosemary scooped up the little dog and headed to the room she shared with her sister to find just the perfect spot for it. A place where it would be safe. Where she could look at it and forever remember this warm bubbly feeling in her belly.

Daddy sat in his favorite chair, reading the paper. She skipped to him. “Daddy, look what Momma gave me. She said I could have it for keeps.”

He put his paper aside and pulled her onto his lap. “My, my what a fine pup you have there.”

Rosemary eyed Jessamine, who sat on the rug playing with her and Rosemary’s dolls. One blonde and the other brown-haired, just like them. Jessamine twisted the blonde doll's hair a little too tight and Rosemary was just about to say so, but then Daddy brushed a curl from Rosemary's face. "Be careful with the little dog. It's breakable."

"Oh, I know, Daddy. I'll be so careful. It's special to Momma, and she gave it to me to take care of. I'm going right now to find a place for it."

In their bedroom, Rosemary cleared off the shelf above her bed and arranged the dog with a few of her other favorite figurines. The perfect spot. Now, even if it fell, it would land cushioned and safe on her bed.

Momma had picked her to care for this special gift. Just her. Rosemary fell back on the bed and couldn't rein in her smile.

Momma's singsong voice lilted through the house. "Girls, time to wash up for dinner."

Rosemary skipped to the bathroom. When she returned, hands freshly washed, Jessamine stood in the doorway of their bedroom. The little dog in her grubby hands.

"Jessamine, put my dog back. It belongs to me. Momma said."

Jessamine glared. "I just wanted to look at it. It sure is an ugly old dog."

"Well, I like it. Which is why Momma gave it to me instead of you." It didn't matter what Jessie said. Rosemary knew how special the little dog was by the way she'd sometimes catch Momma looking at it, like she was in another place and time. "I said to put it back."

Jessamine eyed the dog with a strange expression darkening her angelic features. She lifted it high and let it drop. Rosemary dove forward. The dog seemed to fall in slow motion, but still she couldn't move fast enough. Like in one of those nightmares where it feels like your feet are sucked down by muck.

The porcelain hound hit the linoleum floor with a sickening shatter. Rosemary fell to her knees. Her parents' hurried footsteps vibrated the floor.

"What happened?" Her mother's voice came shrill.

Rosemary couldn't answer. She'd had something precious and hadn't managed to keep it safe for more than a minute.

"I accidentally dropped it." Jessamine's voice came sugary sweet and penitent.

Tears gathered and fell down Rosemary's cheeks. Her father knelt beside her and stroked her back. Words roared, fire-poker hot, inside Rosemary's head. Jessamine did it on purpose. She was jealous because for one second Rosemary had something that

Jessamine didn't.

She clamped her lips down tight to keep the words in. Jessamine would deny the truth. Momma taking Jessamine's word over hers would hurt more than leaving the little dog with justice unserved.

Momma made a tsking sound. Rosemary lifted her head. Her mother propped her hands on her hips. "Well, that's that. Step carefully girls and go to the table. I'll clean this up."

Rosemary's legs didn't want to hold her.

Momma cared about the broken dog. She did. Why did she pretend she didn't?

Daddy helped Rosemary to her feet, and she stepped over the broken pieces, following Jessamine who skipped to the table, humming a happy tune.

Maybe Momma actually gave Rosemary the dog because she didn't want it.

Daddy filled their plates. Before Momma joined them, she opened the trash can and was about to dump the contents inside. But then she paused, closed the lid, and placed the dustpan full of broken bits on top.

With her back turned, Momma dabbed her eyes with a gingham kitchen towel, then sat, her face calm as a still pond on a cool summer day. They bowed their heads and joined hands while Daddy said the blessing.

■ ■ ■ ■

Glory Ann woke in the dead of night. She reached to the place her husband slept and found his space empty. "Clarence?" Glory Ann whispered his name into the dark. She tiptoed down the hall, following the glow of the light. Clarence sat hunched at the kitchen table, his back to her. The lamp from his desk sat on the table next to him.

He glanced up when she entered, glasses perched on his nose.

She shook her head. "I should have known."

He offered her a sheepish smile. "Can't help myself, I guess."

She sat down beside him and surveyed the broken pieces, the bottle of glue, and his tweezers. "You should've thrown it away."

He arched a brow. "You didn't. That was all the information I needed. Poor Rosemary. She was so excited you gave this to her."

Glory Ann knew the truth. He sat there straining his eyes and his patience for Glory Ann. Always, always trying to take her broken pieces and make them whole. "You'd do anything for that girl."

"She had me wrapped around her little

finger from day one."

"Do you think Jessamine did it on purpose?"

He glued another piece of porcelain in place, holding it steady so the bond could form. "Maybe. I hope not. I wish it were easier for them to get along."

"I try so hard to make sure I treat them the same."

He smiled tenderly at her. "But they aren't the same. And maybe that's okay. You'll always see Jimmy when you look at Rosemary, and its full of sweetness and loss all at the same time. Maybe we should stop trying so hard. Just let them be different."

Her chin trembled. "Thank you."

"For what, darlin'?"

"For being the glue." Glory Ann peered into his eyes.

The corners of his mouth tugged downward for a moment, and he placed the glued pieces on the newspaper-covered table. He took her hands. "I know I'm not your first love or greatest romance or any of those things. But I love you and you love me. And that's more than enough for this good ol' country boy."

He stood and switched on the radio and tugged her to her feet. Together they swayed to a static-filled love song.

Long into the night, she swayed in Clarence's arms, never once wishing for the blond-haired, blue-eyed boy she once loved. How could she when she was so loved by this man who held her? He was wrong. This was her greatest love story.

She glanced back at the shattered pieces of the porcelain dog scattered on the table. "Don't put it back together, Clarence. I don't want it to be your job anymore. Trying to hold together pieces of my past."

He released her and smiled, passing her the bottle of glue. "What if we did it together?"

15

Present Day

Sarah perched on a stool behind the checkout counter, nibbling saltines and watching the latest episode of *Married in a Minute* on her phone with her headphones in to escape the lull. She'd never admit to anyone that she watched this melodramatic mess of a show. She couldn't help it. She was obsessed with the backstories of people who would agree to something as crazy as marrying someone after knowing them for only sixty seconds. At any rate, it provided an adequate distraction from her own thoughts.

The front bells jangled. Sarah pressed pause right before the bride walked down the aisle. Ms. Paulette came through the door. She smiled and waved in Sarah's direction. "I heard tell you were back in town. Little Sarah Anderson, carrying on the family legacy."

Sarah stood. "Hi, Ms. Paulette. How are

you today?"

"Fine as frog hair. And you?" She tottered over in her Mary Jane kitten heels and tea-length skirt.

"Doing just fine." Other than the fact that she couldn't eat and she couldn't sleep. Not to mention that in the long watches of the night, she replayed her last conversation with her husband over and over again, dissecting it for a nonexistent message between the lines.

"Aaron —" Words scrabbled in her throat. Words begging him to stay, to let whatever work emergency that pulled him from their anniversary celebration crash and burn. Yearning for him to choose her.

He paused, his handsome face pinched and lined. "Yeah, babe?"

"Never mind."

"Okay."

Aaron. Yeah, babe. Never mind. Okay.

Six words between them, and he was gone.

But that's not what Paulette wanted to hear about. Sarah mentally shook herself back to the present. She sipped her ginger ale and offered an awkward smile.

Paulette tilted her head, studying Sarah. "Did I ever tell you that I was an obstetric nurse in my younger years? I was on duty when your mother and your aunt were born.

And I was there when you were born too. I'm just sad I had to retire." She gestured to Sarah's middle. "How I wish I could be the nurse on duty when you have your little one."

Sarah choked. Ginger ale burned her nose. "Oh, Ms. Paulette, I'm not . . ." Sarah put a hand over her flat stomach. Were all the elderly of Brighton suffering from memory loss?

Paulette tipped her head sideways. "You sure about that, honey? You've got the look about you." She eyed the white plastic pack of saltines and soda beside the register.

"I'm sure. I-I don't know if Mom told you, but I lost my husband a little over a month ago. It's just the grief is why I'm having a hard time eating." Why did she say that? She didn't owe anyone an explanation.

"She did mention it. I am so sorry for your loss. You never know though. Sometimes God blesses us with a bit of sweet in the midst of the bitter bite of loss."

Sweet? How in the world would finding out she was pregnant with the child of a man who'd died right before she had the chance to walk out on him be sweet? Sarah managed a tight smile. "Is there anything I can help you with?"

"No, dear, not at all. Just a few items I need to pick up."

When Ms. Paulette disappeared down the nearest aisle, Sarah picked up a magazine and sat, flipping pages but not registering anything on those brightly colored spreads. The chatter of the patrons entering the store and Nan's cheerful hellos mere background noise to the roaring thoughts inside Sarah's head.

Ms. Paulette was a crazy old lady. No wonder they asked her to retire. Sarah was not, could not, be pregnant. She tried to count back the weeks, looking for any possibility that the retired nurse's words could be true. But the days and weeks blurred together and wouldn't make a time line.

Sarah rang out items for three customers, and greeted a couple more on their way in, but if asked, she couldn't have recalled who those people were. Far too consumed by even the idea that she could be carrying Aaron's child.

Ms. Paulette came through the line. She placed pasta noodles and the necessary ingredients for marinara sauce on the checkout counter.

Sarah smiled but refused to meet the woman's eyes, suddenly filled with the irrational sensation that the woman could read things about her that Sarah didn't want seen. She totaled the purchases and then passed Ms. Paulette her change.

The bells jangled and Clay walked through the door.

Ms. Paulette cleared her throat and laid a slim pink box wrapped in plastic on the counter. "And this, dear, is for you. One line for negative. Two lines for positive."

Face flaming, Sarah lifted her chin in time to see Clay duck around a display, heading for the back of the store.

Sarah stared and ground her teeth. She'd respect her elders like her mother taught her, but that woman was an insufferable busybody.

"It's the most accurate brand, in my opinion. Good luck." Ms. Paulette tottered out the door.

Sarah swiped the accusing box off the counter and tossed it into one of the restock bins before someone caught sight of it. Was there any chance Clay had missed that little exchange?

The walls in the store became oppressive and time ticked too slowly. She needed to find something to do besides stand there with that pink box peeking back at her.

She grabbed the slim phone book and flipped to the newspaper office. No time like the present. Might as well put that ad in the paper for the steak dinner giveaway before the newspaper office closed for the evening. She laughed to herself. When was the last time she'd touched a phone book?

Sarah dialed the number to the newspaper office.

"You've reached *Brighton Daily Post.* This is Sandy speaking, how may I help you?"

Words backlogged in Sarah's throat. She'd expected to have to press one for English then three for the ad office, five for something else.

"H-Hi. My name is Sarah . . ." *Ashby or Anderson? Ashby or Anderson?*

"Hello, are you still there?"

No. "Yes, I'm sorry. Sarah over here at Old Depot Grocery, and I'd like to place an advertisement for a steak dinner giveaway that we're doing next week." She twirled the spiral phone cord around her finger.

"Fantastic. Let me grab our price sheet."

Through the phone, Sandy rattled off an endless string of advertisement options. Ad sizes and costs per line, but it all faded to distant mumbling in her ear. Sarah held the phone so tight in her hand that her knuckles ached as she stared out the window. Ms. Paulette could not be right.

"Ma'am? Ma'am?" The voice blared in

Sarah's ear. How long had Sandy been trying to get her attention?

"I'm sorry, I'm here."

"Did one of those ad options sound good to you? I can repeat them again if you need."

Just then Clay walked to the front. Was he eyeing her middle? She stood straighter, pulling her abdomen flat and angling away from him.

"Ma'am?" The voice came through the line, sounding concerned.

"Uh. The last option you mentioned, that will be fine."

"So to confirm, you would like to run a full-page ad for one week. You're sure?"

Sarah twirled the phone cord so tight around her finger that it throbbed. "Yes, yes. That's fine."

"Shall I charge it to the store's account?"

"Yes. Fine."

"To confirm, the price will be . . ."

Clay leaned on the checkout counter, eyeing her still-paused phone screen with a frozen bride and the title across the middle. *"Married in a Minute?"* he asked. "You're always reading those biographies. I'd have never guessed you were a closet reality show junkie."

Was there something in the air today, causing normally sane people to butt into other people's business? She grabbed her phone and tossed it in her purse, turning her back to escape his blue-green gaze.

"And what would you like the ad to say?"

Sarah rattled off the words she'd memorized. "Giveaway. Steak dinner and fixings for two for the first twenty patrons to arrive on Saturday, July sixth."

"All right. Let me read that back to you to make sure that it's phrased the way you would like it." Sandy droned on in her ear. "Is that exactly like you want it to appear in the paper?"

"Yeah, yeah, it's fine. Thank you so much." Sarah set the phone back into its cradle, hands still shaky from the adrenaline coursing through her from Paulette's words.

Clay braced his hands on the counter, biting his bottom lip. "Sarah, I don't mean to intrude, but —"

"I'm not pregnant."

His face reddened. "Uh. Okay. That's not . . . anyways, about that ad you just —"

Sarah grew hot from head to toe and bile rose in her throat. "Ex-excuse me." She shoved past him and hurried to the bathroom, hand clamped over her mouth.

Thankfully, Sarah hadn't actually vomited, but she did hide in the bathroom long enough to make sure Clay wasn't still there.

She dabbed dampened paper towels against the back of her neck, the evaporation of the liquid cooling her body.

Finally she emerged to find Nan at the register, busy with a handful of customers. When the small crowd trickled away, Nan approached her. "You feeling all right? Clay said you took outta here like a cat with its tail on fire."

Sarah shrugged. "Yeah, I'm fine."

Nan narrowed her eyes at Sarah and then picked up the pregnancy test from behind the counter. "Somebody change their mind about a purchase?"

Sarah bit her lip, trying to keep her expression nonchalant. "Yeah, but I can't spill secrets. Cashier-customer confidentiality and all that."

Nan laughed. "Aw, you're stealing all my fun. Don't you know that half the reason I run this place is to keep up with the inner workings of Brighton?" She walked away to return the box to the shelf.

Sarah sank onto her stool, her breath coming out in a whoosh. She sipped her ginger ale. She absolutely, one hundred percent, could not be pregnant.

Later that evening, just as dusk was falling, Sarah walked out the back doors. Ever since she was a little girl, this view had been her secret treasure. It really wasn't much. An open field lined with trees and a huge maple tree, just off-center, with limbs stretching far and wide. A view that was a dime a dozen in Brighton. But just before nightfall, magic happened. Dusk poured a wash of deep blues and purples all over everything. Blurring all the hard lines of day.

Cicadas' deafening trill filled the air, accompanied by the frogs singing bass and sleepy songbirds warbling good night. Sarah tucked her hands in her pockets and walked toward the fields.

In her eleven years of knowing Aaron, she'd brought him here only once. It wasn't so much that she was embarrassed of Brighton's simplicity. It was more that Sarah had gotten swept up in college life and in the circle Aaron's wealthy family had pulled her into. Traveling the world with them had started as a harmless adventure. She hadn't intentionally tried to be someone she wasn't, but rather felt being with Aaron allowed her to discover new sides of herself. It came down to the fact that there hadn't been a whole lot of opportunities for Kenilworth Sarah and Brighton Sarah to collide.

Until that one summer. They were a year out of college. The year's family trip was supposed to have been a summer spent in the Polynesian islands. But after an argument with his father, Aaron had announced that he wasn't going, so she'd talked him into a week in Brighton instead. That dusky evening, so much like this one, was lasered into her memories.

Sarah had stepped over the long-abandoned train tracks and trekked to the center of the freshly mown hayfield. She'd spun in a slow circle, inhaling the sweet scent in the air while Aaron looked on. He'd been so tense lately. This was exactly the break they needed. In this simple place, they could reestablish that sense of connection that had slipped just out of reach over the past few months.

She stretched her arms out wide. "Isn't this beautiful?"

"Uh-huh." His distracted answer sounded behind her.

Sarah tipped her head back, watching for the first stars to appear, reminding her of standing on the stoop of her apartment discussing marriage on a date the month before. He'd said they'd go ring shopping. But then things had gone sideways with his dad over some work-related disagreement, and there had been no more talks of engagement.

When she turned, Aaron knelt on one

knee. She sucked in a breath. There had been so many picture-perfect moments to pop the question over the years. But he hadn't asked her at the foot of the Eiffel Tower or the Arc de Triomphe. She'd been certain that the middle of the Rialto Bridge would be the place. And then there had been that night in Switzerland with the hauntingly beautiful silhouette of the Matterhorn as their backdrop.

Somehow it would be even more perfect if he asked her right then.

Aaron swiped away the fine coating of dirt from the top of his shoe, and stood, swatting. "Are you ready to go? It's a little hot out here, and the bugs are eating me alive."

"Yeah," she heard herself say. "Nan should have dinner ready by now." The words coming out of her mouth sounded normal, but that effervescence bubbling inside her had gone flat.

As they walked back to the car, he said, "Sarah, there's something I wanted to talk to you about. This thing with Dad isn't working out. I thought I could ride out the tension with him, but it's just been getting worse. And I . . . I think it's time I went out on my own. A buddy of mine from college is interested in partnering with me in a start-up company. He called an hour ago and has found an investor that is really interested in meeting with us. This is our only chance to talk with him before he's out of the country for a month. I know you wanted to stay a few more days, but . . . I mean, we could always come back another time . . ."

"Sure," she'd said, but her heart had cried out. *What about going to Eagle Creek? Or the falls over at Stoney Point? Or the diner where Mr. Sammy makes the best ever Nutella French toast? A menu item he created just for me the day Momma brought me to the diner for a treat after I broke my arm trying to do a handstand on a fence rail in third grade.* It wasn't anything remotely as grand as they'd tasted and seen traveling the world together. But Brighton was something no place on earth could be.

Sarah blinked, loosening herself from that old memory. She returned to the store and walked around to the front. Her mom stood inside, nodding and smiling with a customer.

What would've happened that summer day if she'd said no to Aaron's request, asked him to let his friend take the meeting so she could finally share all the boring, ordinary details of Brighton that were so dear to her? But she hadn't had the courage that day, to ask for more. To tell him that being oblivious to the charm of Brighton was like being blind to a deep part of who she was.

16

September 1977

Rosemary crouched at the shelves, rag moving in slow rhythmic circles. Jessamine roller-skated up and down the aisles, singing "Don't Go Breaking My Heart." The same few lines over and over and over again.

Rosemary growled. "I'm almost done with the top three shelves on this aisle. You know the bottom two are yours. I'm telling Daddy if you don't take those stupid skates off and help me."

The butcher was out, and Daddy was in the back taking his place. Momma was outside talking to the Jefferson Cookie rep. He came in every week with those big tubs of lemon cookies. Daddy always let her and Jessamine have the first two off the top after they finished their weekly shelf cleaning. Her mouth watered at the thought of the sweet-tart goodness melting on her tongue.

Jessamine skated past again, crouching

and dragging her fingertips on the wood floor. Momma would skin Jessie's hide if somebody came in and caught her sister treating the shop aisles like a rink while the store was open. She had half a mind to go tell Daddy right then, if she didn't have to hear Jessie whine the rest of the day about her being a tattletale. But, by golly, Rosemary wanted those cookies. Now, not later.

"You're the youngest. You get bottom shelf duties, and you know it." Now that Jessamine was old enough to work too, Rosemary had self-promoted to upper shelves.

Jessamine slid to a stop. "You're so bossy. You want 'em done this instant, do it yourself. I want to skate before Momma comes back. I gotta sneak a little fun while I've got the chance."

The bell jangled. Rosemary craned her neck to spy who entered. Not Momma. Just scrawny Sammy Hall. A boy from her grade who always came to school in raggedy clothes with a ring of dirt behind his neck. Mean little slits for eyes.

Rosemary continued dusting, listening to the sound of Sammy's feet squeaking the floorboards as he paced up and down the candy aisle. Jessamine had moved her skating to another aisle, the rumble of her wheels fainter now.

Rosemary strode to the aisle where Sammy stood, slipping his hand in his pocket. He started when her foot landed on a squeaky board.

His eyes widened.

"Sammy Hall, don't even try it." Rosemary sucked a lungful of air and yelled for her father at the top of her lungs. "Daddy!"

Sammy ran for the door, but before he could reach it, Jessamine came flying like a speed skater across the front of the store and tackled him into the tobacco display. A stack of Skoal cans escaped their box and rolled across the floor. The scuffling pair thrashed on the floor.

Jessamine cried out as he pinched and kicked her, trying to get free. Rosemary ran to her aid, pinning him to the floor, hollering for her daddy to come all the while.

"Girls!" her mother shrieked. Rosemary twisted to find her white-faced mother behind her. The cookie man smirked at her side.

Still Sammy and Jessamine thrashed, so Rosemary refused to move.

"Enough." The low, steady tone of her father's voice made her jump to her feet. Jessamine stopped her fighting and stood clumsily on her skates.

Sammy stared wide-eyed at the towering

man in his red-streaked butcher's apron, with a storm brewing in his eyes. The boy scrambled to stand, knees visibly quaking. Blood dripped from one of his nostrils, and he smeared it across his face when he swiped with his sleeve.

"What is going on here?" Daddy crossed his hands over his chest.

Rosemary's own knees felt on the mushy side, even knowing the gentleness behind this huge man in a bloody apron.

Jessamine pointed at Sammy. Half of her brown hair had escaped from her ponytail and was stuck all over her face. "That boy stole candy, and I stopped him."

"That right, son?" Daddy asked.

Sammy dug in his stuffed pockets and held out a handful of Pop Rocks and Everlasting Gobstoppers in shaking hands. "Are you gonna call the police?"

"I'm not going to call the police. I'm going to call your parents."

The grubby boy blanched. "Please don't do that. I'll do anything you want."

"What's your name?" Daddy stepped closer, his hulking figure dwarfing the stick-thin boy.

"S-Sammy. Sammy Hall."

His mouth stretched in a line. "Roger Hall's boy?"

Sammy nodded and hung his head.

The sternness softened on Daddy's face. "Come with me to my office, and we can talk this over."

Sammy followed her father like he walked to his own execution.

Momma propped her hands on her hips and leveled a glare at them. "Girls, get your rear ends to the bathroom to freshen up before the evening rush starts. And then straighten up this mess."

Jessamine skated toward the back.

"And Jessamine," said Momma, "if I ever catch you skating in my store again while the open sign is turned, I'll tan your hide."

As the girls headed to the washroom, the cookie man chortled. "I don't know, Glory Ann, you might want to reconsider. Store security detail on roller skates? I think it could work. Getting tackled by fierce little spitfires like your daughters might be a mighty big crime deterrent."

The next day the delivery truck pulled in with a roar and a hiss. Rosemary stuffed the last of her pimento cheese sandwich in her mouth and gulped it down with a glass of milk.

The delivery ran every Wednesday after school. Out of the woodwork, the extra high schoolers Dad hired for delivery days showed up, and they started the hours-long process of getting everything unloaded, sorted, and stocked.

Rosemary bounded outside. It was her favorite day of the week. Stocking was an all-hands-on-deck event.

Momma always stayed home the first half of delivery day and cooked up a great big supper for everyone. Later they'd all crowd around the picnic tables outside and eat pot roast and corn bread until they were full to popping.

Jessamine usually stayed with Momma, so it was just Rosemary, Daddy, and the high school crew. The older kids talked to her just like she was one of them. While Rosemary wasn't one of the popular kids in the sixth grade, she was sure that if her classmates saw the way the high school kids treated her, it would elevate her social status.

Sammy Hall waltzed out back where the rest of them waited to start unloading the truck like he owned the place. Rosemary's jaw dropped.

She marched to him until they stood toe to toe. "You better get on outta here. My daddy don't stand for thieves."

Sammy smirked. "I've got just as much right to be here as you. I work here now."

"He hired you?" Her voice went high, and her shoulders and cheeks grew fire-poker hot. This had to be some mistake.

Rosemary spun on her heel, searching out her father. He stood next to the delivery driver, head down, looking over the invoice. Rosemary paced back and forth. Several stock boys were already lined up at the back of the truck, setting up the roller conveyer ramp, ready to start the assembly line of unloading and sliding the crates down the track into the stockroom.

As her father finished, he noticed her pacing. "Rosemary, what are you doing? Why aren't you in the stockroom?"

She lifted her arms and let them drop at her side. "You hired Sammy Hall? He's a thief." And a runt. And too young. Something about another kid her age working there rubbed the shine right off delivery day.

Several heads pivoted their direction.

"Lower your voice." He stepped to her. "You don't know a thing about what that boy goes through. Not that I owe you an explanation for my decision, but I hope I can teach you a little something from this, so listen close." Daddy knelt, bringing his eye level closer to hers. "He sees you and this store stocked full of things he has precious little of at home. From his perspective we're sitting on a treasure trove, and it wouldn't hurt us one bit if he swipes a little off the top. But if he gets a chance to put his hands to work, to see what it takes to have what we have, he gets two things. One, he learns about the work it takes for this little store to survive. Two, he gets to see a world beyond what he has at home. A world in which hard work and diligence actually pay off." He took her hands and squeezed them before standing. "Now not another word about it. And I better not catch you even looking sideways at that boy, do you understand me?"

His tone was firm but brimmed with compassion.

17

Present Day

Sarah sat in her mother's kitchen, the world beyond the windows pitch-dark. Exhaustion weighed her body and her brain felt like it was made of congealed oatmeal. Falling asleep should be a breeze. And yet whenever she closed her eyes, all she could see was Aaron's face. In the quiet of the night, memories, both good and bad, came knocking. Tapping, tapping until she'd go mad if she lay there another second.

She looked up at the shelves that ran around the wall about a foot from the ceiling. Covered in little chicken figurines. Blue hens. Pink hens. Yellow. Short and squat. Skinny and long-legged. Mom and her hen obsession.

At least it had always made buying her Christmas and birthday presents easy.

Sarah stood and poured herself a mug of milk and set it in the microwave. The timer ticked down while the mug spun on the turntable.

She opened the door before the microwave had a chance to beep. The last thing she needed was to wake someone. Dad left tomorrow and needed his rest. Mom would have questions about the future Sarah refused to consider.

She settled back in the kitchen chair and sipped her warmed milk, wrinkling her nose. It was kind of gross, yet somehow soothing. Nan swore by warm milk.

What she really needed was something to busy herself with. She eyed the shelves. Surely Mom didn't get around to dusting all that. Sarah retrieved a folding stepladder from the nook beside the refrigerator. Armed with a dustrag, she mounted the ladder.

One by one she wiped the fine layer of dust from each of the hens. She worked her way around the room. Thankful to no longer be lying in bed while the night crawled by minute by minute.

Sarah paused. She should stop ignoring her realtor's phone calls and commit to selling the house. Maybe that was the next step in gaining some closure.

In the corner, tucked out of view, she discovered one figurine that didn't match the rest. A blue hound dog. Cracks marred the surface. Some fine lines. Others, gaps that had been filled in with glue. One of the ears was missing a long sliver of porcelain.

She lifted it from the shelf. "What are you doing up here, little guy?" It sure didn't match the rest of Mom's collection. The damaged trinket wasn't the type of thing her mother would hang on to.

Sarah placed the little dog back in his place.

"What in heaven's name are you doing up there?"

Sarah jolted and she grabbed the shelf to steady herself. Heart thudding in her chest, she gave her mother a limp smile. "Couldn't sleep, Momma." Her vision fuzzed, and she blinked. She took a few wobbly steps down the short ladder. The floor tipped slightly under her feet, and she took a couple unsteady strides before returning to her seat at the table.

"Are you feeling all right? You just went real peaked."

Sarah waved her hand. "I'm fine. You startled me."

"I think you need to see a doctor."

Sarah shook her head. "Really, I'm fine."

Mom sat and placed a hand over Sarah's. "You barely eat. You're up all hours of the night. You don't look well. You're grieving yourself sick. The doctor might be able to prescribe you something to help."

The warm milk in her stomach soured. What would happen if she confessed the truth? What she was going through was not the normal grief a wife should feel at the loss of her husband. She was angry. Angry at all the somedays he'd promised while working away the time they'd had. Angry at herself for letting him. That niggling fear that whispered that if she asked him to prioritize their relationship over his unending need to prove himself to an estranged father, her words wouldn't have changed anything.

Here in Brighton, she was far less lonely than she'd been in years. And yet restlessness still stirred inside her, keeping her from peace while the rest of the world slept.

"Maybe there isn't anything physically wrong with you, but there will be if you don't take care of yourself." Mom's grip tightened on Sarah's hand. "Please don't put this off. If you won't do it for yourself, do it for me."

"Mom." She wanted to argue, but tears glistened in her mother's eyes. "Okay. I'll make an appointment tomorrow."

"Good. Nothing good comes from putting things off when you get a sense that something isn't right." Her mother stood and kissed the top of her head. "I'll miss you, but it'll be good for you to get back to your normal routine."

Sarah shook her head. "I'm not leaving Brighton."

"Your dad is back on the road tomorrow. I thought . . . I thought that when he went back, you'd . . ."

Sarah bounced her foot. Should she drag on this charade that her visit was in any way temporary or just rip the Band-Aid off?

"Sarah, you should see your primary care physician in Kenilworth. A doctor who already knows you. You need to get home and rest and process all this and stop wasting your energy at the store."

Wasting my energy at the store? As a child, Sarah had loved being at Old Depot, working side by side with Mom and Nan. But Mom always nudged her out the door to go to piano lessons. Or to sports teams. Always sandwiching whatever it was with lines like, "You need to" and "not wasting your time at the store."

Sarah straightened her shoulders. "I am where I want to be, doing what I want to do. This makes me happy."

"Sarah . . . you're not happy."

"Mom, stop."

"How much longer can you afford to put your life on hold here? A week? Two?"

Sarah swallowed. "I'm staying. Permanently."

Color drained from her mother's face and she stepped forward to gently grip Sarah's upper arms. "You were meant for more than what Brighton can offer."

What if she wasn't? The ill-fitting life Mom insisted she needed had rubbed blisters on her heart long before Aaron's death. "I'm going to lie down."

Before leaving for college, had Sarah ever really wanted a life outside of Brighton? Or had it been Mom's insistent nudging that put her on that path to begin with? What Sarah never understood was why her mother had been so intent on remaining at a store she'd practically shoved Sarah out of.

Glory Ann unlocked the front door and flipped the sign to open. She looked over the sparkling floors and the dusted shelves, with contents lined up like neat little rows of soldiers, and let out a satisfied sigh. Old Depot Grocery looking as it should with Sarah's help.

The trill of the phone punctured the

silence. "Old Depot Grocery, this is Glory Ann."

"Did Sarah ever take that pregnancy test?"

Glory Ann shook her head. "Paulette, you scoundrel. I had a feeling that was you. Quit tormenting that poor girl. She has enough to deal with." In the forty years of knowing Paulette, Glory Ann had never seen her shy away from an opportunity to interfere in other people's affairs.

"You said yourself you thought she was in denial. Going around nibbling saltines and clinging to her ginger ale like a wino to a bottle. I was just trying to nudge her in the right direction."

"She'll sort everything out without our help. Speaking of people needing help, are you able to take Mable to the doctor this week, or should I get Rosemary to cover my shift?" After all the convincing it had taken to get Mable to see a specialist about her memory issues, there was no way they could let her go alone to hear the doctor's prognosis.

"I can take her. Welp, it looks like Jonny and Emma are having another row. She's throwing his clothes out on the lawn again. I'll ring you later and tell you the final outcome."

Glory Ann laughed lightly as she hung up

the phone. Good old Paulette, always keeping her and Mable on the up-and-up.

Glory Ann offered up a quick prayer for Mable as she straightened the newspaper stack. She didn't mind the idea of growing older one bit. It was a privilege to see this much life. But the thought of losing her memories? That was a beast she couldn't fathom facing.

Rosemary came through the door. "Just you and me this morning. Sarah is finally seeing a doctor."

"Oh good."

"She's trying to hide her pain by working here and cleaning my house from top to bottom. Not once have I been able to get her to talk about Aaron. Grief is eating her from the inside out."

Glory Ann lifted her shoulders. "We all handle our losses in different ways." Neither of them had any room to judge.

Rosemary pressed the heel of her palms to her cheekbones. "Last night she told me she wants to stay here. She needs to get back home to Illinois before she ends up stuck in a rut."

Glory Ann blew out a breath. *This again.* "Why have you always pushed her so hard?"

Rosemary stiffened. "It wasn't healthy the way she used to plant herself here. Using this place like some hideaway from the rest of the world. Fourteen-year-olds should be begging to go to the movies and their friends' parties. But all she wanted to do was hang around here, sweeping and dusting and restocking shelves." She busied herself straightening the boxes of gum, mints, and ChapStick on the shelves beside the checkout line, even though they were already in perfect order. "If she's not careful, she'll fall right back into the same pattern. There is no future for her here."

A weight settled on Glory Ann's chest. Why did it scare Rosemary so badly that Sarah was so much like her? "Let your daughter live her life. So what if she stays and it's a mistake? She can leave and start new any time she wants."

Did the message hit its mark? Did Rosemary recognize she meant it for her too? That if staying beside her all these years had been a mistake, Rosemary could still choose a different path. She didn't have to close the store to be free.

18

June 1982

Rosemary typed in the prices on the old register, carefully ringing up Mrs. Johnson's hefty order. Apparently it took a whole grocery store to feed her brood.

Mom and Dad had finally entrusted her to run the store solo for a little while, and Rosemary would not make a mistake. At the end of the day, everything in the cash drawer would match up perfectly with what was sold.

She gave Mrs. Johnson her receipt and helped her to the Ford Cortina with her bags.

After placing her groceries in the back seat, Mrs. Johnson jerked her thumb over her shoulder. "Who is that man over there? You know him?"

Rosemary looked past her. A man paced the train tracks. Tall and too skinny. Scruffy. He seemed like he was mumbling to himself. A daisy pinched between his fingers. "I have no idea," she said.

"Well, keep an eye out for him. He's been pacing those tracks since I pulled up half an hour ago."

Rosemary nodded. The skin at the nape of her neck prickled, and she ran a hand over it to rub the sensation away. Strange faces weren't common in Brighton. Sometimes boys from her school loitered out there kicking cans, but never anyone remotely dangerous.

She returned to her post at the register. Mom and Dad had left to go to lunch, they'd be back soon. The guy out there wasn't causing any problems. Yet. She squared her shoulders. No need to worry.

Waiting for the current customer to approach the register, Rosemary admired her freshly painted pink nails. Maybe Momma would let her try a little makeup next, like the women on the glossy magazines Rosemary snuck and read when the store went quiet.

Jessamine burst through the door, passing the last customer in the store. "Hey, sis!" Her cheeks were flushed and her smile wide. She'd spent Friday night at her friend's house. No doubt up half the night whispering about which boys they liked.

Rosemary closed the magazine and stashed it under the counter. "Did you see an old guy outside?"

Jessamine shrugged. "Yeah. He looked sad." She continued on past the checkout counter. "I'm going to make him a sandwich."

"What? No. We don't know him. And Mom and Dad won't be back for another half hour."

Jessie grinned. "Aww come on, Rosemary. He looks too tired and sad to cause any trouble. Remember that Good Samaritan story from Sunday school last week. Here's our chance."

Rosemary groaned and her sister skipped over to the deli counter in the back. Everything was always a grand adventure to Jessamine. Her devil-may-care attitude would end up being the death of them both. Rosemary rang out the last lingering customer. There probably wouldn't be many more until later in the afternoon.

Jessamine came to the front of the store, balancing a paper plate with three sandwiches stacked on top of each other and a can of cola. "Hey, Rosemary, grab two more drinks and follow me, why don't you?"

Rosemary's eyes went wide. Surely, she didn't intend for them to picnic with the guy. She huffed and grabbed two more cans of cola. The store was empty for the moment, and somebody had to watch out for Jessamine.

"Hi there!" Jessamine called out to the man who now sat on one of the train track rails. A wilted daisy lay at his feet. He lifted his head.

"You looked hungry, and we are too. Would you like to eat with us?"

His brow creased and he stared at the plate of sandwiches as if trying to make sense of why two teenage girls would be intruding into his life in such a way.

"Go on, take one. My name is Jessamine, and this is my sister, Rosemary. What's yours?"

His mouth opened and closed. "It's not important. Thank you for the sandwich." He carefully plucked the egg salad sandwich from the top without touching the others.

Jessamine set the cola at his feet and sat on the ground across from him. "This is our mom and dad's store. We can run it all by ourselves." She spoke as if she'd laid the foundation of the building herself.

Rosemary rolled her eyes and ate her sandwich standing. Her little sister floated in and out of Old Depot Grocery like a disoriented butterfly.

Jessamine took a bite of her sandwich and spoke around it. "You aren't from here. Whatcha doing in Brighton?"

Rosemary cringed at her sister's terrible manners.

The man squinted his eyes, staring hard. "Are you . . . are you Glory Ann's daughters?"

"We are!" Jessamine grinned from ear to ear like she'd just discovered a long-lost friend.

Rosemary's pulse increased at the sound of her mother's name on this stranger's lips. "How do you know our mother?" If he knew their mother, why was he loitering on the tracks instead of coming inside?

His expression crumpled, constricting Rosemary's heart.

"I shouldn't be here." He scrubbed a hand over his face and stood, uneaten sandwich in one hand. Wilted flower still at his feet. "Thank you for lunch."

He hurried away, but then he turned back. "Is she happy? Glory Ann?"

What an odd question. Rosemary nodded, and the lines around his face relaxed a fraction.

"I'm glad." He directed his gaze at her. "I won't bother you anymore. I just needed to make sure she was okay."

"Well, that was weird." Jessamine stood and bounced back toward the front door, not a care in the world, while Rosemary's heart thumped too loudly in her chest. She reentered the store and perched on the stool.

It was so strange, the thought of her mother having a life and acquaintances outside the little fishbowl of Brighton. That she would know this bedraggled man who wore his sorrow like a cloak. Faraway memories flickered in her mind.

A long car trip, looking at the back of her mother's head and the way her dark curls glistened in the sunlight. Rosemary had soaked up those moments in which her mother was completely hers. There were other people connected with these trips, but they were only foggy, incomplete pictures, like the teacher from the Charlie Brown specials with the "wah, wah, wah" voice. And a house with thick beige carpet. And warm home-baked desserts. And the smell of coffee brewing.

Rosemary shook herself. Was the stranger who'd appeared connected to those forgotten people? Or maybe he was related to Momma. She never spoke about her parents, but she received a card from them every Christmas. Rosemary always slipped them out of the mail stack before Momma could toss them. They always said the same thing. "We love you. We'll try to visit soon." But they never came.

Mom and Dad came through the door. Both of them smiling and relaxed.

"How did everything go, Rosemary?" Her Dad motioned to the register.

"Just fine."

"Good girl. I knew you'd do great." He walked to the back of the store.

"Momma?"

"Yes, sweetie?"

"A man was here. Outside on the tracks. He knew you." Rosemary described him. From his unkempt, broken appearance to his sky-colored eyes.

Her mother frowned and her brow creased. A look of confusion, not displeasure. She shook her head. "I have absolutely no idea who it could have been. Let me know if you see him again. You and Jessamine ought not approach wanderers. He may not have even known me. Just known my name from overhearing conversations around town and acted familiar to lure you and Jessie closer."

Ordinarily, Rosemary would have sided with her mother. But after meeting this wary stranger, somehow she knew he'd spoken the truth. All he'd wanted was to make sure Momma was okay.

19

Present Day

This could not be happening. When she'd gone into the doctor's office, she expected a prescription for antidepressants. Not this. Sarah gripped the steering wheel, gasping for air as she drove past stretches of fallow land. Land that had once been filled with unending rows of crops.

How? How could she be pregnant? Well, she knew *how* — it must have been that one night, a couple weeks before Aaron's death. So sick of the distance between them and feeling powerless, she'd been desperate to capture his attention.

The world would see her child as a proof of love for her husband. But Sarah would always know it was actually a reminder of just how broken they'd been.

A car blew past her on the two-lane road. Sarah glanced at her speedometer. She was traveling a shade under the speed limit. She shook her head. Crawling home wouldn't stop time from marching forward. She pressed the gas pedal harder, but her car only responded with a slight shudder, no increase in speed.

And then everything went quiet.

Sarah veered to the shoulder, struggling without the aid of power steering or brakes. Why was this happening? Today of all days.

She stared at the gas gauge. The needle below E. Sarah slapped her hands on the steering wheel until her palms stung. "Stupid, stupid, stupid." Pinpricks burned behind her eyes.

She reached into her purse for her phone, but it wasn't there. She must have left it on her nightstand still on the charger. Sarah stared out at the empty road and then rested her head on the steering wheel. Might as well get walking.

This would be fun. Trekking the asphalt road in her skirt and heels with the temperature pressing ninety. Had she really thought nice clothes, shoes, and styled hair could shield her from whatever the doctor might say?

Purse over her arm, Sarah walked. Her heels crunched on the fine grit coating the shoulder. After she walked for half an hour, her knees trembled and sweat had soaked through her filmy white blouse. She longed to remove her pinching shoes, but the asphalt would sear her skin.

In the distance a dirt cloud rose. She squinted. A tractor rolled down the side of the road. Only in Tennessee would a tractor look like a rescue vehicle.

The slowing tractor veered her direction and rumbled to a stop next to her. Sarah waved away the dust swirling in the air. A man in a crumpled hat appeared through the cloud. Blue-green eyes peered down in concern.

"Sarah? Are you okay?"

Of all people it had to be him. The last time she'd spoken to Clay she'd blurted out she wasn't pregnant, and then ran away to avoid puking on his cowboy boots. She shrugged and propped her hands on her hips, willing her false-confidence smile not to wobble. "Sure, fine. Just thought I'd take a stroll on this lovely temperate day." A bead of sweat dripped down her forehead and onto her nose. She thumbed the droplet away.

Clay cut the engine and jumped down. He looked past her, toward the direction she'd traveled from. "Did ya have car trouble?"

She inwardly groaned, not wanting to

admit her silly mistake. Her knees shook, and her smile dissolved as she swallowed the rising acid in her throat. She was dehydrated, overheated, and exhausted. Humiliated or not, she needed Clay's help.

She thumbed behind her. "I ran out of gas. My car is about a mile that way. I'm just walking to get some fuel."

"That I can help with. Hop aboard."

She turned to the big red tractor with tires almost as tall as her. "On that thing?"

He shrugged. "Well, my magic carpet is in the cleaners and my white horse is at the vet, so . . ."

A corner of her mouth curled up. "Ha, ha. Real cute."

"A friend of mine borrowed my tractor, so I was just on my way home with it. We can stop at my place and take my jeep to get gas." He flicked a glance over her, his forehead creasing. "And get you some water."

Sarah stepped to the tractor, but her ankle rolled beneath her. He caught her elbow as it dipped, saving her from injuring herself.

"Come on. Let me give you a hand."

A moment later she perched on the tiny fold-down buddy seat, unavoidably close to Clay in the tiny space, as they rolled down a long country road. They turned onto a residential street. Heads of front porch–sitting elderly people followed the tractor as it rumbled down their street. She stared at the ground moving past the huge wheels below. Clay lifted a hand and waved like they were in some sort of parade.

"Would you stop drawing attention to us?" She had to shout to be heard over the noise of the engine.

His inaudible laughter shook his shoulders. He leaned close to her ear to be heard. "I'm driving a roaring red tractor with a pretty girl perched next to me. Fairly sure it's not my waving catchin' their attention." He shrugged. "You might as well look up and smile back and have a little fun with it. They're thrilled to death. This will give them gossip fodder for at least a week, or until the next tractor rolls through town bearing a damsel in distress."

She smirked and waved at a nosy neighbor. "Do you make it a habit, riding women through town on your tractor?"

His shoulders shook with laughter again. "No, *ma'am.* I'm pretty sure this is a first. Besides this is completely, one hundred percent illegal. You're not supposed to have a passenger on the road."

She leaned closer to Clay, resisting the urge to grip his arm. If it was illegal, there was probably a reason for it.

He spoke close to her ear. "Don't worry. Everything is gonna be just fine."

There was such surety in his tone that the tension that had bunched up her shoulders ever since she'd walked out of the doctor's office eased.

They traded the residential road for a long, straight dirt path. Clouds of red dust rose around them. After about a mile, Clay pulled the tractor to a stop in front of a weathered barn and a gray farmhouse with a wide, sweeping porch.

He helped her down and walked her to the porch. He didn't touch her as they walked, but she couldn't help but notice how close he lingered.

"I'm not going to fall over, you know."

He laughed softly. "Well, not to be rude, but you look like a puff of wind could do you in. Why don't you have a seat on the rocker right there, and I'll bring you a glass of water."

She sat, smiling softly as the screen door smacked closed behind him, pulled by squawking spring hinges. The fan overhead began to spin, and a soft breeze blew across her sweat-sticky skin.

The house was situated on a slight hill. Rows and rows of crops in one field and another hill mottled with black cows filled her view below. Clay reappeared, offering her a chilled glass.

She let out an involuntary sigh of relief as the icy cold water hit her tongue and did her best not to gulp it like a thirsty hound dog. She rested her head back against the rocker. "Thank you."

"Of course. If you want to go in and freshen up before we head out, there's clean washrags under the sink. Bathroom is the first door on the left." He settled on a rocker opposite her.

She stood hesitantly and entered the farmhouse. It was more well-furnished than she expected from a single country boy but definitely lacked any traces of a feminine touch. A photograph on the mantel of the stone fireplace snagged her attention as she passed. Clay and three other men in military gear stood together, with what looked to be desert behind them. Wide grins on all of their faces.

After she spent a few minutes wiping the grit from her face and neck, she met Clay back outside. "You served in the military?"

A muscle ticked in his jaw. He bowed his head as he slid his feet into a less ragged pair of boots. "I did. Served in Afghanistan for a couple tours." He lifted his gaze and shrugged. "Farming is more my speed though. At least now that your grandma pointed me in the right direction and got me connected with some local farming associations."

She sat in a rocker across from him. "So you haven't always farmed?"

He shook his head and flashed a crooked smile. "Nope. I was a regular city slicker compared to what I know now. This was my uncle's land, and he passed it on to me about seven years ago. Brighton seemed a nice place to get a fresh start." His Adam's apple dipped and rose as he surveyed the field below the house.

She felt the sudden urge to say something to ease the tension playing across his features. "I feel the exact same way about Old Depot." She offered a gentle smile. "I'm guessing you've heard about my husband."

He looked back at her and nodded. She could see the "I'm sorry for your loss" already forming on his lips.

For some reason she couldn't stomach getting those same undeserved condolences from Clay. "Marrying Aaron was a mistake." Her eyes went wide. That was not supposed to be spoken aloud to anyone. Ever. Much less to a man she barely knew.

If he was shocked by her words, he didn't

show it. "Our losses are an important part of our story, too, Sarah. We can't go back and edit our lives, thinking we could've avoided the loss. Loss is a part of living." He stood and walked to where she sat in the rocker and placed a hand on her shoulder. "I know it hurts. Losing someone we care about feels like a hole gets knocked out of the middle of us. And the pain sometimes eclipses the love we had for them, but —"

"I was going to leave him that night." She gasped from the pain of speaking those words aloud, but she couldn't shut off their flow. "All those people comforting me at the funeral, feeling sorry for his poor little wife. I didn't deserve it. Not when I had been packing my bags in our bedroom at the same time he was trapped in his car breathing his last breaths, alone on some rain-slicked back r-road." She swiped her arm across her eyes and gulped in oxygen.

"It's not even like I was leaving because we fought all the time. I just felt so stuck," she continued. "Married people aren't supposed to suffer from loneliness. Maybe I thought me leaving might finally get his attention." She gripped her knees as sobs welled in her chest, choking her words that she was just as powerless to stop as her sobs. "At the funeral people went on and on about how wonderful he was. Kind. Attentive. But their words just . . . just . . . *hurt.* It wasn't fair. His coworkers got the best parts of him. And I — I just got his leftovers."

Clay pulled his chair close to her and sat holding her hands when the tightness in her chest cut off her words. She was making an absolute fool of herself in front of this man, but she couldn't seem to stop.

Sarah shook her head. "I sound so petty."

"Maybe you and Aaron both made mistakes you can't undo, but you still have breath in your lungs and life to live. You have the chance for that fresh start you're craving. And you don't have to feel guilty about that. I've learned the hard way that punishing yourself doesn't help anyone."

20

August 1982

Rosemary entered the store Saturday morning a little breathless. She'd stayed up too late studying for finals and overslept.

"Rosemary, there is a whole mess of bottles that need to go back in the cola room. The Coke man comes tomorrow, and I don't want those empty bottles sitting around the store a whole 'nother week." Momma glared at her from the register.

"Why can't Jessie do it?"

Jessie sat on the floor of a nearby aisle stocking cans, smug as a cat in front of a milk saucer. " 'Cause I'm busy. First on the job gets first pick, remember."

Rosemary glowered. She often saved the worst jobs for her tardy sister.

The cola room was the worst place at Old Depot. It was a walled-in area out back where crates and crates of sticky glass bottles were stacked sky-high, waiting to be returned each week. People tended to store them up at home until they amassed a substantial amount, wanting to get their bottle refund money all at once.

Rosemary loaded the bottles waiting by the register and headed out back, the glass clinking with her stride. Several more sacksful waited in the storeroom, ready to be sorted and crated.

It was only ten in the morning, but already the late-summer heat descended like Satan's breath on her neck. Rosemary craned, trying to stack the crate on top of an existing tower. Yellow jackets buzzed around her head, hungry for the sugary residue in the bottom of the bottles. The infernal things dove at her no matter how much she swatted.

She returned to the cool of the stockroom and sorted bottles by type and size, placing them carefully in their crates. When she finished, she stacked one plastic crate on top of the other and leaned against the huge metal door to open it.

Momma got so mad if she broke any of them. They paid the customer as soon as they returned the bottle. But if it didn't make it back to the bottling company intact, that meant the store lost out.

Rosemary squatted to set the stacked

crates down. Glass rattled and sweat trickled down her back. Just as the crate touched pavement, she heard a bloodcurdling scream. Her sister's scream. Then the squeal of car tires.

Rosemary settled the clanking glass and sprinted to the front of the store. Jessamine stood red-faced in the parking lot. "They stole the ice again."

"Those idiotic boys." Rosemary took off running, yelling at them to stop. Some little voice in the back of her head told her to quit making a fool of herself, chasing cars down the road on foot all for a fifty-cent bag of ice. But rationality didn't have a thing to do with it. She was sick of her family's store bearing the brunt of childish pranks.

Her sneakers slapped the pavement and her lungs burned. How was she doing it? Actually gaining ground?

Oh. Brake lights. They'd stopped. They'd actually stopped. Now what would they do? Laugh in her face and speed off, most likely.

Rosemary pulled herself to her full five-foot-five height and tried to channel the intimidation her gentle giant father brought with his sheer size alone. She marched to the idling car.

Her jaw dropped when she saw the boy

behind the wheel enduring the passengers' jeers.

"Bo Anderson? I thought better of you than this." She'd never imagined he'd be running around with this group of older guys who were known for stirring up trouble. Most of it worse than swiping ice.

He ducked his chin and his cheeks reddened.

"Ooooo . . . somebody's in trouble."

Rosemary crouched and fixed her glare on the boy in the front passenger seat. "I oughta call the law on all y'all. That's theft."

"Oh, come on. Like they'd care. It's one bag of ice," the boy said.

She fixed her attention back on Bo. "I didn't think this was your crowd." Like her, Bo sometimes seemed on the fringes of social circles, not quite knowing where he fit. It seemed he was trying out a new group and this was some sort of initiation.

He lifted the ice bag from the center console.

"Bo, if you give her the ice, it don't count. It was this or turpentining Ms. Paulette's cat."

Bo swallowed hard but handed over the ice.

A boy from the back seat laughed. "This boy's *whipped.*"

Rosemary took the ice but wavered. Maybe she should hand it back if it kept the cat safe. She leveled another glare at Bo. "If I hear of anything happening to that cat, I swear I'll never speak to you again." As if that threat mattered to him.

He shook his head, his face still red. "I won't."

She flicked a glance over her shoulder. "You're better than this." A remembrance flickered in her memory. A remembrance that made his "harmless" theft all the worse. She marched back to the car, full of enough fire to melt the ice in the bag. "I know this ice might seem like no big deal, but after all the kindness my father has done to your family, you'd think you'd show a little decency. All that credit he extends to y'all, even knowing you'll only pay a fraction at a time before you rack up more debt. You're stealing from someone who has shown you and your kin so much grace."

Bo's mouth opened and closed. Even the raucous crew in the car had gone silent.

Rosemary marched away, triumph swelling in her chest. Her mouth stretched wide, for once feeling as though she'd won.

Her steps slowed as she spied her father just a little bit away, standing near the side of the road. He must have witnessed the whole thing.

She lifted the bag in the air with a wide grin. "I got our ice back."

But his expression didn't match her mood. "Rosemary Clearwater, don't ever let me catch you treating another person like that. The credit I extend is between me and my customers and is never to be thrown in that family's face. Do you understand me?"

Her shoulders curled in. "Yes, sir." Her whisper pushed past the tightness in her throat.

"The Good Book has a lot to say about giving. And about avoiding the bread of a selfish man. Old Depot Grocery isn't the selfish man of Proverbs. We don't give and lord it over people, forcing them to vomit it out for all to see what we gave them. We don't give store credit with the perspective of a lender. We give. And if it so happens they repay, we count it a blessing. I give carefully, Rosemary, as I can afford to do so. It might mean less lining my pockets, but my heart is fuller for it." He nodded at the bag of ice in her hands. "Let's get that put away. I don't want your valiant efforts to chase down the assailants to go to waste."

She chanced a look at him. There was a twinkle in his eyes. He patted her shoulder and together they walked back to the store.

"But, Dad, what if the people never pay back their credit and they are just taking advantage of you? You know, spending their money on other things instead."

"Sweetie, that's between them and the Lord. And I trust God to take care of us. While some years have been leaner than others, we've always had what we needed. Sometimes I have to say no when people ask. But if it is in my power to help, I do it."

She placed the ice back in the cooler. Would she ever be like him? He always seemed to overflow with kindness, confident that there would always be enough to go around for everyone while she grasped tight to whatever she got ahold of.

Though he'd been disappointed, angry even, at the words she'd said, he allowed her to feel remorse for the way she'd behaved, and instead of talking down to her, he put her up on his shoulders, giving her a broader view of things.

21

Present Day

Sarah walked up her front steps, watching the moths beat themselves against the glass of the porch light. Her body ached for a warm shower to wash away the dried sweat and grit that clung to her skin.

After she'd unintentionally poured her heart out to Clay, including the news of her pregnancy, he'd helped her take care of her car. He remained so unruffled, despite her buckets of tears and the things she'd blurted out that were never meant to be voiced aloud. Did they teach him that in the military? To not only stay calm under fire in a war-torn country but also in the presence of a dehydrated pregnant woman on the verge of a mental breakdown?

Despite her fatigue she chuckled imagining what that training exercise would entail.

She inserted her key and opened the front door. A shower first, and then maybe she'd confess the doctor's diagnosis to Mom.

She closed the door and locked up. The house was too empty with Daddy back on the road with his annoyingly adorable canine sidekick.

"Sarah, dear, that you?"

"Yeah, Mom." She followed her mother's voice to the living room.

"I'd be about worried out of my mind if I hadn't caught wind of the latest news." Her mother arched an eyebrow. "Somethin' about my daughter riding around town on Clay Watson's tractor." Her mother stilled her rocker and her knitting hands.

"Mom —"

Mom smirked. "I know you ran out of gas. I'm just teasing. I'm just glad he came along when he did and you weren't stuck walking all the way. Seriously, child, where is your cell?"

"I forgot it."

"What did the doctor have to say?"

Sarah looked away. If she told her the truth, Mom would spring into action, armed with all her opinions. Sarah would tell her the full story. Just not tonight. "She said that I'm physically in good health, but that my body is going through a lot. To give myself permission to rest if I need it."

Mom tucked her knitting in the basket at

her feet, shaking her head. "I told you, you were working too hard at the store."

"I'm not doing much. Sitting at the checkout counter. Planning a few events to get traffic up."

"Things that don't need doing."

Better than spending her time stewing in regret. "Why are you so against me being there?"

"You're knowingly investing your energy in a failing venture. It makes no sense."

"Some of my happiest memories are at that store. Did you know that? Working beside you and Nan. Feeling like I was a part of something bigger than myself.

"No matter how tough my school day was, I could walk in those doors and it was like I became free from whatever schoolgirl drama was bothering me that day. You've spent your whole life there. You must have loved it at some point. What changed?"

Mom flicked her hand in the air, waving away Sarah's words. "My decision to sell has nothing to do with memories and days gone by. It's about stewarding our resources. My father never meant for us to struggle when we didn't have to for the sake of memories. If he were here, and knew what I know, he'd support us selling."

Sarah leaned in, hungry for this piece of

her mother's story. Longing for her to say more about the grandfather she'd never met who'd helped shape her mother into the strong woman she was today. Instead her mother pulled her yarn back out of the basket and resumed knitting.

"It was his store first, right? Before he met Nan. Does the store help you feel close to him?"

She didn't want to hurt her mother by digging into something so obviously painful, but Sarah needed to know her journey. Being in her and Aaron's home didn't make her feel close to Aaron, it just reiterated the space that had been between them. If she learned from her mother's experiences navigating loss, maybe Sarah could find her own way forward too.

Mom's hands paused. "Letting go is never easy. Hanging on to little keepsakes is fine, but a business is not a keepsake. And that is all I'm saying about it."

Sarah went to the shower and cranked the water as hot as she could stand it and stood under the spray until the heat in the steamy bathroom made her light-headed. Why wouldn't Mom answer her questions?

Wrapped in a fresh-from-the-dryer towel, Sarah placed her hand on her flat lower stomach, trying to accept the reality that a little person grew in there. She trudged to her room and dressed in pajamas. It was only seven in the evening, but it felt like midnight. She went to the kitchen for a glass of water. On the way back she picked up the portable phone from the receiver.

Maybe Mom wouldn't reveal her past or give Sarah some clue why she was so ready to let go of a place she'd dedicated her life to, but maybe Aunt Jessie would spill the beans.

"Hello, Rosemary. This is unexpected."

"Actually, it's Sarah. I'm in Brighton with Mom and wanted to give you a call."

The next morning, Sarah sat in the back at the deli counter with an unopened book on her lap. Over and over again her mind drifted back to her phone conversation with Aunt Jessie the night before.

"If she didn't really like being there, why'd she stay, Aunt Jessie? Why didn't she move across the country like you did? Or just stop working in the store and do something new with her life."

Aunt Jessie's heavy sigh had come through the line. "There came a time, right before she graduated high school, that I thought she'd do that very thing. And . . ."

"And what?"

"And for the first time in her life, something let loose in Rosemary and she did what she wanted instead of what everyone expected, and the consequences shattered her world. Our world. She's spent the rest of her life trying to make up for it, I think. The only thing I don't understand is what in the world has made her switch paces all of the sudden and want to sell the store —"

"Sarah? Is that you?"

Sarah was shaken out of her trance by the shocked tone. Her childhood best friend stood on the other side of the deli counter with a pudgy baby in her arms. "Libby?" Libby was one of her few friends who stayed around Brighton after high school.

Libby let out a squeal and the baby in her arms squirmed when she squeezed a little tighter. "I'd heard it through the grapevine that you were back in town. I just had to come see it to believe it!"

Sarah dropped her book into her tote and rounded the counter. Libby stood with one baby on her hip and twin toddlers clinging to each leg. She pulled Sarah into a one-armed hug. A sweet and sour scent of baby powder and spit-up lingered in the fabric of her friend's shirt.

Libby let her go and grinned at her. "It's so good to see you."

Sarah winced. "I'm sorry. I should have called you before now. I've just been a little preoccupied." Sarah nudged the toe of her tennis shoe on the wood floor, rubbing out a scuff on the finish.

"Oh, honey. Don't you worry about it." Libby nodded to the baby in her arms and then the twins. "I would have been over here sooner, but the twins came down with hand, foot, and mouth. And of course passed it to baby Caroline. My older two at least already had it when they were real little, so they didn't get it again. Whew. That virus is nothing but torture. But we're all right as rain now, thank goodness. The older two are at school right now. I have to go pick them up in an hour."

"I can't believe you're a mother of five." Sarah smiled gently at the little boys who eyed her suspiciously.

Mom walked up behind Libby with her lips pursed and head shaking as she passed. How well Sarah could read that look on her face. *See, Sarah, this would have been you if you'd stayed.* Sarah looked at her friend. Her hair was mussed, and there were purplish circles under her eyes. A yellowish stain marred the shoulder of her oversized white T-shirt.

"I don't know how you manage. You sure

have your hands full."

Libby smiled. "I sure do. I feel crazier than a betsy bug most days trying to keep them all clothed, fed, and behavin', but I wouldn't have it any other way."

"Are you doing any shopping today, or were you just in for a visit?"

Libby shifted the baby on her hip, who cooed and looked at Sarah with her wide eyes. "I've got to pick up a few things. Your grandmama has been bringing us groceries since the littles have been sick, but I finally convinced her we were all well enough to be doing our own shopping again."

"The store is pretty quiet. Why don't I grab a buggy for you and then I can carry Caroline so your hands will be free while you shop." When Sarah returned with a cart, Libby passed the baby to her and then lifted one toddler into the seat and one into the large basket of the cart.

Baby Caroline nuzzled against her chest, and Sarah inhaled her sweet baby scent. The baby gripped a fistful of Sarah's long blonde hair and popped it in her mouth. While following Libby and her steady stream of conversation, Sarah carefully unwound her slobbery strands of hair from the baby's pudgy fingers.

Sarah used to do this all the time when

she was a high schooler — assist moms with their little ones while they shopped, day-dreaming about having a houseful of babies when she grew up.

"Lib, when you were pregnant with your babies, did you automatically feel connected to them?"

Libby turned to her as she dropped a jumbo bag of generic cereal into her cart next to her little boy. She shrugged. "Each one was different. I mean, most of the time I was in love — Charlie, stop crushing the cereal — the minute I saw those two little lines on my pregnancy test. But Caroline was different.

"I didn't admit it to anyone, of course, but she was a surprise I found out about right after Momma passed. Plus, mine and Ben's marriage was going through a rough patch and I had the other four I was trying to take care of. Goodness, even after she was born it took us a month or two to find our rhythm." Libby reached out and stroked the baby's cheek. "We just needed a little time to get to know each other, is all."

Sarah released a breath. Time. Maybe that's what Sarah needed too. Just because she'd struggled so much to connect with Aaron didn't mean that was doomed to be repeated with his child.

Libby put a hand over her mouth and giggled. "Goodness gracious. I'm just a-blabbin' away, aren't I? I don't get out among the grown-ups enough. I'm a little starved for real conversation."

Sarah smiled. "Well, maybe we need to remedy that. I could use a friend."

22

March 1983

The ticking of her Timex seemed to echo in the quiet store. Two hours until closing. Ordinarily she enjoyed having it all to herself. Pretending it was hers to run.

But tonight, Brian Olsen had asked Rosemary to go with him to the party over on Johnson Mill Road. *Brian.* The boy half the female population of their small high school mooned over. Rosemary was never the one the boys paid attention to. So unlike her sister who seemed to draw people to her like bees to a honeysuckle bush.

Rosemary might not have Jessie's charisma and free-spirited ways, or her great big, larger-than-life dreams, but she had cornered the market on dependability and hard work. And if that meant she missed out on things like the most popular boy in school asking her to be his date at the party because it was her day to close up, so be it.

It wasn't as though she could ask her parents for a night off so she could go to a party they'd never approve of in the first place.

The shrill phone ring jolted her out of her musing.

"Old Depot Grocery. How may I help you?"

"Ma'am, do you have Prince Albert in a can?" The craggy voice came through the phone.

Rosemary looked to the tobacco aisle and rolled her eyes skyward. "Yes. Yes, we do."

"Then you better let him outta there. He can't breathe!" Maniacal laughter filled Rosemary's ears and then the click of the disconnect on the other end of the line. She groaned and put the phone back in the cradle.

Another highlight of closing Friday night. The prank calls. The least they could do was come up with something a little more original.

Another hour ticked by. No one had entered in hours. But she'd fielded four more prank calls. Yes, her refrigerator was running, but no she wasn't too worried about catching it. This was her Friday night, while somewhere on a secluded piece of property her friends were huddled around a bonfire with somebody's boom box blasting. Laughing and dancing.

She reached in her purse and pulled out the acceptance letter from the University of Tennessee. Her grades were good, and her school counselor encouraged her to apply despite Rosemary's assertion that she had no plans for college. Why go when she had no idea who or what she wanted to be? But when she'd found this in the mailbox this afternoon, the idea of leaving Brighton and seeking out dreams of her own had sent her mind buzzing with possibilities.

Rosemary tidied the checkout area. Walked the aisles to make sure everything was in place. Never mind the fact she'd already done it two hours ago. The glass on the deli display was already shining and smudge-free, matching the sparkling glass on the front of the building.

All the while she daydreamed about a fictitious life in which she started over in a new city. A college girl surrounded with friends. The kind of girl that guys wanted.

An image of Brian's ready smile flashed in her mind, taking over her college-life daydreams. The way he'd looked into her eyes and squeezed her hand when he'd asked her to go out with him tonight. Warmth found its way to her cheeks.

Temptation had pulled hard, but the reality of her parents' expectations pulled harder. Cathy gave her an earful about it all afternoon when Rosemary had told Brian she couldn't go with him.

"This is a once in a never invitation, Rosemary." Then her friend dragged her by the hand back to Brian and elbowed her until she muttered that she'd try to come.

It was only nine. Surely the party was just getting started. It wouldn't be that big of a deal if she closed up a little early. Rosemary went to the front of the store and flipped the sign. What was the point of sitting here rotting away her senior year in an empty store?

Just this one time she should simply do what she wanted without tying herself in knots trying to make perfect decisions. To never let anyone down. Except in all this striving, maybe she had been letting someone down. Herself.

Rosemary grabbed the phone and dialed her best friend's number. "Hey, Cath. I decided to go. Will you come pick me up? I don't want to show up by myself."

Fifteen minutes later, Cathy's car pulled into the lot. Rosemary double-checked that all the lights were out and the door was locked behind her. She gave a long look at the phone on the wall. She should probably call home and let them know she was leaving early. But these were the types of gatherings their blustery preacher warned against on Sunday mornings. Though Momma and Daddy never commented, she was pretty sure they agreed.

Cathy laid on the car horn, causing Rosemary to jolt and shriek.

She scurried to the car and plopped into the passenger seat. "I can't believe I'm doing this."

Cathy laughed. "You rebel, you. Closing up an hour early on a Friday night. You better watch out, the whole world might tip on its axis or something." She passed her a makeup bag. "Here, I just got some new eyeshadow colors."

In the dim light of the streetlamps, Rosemary smeared her lids with bold color and layered her mascara thick. Far more makeup than Momma would approve of. She pulled a comb from her purse and teased her blonde curls a little higher. Tonight was the night to go all in. To dare to stand out. Break out of her taupe existence. All she had to do was pretend to be Jessamine for a couple of hours and maybe that craving inside her, that hunger to be seen, would quiet, if only for a little while.

They bounced down a rutted path through a fallow field, radio blasting. Soon the glow of the bonfire crept into view. Cathy and Rosemary giggled, anticipation turning them giddy.

Tales of these parties had to be inflated rumors and it was more than likely just a bit of mischief and sowing wild oats. Brighton was a pretty tame place. Still, neither Cathy nor Rosemary dared venture to one of these backcountry parties until now.

They climbed out of the car and wove through the crowd. Couples paired off and slipped into the cornstalks for privacy. Music blared.

Cathy grabbed Rosemary's hand and pulled her up short. Seated on a large log in front of the bonfire was a couple wrapped in an embrace.

Brian. There was no mistaking him. Not after spending the entire school year sitting behind him in chemistry admiring his thick brown hair and the slope of his broad shoulders in his letterman jacket, all the while doodling his name in her notebook. The girl he had in his arms, kissing too passionately for any amount of decency, wore a jean jacket all too familiar. Rosemary's jean jacket.

"Jessamine Clearwater!" At Rosemary's

screech, the couple broke apart. What was her little sister doing here? Making out with a senior classman.

Jessamine's face crimsoned and her jaw clenched.

"Do Momma and Daddy know you're here? With that boy? He's much too old for you."

"Mind your own business. What are you doing here anyway? Aren't you too goody-two-shoes for this scene?"

Rosemary stood closer, having a slight height advantage on her sister. She wrinkled her nose. "You smell like beer. We're leaving."

Brian edged away, letting himself melt into the crowd that was gathering to witness the source of the feminine screeching.

"I am not leaving. I'm having fun," said Jessamine. "And I didn't drink anything. Some guy spilled his cup on me while we were dancing."

Rosemary clenched her jaw. "Brian invited me to go with him. Not you."

Jessamine smirked. "No, Brian asked you because he thought our parents might let me come if you came." She shook her head. "It was a stupid idea. I tried to tell him that you worked closing on Fridays and that you'd never blow off a responsibility like that. So I told Mom and Dad that I was sleeping over at Jennifer's house. Piece of cake."

Cathy squeezed Rosemary's shoulder, and Rosemary blinked back the hot tears gathering behind her eyes. It was always Jessamine everyone wanted. How dense could she be, thinking that all of a sudden her out-of-her-league crush had eyes for her?

Rosemary grabbed a beer from the cooler and knocked it back. She grimaced and choked but kept drinking. When she finished the first beer, she grabbed another. Winding her way through the throng, sick to death of always being on the outside, she tried with everything in her to get lost in the crowd.

Time passed in a blur that throbbed like a drumbeat.

Someone grabbed her by the shoulders as she stumbled over a log by the bonfire. "What are you doing? This isn't you."

Rosemary blinked, trying to clear her blurred vision. Cathy stood in front of her, blocking her way.

"Cath, I've been going about my life the wrong way all along. Maybe it's better to just do the next thing that pops into your head. To stop thinking so hard."

Cathy wrinkled her nose. "Let's just go. I'll sneak you into my room and call your parents to let them know you're staying over. You can't go home like this."

Rosemary jerked away, and the ground beneath her seemed to tip. She fought for balance.

In the distance police sirens sounded. Everybody froze. Someone doused the fire, filling the air with smoke and ash. A few people ran for their cars. Others disappeared in the field.

But the sirens passed by. The crowd murmured. A little later they heard the sound of the firetrucks' wail. Everyone stood locked in place. Something terrible had happened. Whatever it was, it affected someone there. Maybe all of them. That's the way it was in Brighton. For better or for worse.

Headlights bounced down the rutted dirt road that cut between fields. A pickup slid to a stop.

Bo Anderson, who had traded ice stealing for volunteering with the fire department, jumped out of his truck. He peered into the smoky dark. "Rosemary? Jessamine? Y'all here? Your momma's lookin' for ya. She's in a right state."

Rosemary stumbled forward, followed by her sister, whose shirt was twisted and hair was full of twigs. Rosemary's head pounded and her stomach roiled. “What’s going on, Bo? What’s happened?”

He brought a shaky hand to his forehead and looked into the crowd as if desperate for someone else to appear to answer her question. He stepped close. “Somebody broke into y’all’s store. There’s a lot of police there. I don’t know everything, but your momma seemed to think you was at the store and she’s in a real panic.”

“Where . . . where’s Daddy?” Rosemary swayed, and Cathy gripped her elbow.

Bo stared into her eyes, his face pale as moonlight. “I think you better come with me.”

23

Present Day

Saturday morning Sarah walked to the store instead of driving, seeking space to explore her frantic thoughts without her mother's hovering. Sarah might be able to ignore the life she'd had in the past and it would obediently fade into obscurity, but this pregnancy would not work the same way. This . . . this baby . . .

Right now this baby was the size of a kidney bean, tucked safely away where no one had to know. But in a few more weeks, details of her life would once again be on display. Just when people in Brighton had finally started to treat her normally, that pity would creep back into their expression when they heard the news of her unborn child who would never know its father.

At least for today it could remain her secret.

It was a big day for the store. She hoped.

If everything had gone according to plan, people had seen the newspaper ad and were lined up at the door, eager to put their name in the drawing for that steak dinner for two. This was a great chance to reconnect with patrons who'd drifted to the new store, to remind the community why Old Depot Grocery was so precious. Why they all needed it to stay.

Sarah crested the little hill. The parking lot was nearly full. She resisted the urge to punch the air in triumph. One step forward in saving Old Depot. Now to keep these people coming back.

When she reached the bottom of the hill, her mother came out to meet her, a scowl crimping her face. She flung her arms out to the side. "What have you done? Why in the world did you think this was a good idea?"

Sarah gestured to the full parking lot. "I've attracted a lot of traffic to the store this morning. This is proof that we can turn things around. There's still hope."

Her mother kneaded her forehead. "We can't afford this. It won't do us any good if your plan to get people to the store bankrupts us in the process. Did you realize that you took out a full-page ad for a week? There went four hundred dollars we didn't have. I know you're used to a different lifestyle, but we don't have that kind of cash lying around."

Sarah's stomach churned. Had she really agreed to pay that much? Her mind went back to the phone call. Her shoulders crept higher. She'd been distracted by Ms. Paulette's claim that she was pregnant, instead of giving the ad agent on the phone her full attention. "I made a mistake when I placed the ad. I'm sorry."

"Well, we've got bigger problems than that." She jerked her thumb over her shoulder. "You see all those people over there? The first twenty who arrived are all wondering where their steak dinners for two are."

Sarah's stomach dropped like she was a passenger on a plunging roller coaster. "No, no, no. The first twenty shoppers would be entered into a giveaway for one steak dinner for two."

Rosemary held out the paper. "Well, that wasn't clear enough from the ad."

Sarah scanned the words in huge bold letters. Giveaway. *Steak Dinner Fixings for Two for the First Twenty Patrons to Arrive on Saturday, July 6th.* Sarah stared, willing the printed words to change. "I'm so sorry."

"Nineteen people over there are about to get a real bad taste in their mouth." Her mother pivoted and walked toward the store.

"Mom, wait."

She turned.

"How many steaks do we have in stock?"

Mom put her hands on her hips. "Fifteen, I think. But still, we can't afford to just empty our stock. There's nothing left for the paying customers to buy."

"I can fix this. Just . . . tell them that the delivery was delayed. Tell them it is on the way."

"Holding them here longer will just make them angrier. Even if you can magically make forty steaks appear, we can't afford that."

Sarah lifted her chin. This was something she did have the power to fix. "I'll make this right on my dime, not Old Depot's. And I'll pay back what I spent on the ad. If they can't wait, get their addresses and I'll deliver them myself."

"But where are you going to get that many steaks?"

Sarah grimaced. "I guess I'm headed to the Shop n' Go."

Rosemary propped herself against the stool behind the checkout counter. Half-sitting, half-standing, unwilling to fully give in to the extra support she needed. She massaged her hands, praying for strength and sensation to increase in her joints.

Her mother and her daughter stood on the other side of the glass, passing out boxes of steaks and sides to the "winners" of the giveaway gone wrong. She'd be willing to wager Sarah hadn't admitted the mix-up to Momma, nor where the steaks had come from.

That was part of the problem. Momma should have known that they didn't have that many steaks in stock or the profit margins to give away that much food, but she just wanted to go on living in a fairyland, convinced that things would just "work out" if they kept working hard enough.

The foot traffic had been great today. If you didn't count the fact that Sarah's efforts had cost far more than what they made. Events like this every weekend, practically begging people to shop here, was no way to run a store.

That business model was about as dependable as Rosemary's health. Though the doctor said her condition might not get much worse, it could just as likely go into a rapid decline. She could still succeed in the goals she'd worked a lifetime for if the store sold — she could make sure Sarah didn't get stuck here and that Momma was provided for. Best to make plans now before her failing health forced her hand, even if Momma and Sarah thought she was letting them all down.

Rosemary flipped over the open sign and closed out the cash register for the evening.

She waved goodbye to her mother and daughter, who still chatted in the parking lot with the last of the giveaway winners who'd returned for their gift. Rosemary settled into her car and then drove west with the windows down, squinting against the glare of the sun making its descent.

She pulled into the gravel lot near the place her daddy was buried. It was a nice cemetery. A little out of the way of most of the town traffic. There was a stream and weeping willows. Frogs croaked out their evening song. Lightning bugs flashed.

Rosemary loved this time of year. When the days lingered long and there was time to savor the sights and sounds of a day coming to a close before darkness dropped. She strolled through the rows of headstones, almost all the names familiar to her.

Maybe life here cramped and chafed sometimes, but would she have done things differently if that horrible night hadn't happened? Probably not. She still would have married the boy who reminded her so much of her father. And she would have stayed.

She settled on the stone bench next to her father's grave. Her mother probably had it put there because she knew how many hours Rosemary would have to sit with him before she could forgive herself.

A forgiveness that still eluded her to this day. Which is why every Saturday she still came. Because no matter how hard she worked, devoting her life to the store in his stead hadn't brought the peace she craved.

When the store sold, this would be all she had left. Sitting by her father's grave. Talking to his headstone like he'd talk back.

"Daddy, I don't know what I'm going to do. Momma's so mad at me. She thinks I don't care about Old Depot closing. That I'm callous and cold. But I'm just trying to be strong. Just like she always was when loss came her way. She'd pull up her bootstraps and dig in harder. This is my way of digging in. They think I'm quitting, but I'm just trying to take care of things. I can't do it by working like Momma did. But I can do it by letting go."

She stared at the gray granite. But it didn't talk back. Other than the words engraved in the stone. *Loving husband and father.* A minuscule phrase to describe the man he was.

"But it hurts in ways I can't admit to them. I'm losing another piece of you I'll never be able to get back."

24

March 1983

Yellow crime scene tape. Shattered glass. Flashing blue lights. Two missing daughters. The still form waiting beneath the sheet on the other side of the glass of Old Depot Grocery. Glory Ann's bones rattled with her trembling. Someone placed a wool blanket over her shoulders that pricked at her skin.

Lights and sounds blared too loud. She was frozen in place, unable to leave Clarence. The authorities assured her they were working to locate her daughters.

Jessie hadn't been at her friend's house. Rosemary should have been here at the store. If she'd been there closing up, it could have been her under that sheet. Which is why Clarence rushed in. Heedless and fierce, his buddy Frank had said, Clarence had burst in through the door when they witnessed a man's silhouetted figure slinking through the darkened aisles.

She shuddered. Brighton had always been so safe.

Someone brought her a steaming mug of some liquid that had no taste and scalded her tongue.

A rusty gray pickup truck pulled off the shoulder of the road. Jessamine appeared, followed by Rosemary and her friend Cathy.

The mug fell from Glory Ann's hands, shattering and splashing steaming liquid against her stocking-clad legs. She ran to them and pulled her daughters into her arms. Her life. Her everything.

Bo Anderson stood a short distance back, head bowed and hands clasped behind his back.

Rosemary smelled of alcohol. And her hair was a mess. "Where have you been? There was a break-in." Glory Ann's throat tightened, clipping her words. "You . . . you were missing. We —"

Rosemary was pale as the fog floating in the air. Her wide eyes darted, searching. Searching for the man who was always her hero.

"Where's Daddy? I don't see Dad."

Glory Ann couldn't find the words. She knew them. But they refused to string together and leave her lips.

Rosemary trembled. Her voice rose as she

continued to repeat herself, and then called out for him. "Dad? Dad!"

Officers turned and stared.

Jessamine wept and clung to Rosemary's arm, somehow grasping what Glory Ann's silence spoke.

One of the officers removed his hat and approached, compassion softening his expression. Not one of the men from Brighton, but one from a neighboring county who must have come in for support.

He reached for Rosemary and Jessamine's hands. "Are you Clarence Clearwater's daughters?"

Trembling and sniffling they nodded.

"I'm so sorry to inform you that your father was killed in the line of duty."

Rosemary gasped for air. "Line of d-duty? There's some mistake. He's not an officer."

The man swallowed, and a muscle jumped in his jaw. "In the line of fatherhood. As I understand it, he bravely rushed into danger in order to protect one of his children. Unfortunately, he sacrificed his life in the process. The assailant was armed and startled by Mr. Clearwater rushing into the room. At that time, he discharged his weapon and Mr. Clearwater . . . your father succumbed to his injuries. I'm so sorry."

Rosemary dropped to her knees and Jessamine followed. Glory Ann was still frozen in place. Keening filled her ears. Did it pour from the ache in her chest or from one of her daughters?

She wrapped her arms around her middle. No matter how many times she faced loss in this life, there was no way to shake the shock. The suddenness. Of having someone and then in the blink of an eye they're gone with no way to rewind time. To reach back to regain her grasp on that last ordinary, everyday moment that she'd let slip past like it held no weight.

His smile and wink, and *I'll see you in a little while* were gone.

This wasn't real.

Tomorrow morning she'd roll over and stretch in her bed, and Clarence's large, warm presence would fill the space next to her. Relief would wash over her as the horror would fade, replaced by the reality that all the people she loved were safe and sound.

Rosemary curled into the back of her father's closet. People filled every other nook in her family home. There was just too much noise. Too many voices swelling in a senseless cacophony. Days had marched forward, bringing events she wasn't ready to face. She just needed everything to stop.

Or rewind. Forward didn't make sense without him.

She reached up and pulled a sherpa-lined flannel shirt he wore on the coldest days from a hanger and wrapped it around herself like a blanket.

If Dad were here, what would he say? She was the reliable one. The one he trusted with the important things.

But now he wasn't here. Because of her.

Muffled by walls and conversation, she heard her mother call her name. But she could not move. If she stayed in this spot, maybe time would somehow freeze and she could hold this moment, inhaling the shirt that still held the faintest scent of her father, and imagine that her body heat rising beneath his flannel was his comforting warmth.

Minutes or hours slipped past. She didn't know which. Shadows beyond the closet door lengthened and grew until they melded together and became the dark. The faint buzz of the mourners faded. Rosemary drifted between blurred lines of waking and sleeping.

The bedroom door squeaked open, spilling in yellow light from the hall. Her mother's shadow preceded her. She sank onto the bed, sitting ramrod straight. Then little by little her posture softened, sobs shaking her rigid frame until it melted into a curled form on the mattress. Momma's hand reached to the side her father slept on, and she grasped at the wedding ring quilt, clutching it tight.

A moment not meant for Rosemary to witness. Should she stay until grief consumed her mother, pulling her into sleep, or should she stand and join her? Tuck into the empty space on the bed and hold one another instead of losing themselves in voids once filled by a man they loved.

Rosemary emerged from the closet, stiff and aching. "Momma." Her voice came out hoarse and cracked.

Her mother started. She pulled herself upright, her tear-streaked face illuminated by moonlight. She swiped her nose with the back of her hand. "Rosemary? What in heaven's name are you doing in here? Why didn't you come when I called?"

"I just . . . I couldn't. I needed space."

Her mother's jaw clenched. "Space?" She shook her head. "People were here to honor your father, and you were nowhere to be found. You, of all people, should have been there."

Because he gave his life for hers? Rosemary repeatedly tightened and released her fists, trying to give her crashing emotions an outlet.

"I always thought you'd be the one to set an example for Jessamine. You were the responsible one. The steady one. I never thought it'd be you leading her astray."

Weights compressed Rosemary's chest. "Astray?"

"Lying, sneaking around at a party you know your father and I wouldn't have approved of. I smelled the alcohol on you that night. Your father was rushing into the building you were supposed to be in. And you were out getting *drunk.*"

Rosemary reeled, her mother's words cutting soul deep. "You wish I'd been there, don't you?"

Her mother buried her face in her trembling hands. "No. No, I just wish you would have called and told us you were going to leave. It was all so preventable. That's the thing I can't stomach about this."

Rosemary backed from the room, gasping for oxygen.

Words followed her out the door. "I've always tried to teach you girls to be honest. To communicate. Secrets cause damage. And sometimes that damage can't be undone."

Arms wrapped around her middle, Rosemary stumbled to her bedroom. She couldn't stay here. Not after the words her mother uttered, letting them loose into the air where they couldn't be called back. Things Rosemary could never unhear. This was why she couldn't face the people who came to their house after they'd put her Daddy, the man who had always been her Superman, into the ground.

To hear those words from her mother's mouth, that it really was her fault he died, was too much. But where could she go? Rosemary dug into her keepsake box and pulled out an old envelope and ran her fingers over the address she'd never been to. She left a note and collected the savings she'd squirreled away in the wooden box she kept underneath her bed.

She grabbed her car keys. On the way out of the house, she spied her sister staring at the blank television screen. Rosemary wrapped her in a hug. "Jessie, I need to leave for a little while. I'll be back. But I've got to get out of here before I lose my mind. I just . . . I think it would be better if Mom didn't have to look at me."

Her sister blinked her swollen eyes. "Where?"

"Grandma and Granddad Hawthorne." Who knew if they'd even let her in the door?

She was a stranger to them. Because of some long-standing rift between her mother and her parents that Rosemary didn't understand. It'd probably only make her mother angrier, her leaving. But she had to get out of Brighton.

25

Present Day

Sarah sat at the kitchen table watching her mother, who stood with the phone to her ear. After a polite greeting, Mom narrowed her eyes, and her stance went cockeyed. "Uh-huh. Sarah is here. How did you get this number?"

Sarah's spine stiffened.

Her mother turned from where the phone cord tethered her to the wall. Something in her expression constricted Sarah's chest. "It's for you. Your realtor, she says."

Sarah's eyes darted in search of the wireless phone, a million emotions crashing and colliding inside of her. She could not do this under her mother's scrutiny. "Where's the portable?"

"Probably on the charger in the living room."

Sarah hurried to the living room and pressed the phone to her ear. "Hi, Marcie."

She returned to the kitchen. Her mother still stood by the wall with the phone up to her ear, listening as Marcie gave her a dressing down about hiring her as her realtor and then dropping off the face of the earth before all the details were finalized.

Sarah covered the mouthpiece with her hand. "Hang it up."

Mom gave a sheepish shrug and returned the phone to its cradle. Sarah headed toward her old bedroom. Her mother's presence followed behind her, straightening already tidy throw pillows. Closing open doors in the hallway.

Sarah went into her bedroom and shut the door. Her mom might not be the type to listen in after she'd been told not to, but she wasn't above lingering close enough to glean any details that might float beneath the bedroom door. Those were fair game.

"I'm sorry to turn into a stalker, but I've tried calling your cell about a hundred times. Why haven't you returned my calls?"

Sarah plopped onto the twin bed. "I've just been going through some things." If she explained the mental weight that settled over her every time she thought about returning her calls, she'd sound like an insane person.

"Of course. Of course. I totally get it. But

the market is hot right now. Especially in your neighborhood. A house down the street just sold well above market value. But I've got to be able to reach you. I've got to get people coming through the doors."

Bands tightened around Sarah's chest as flashes of her life with Aaron played in her mind. Not the stark loneliness. Sweeter memories that had been sneaking into her consciousness while she ate dinner with her parents or stocked cans and stacked the milk delivery on the hand truck. Like when Aaron left her notes while she showered, scrawling "I love you" in the condensation on the mirror.

Then there was the day they'd closed on the house, when he'd carried her across the threshold and chased her up the curved staircase, tickling her ribs. Picnicking in the unfurnished dining room, eating Chinese takeout straight from the box.

They'd had moments, good moments, where they connected. But those feelings had slipped through her fingers like water in her cupped hands.

"Sarah? Are you still there?"

She tried to clear the knot in her throat. "Yeah, sorry. I didn't catch the last thing you said."

"I said there could be a bidding war based

on the level of interest for houses in that area. Isn't that great?"

Memories, sad, sweet, angry, and desolate, collided inside her mind. Her lungs became stone. "I can't do this." The words escaped in a breathless whisper.

Marcie's excited chatter ceased like a faucet being shut off. "I think we must have a bad connection. It sounded like you said you didn't want to sell."

Sarah rubbed the throbbing ache between her eyebrows. "No. I — I do want to sell. Reality just hit me all of the sudden. And it was . . . a lot."

"O-kay."

"Yes. I want to sell the house."

"I think you should consider raising the price we initially talked about. You could walk away with a nice chunk of change to start over someplace new, but it's all contingent on buyers liking what they see on the walk-through. When can I show it?"

Sarah ended her call with her realtor with promises to start returning her calls and making real plans. She either needed to get back to Virginia or hire a company to clean the place out. She recoiled at the thought of someone walking in and finding the food left to mold and the shattered crystal littering the dining room. Personal paperwork and photographs strewn across the closet floor.

She slumped against the pile of pillows carefully arranged against the headboard. When Aaron died, one of the first things she'd found the energy to do was to call their realtor. At the time, letting go of the house seemed a clear first step.

But as the weeks had marched on, it became easier to pretend her Chicago responsibilities didn't exist.

A light tap sounded on the door, and her mother cracked it open before she had the chance to answer. Mom wrung her hands. "Please don't do this."

Despite her mother's downcast expression, Sarah smiled. "Don't you see? I can use the profit from the house to help the store. We don't have to close."

Her mother stiffened. "You will not invest a dime of that money on the store. If you sell, and I don't advise it, that money is seed money to help you start fresh. To buy you a new place and pay your bills while you get settled. But you will not waste it on that store, not when we should be selling it for a tidy profit. That place is a money pit."

Sarah's pulse pounded in her ears. "You talk like you know what I need, but you don't have a clue. I've been trying to tell you, and you keep pushing me away. All I ever wanted was to work that store with you and Nan. Why is that never enough for you? What is so wrong about me wanting the life you had? What's so wrong with being *you*?"

Her mother's chin dropped and moisture glistened in her eyes, but in an instant she straightened and blinked it away. "I'm trying to help you see beyond what's right in front of you. Trust me when I say that it's time to let the store go. Don't give away the best years of your life just to make things easy for your grandma. Lord knows I've done enough of that for all of us."

Recoiling from her mother's callous words, Sarah stalked past her and out of the room.

The next day, Sarah sat on her bed swinging her foot back and forth, trying to plan her next steps. No matter what, it was time to get her own place. Or move in with Nan.

Mom had left to meet with a delivery truck to sort out a small order of produce. The tension from their argument still laced the air, but Mom hadn't voiced her opinion any further. Sarah sighed and chewed a ragged edge of her fingernail.

Her gaze found her latest selection from the library opened facedown on her bed to hold its place in Louis Zamperini's life story. What if . . . what if she could compile the store's life story? Bits from her life, and Mom's, and Nan's. Words from the people of Brighton who loved the place as much as she did. Newspaper clippings. Old photos. Maybe it wouldn't be enough to sway Mom into believing the store was worth Sarah investing in, but at the very least the scrapbook would make a nice gift for Nan.

When her perusal of the house yielded only an old photograph of Mom and Aunt Jessie as children standing in front of the store and another of Mom and Dad working the checkout counter, Sarah pulled down the attic access ladder and climbed.

At the top, she illuminated the attic space with her phone's flashlight. Ducking slightly, she passed the plastic bins of Christmas decorations. She shivered as a spider skittered away from her bright light. "I hope you don't have any friends up here."

She sifted through boxes and bins, looking through her childhood memorabilia — favorite outfits and homemade princess dresses. A faded child-sized version of the store apron. She pulled a little handprint Thanksgiving turkey from a stack of saved elementary school papers. The palm and thumb painted brown and each finger a different color. Sarah placed her adult hand over the print, her fingers stretching far past the turkey feathers. Stapled to it was another page titled "When I Grow Up." She traced her fingers over her unpracticed first grade handwriting. *I want to work at Old Depot and take care of the town just like Nan.*

She found another box to dig through. This one from later in life. She dug out her National Honor Society stole and mortarboard from her high school graduation. Beneath that was her slim yearbook. She flipped through the senior section, laughing at the silly memories she'd made. Brighton hadn't always been easy to live in, with the whole town always watching your every move, but there was something nice about living in a place where everybody really did know your name. She found her senior picture. Beside each photo was a place for favorite quotes and life goals. Sarah stared at the words printed beneath her name. *Life is either a daring adventure or nothing — Helen Keller.*

She slapped the book shut and stiffened. As much as she admired Helen Keller, her chosen senior quote didn't even fit the person she was. Sarah ground her teeth. It sounded like something her mother would have picked out for her.

A lot of life had happened between that little handprint and the woman she was today. What would that little girl who'd so carefully placed her painted hand so as not to smudge the printed turkey think about her now?

Sarah sighed and shook her head, placing everything back in the storage bin.

A large trunk sat separate from the rest, as if it had been exiled by its companions. Sarah sat in front of it next. Locked.

She dialed her dad's number. He answered on the third ring. "Hey, sweetheart. How are you faring?"

"I'm not bothering you, am I?"

"Not at all. Just stopped to eat. What's up?"

"I was picking through the attic, thinking about putting together a scrapbook about Old Depot for Nan, and I found this old trunk sitting by itself. It's locked."

"It's your mother's. She had me haul the heavy thing up there right when we moved in. I don't know what all she had in there. Things from her childhood, I reckon. I don't even know if she still has the key."

A locked box that Dad didn't even have access to? Sarah nudged the padlock. If Sarah cracked open the box, would she gain entry to the shut-away bits of her mother's heart and be able to draw them out? To finally understand why a mother who loved her daughter so much also worked so hard to keep her out of Brighton.

26

March 1983

Grandma and Granddad Hawthorne lived on a street lined with cottages that all looked the same except for the color. Matching stone front walks. Trellised gardens in the backyards.

Her grandparents were old and bent. Their expressions perpetually a bit resigned. Not at all how she'd pictured them based on Mom's sparse descriptions. Of how rigid and unyielding they were. Maybe that was true at one point, but now it appeared the years had not been kind. Or perhaps it was they who had not been kind to the years.

Today Rosemary knelt in her grandparents' flower garden, clearing out the debris from last year's blooms. Rosemary stood and brushed the dirt off her hands. When she'd appeared on their doorstep, they'd stared at her like she was a phantom figure.

"Rosemary," she'd said, trying to explain who she was to the elderly man in front of her. "Your granddaughter. Glory Ann's oldest."

Her grandmother stepped from behind her husband and grasped Rosemary's hands. Her grandmother's chin had quivered as she spoke. "We know who you are. Why have you come? What's happened to Glory Ann?"

"N-nothing's happened to my mother." Pent-up tears broke loose. "M-my father. I killed my father."

Eyes darting over her shoulder to the houses behind Rosemary, they pulled her into the house, wrapped her in a blanket, and filled her with hot tea until words followed, assuring them they weren't, in fact, harboring a fugitive.

And they'd let her stay. So she'd spent the past few days hiding away in Humboldt, trying to make herself useful. Momma had called. At least Rosemary assumed that was who was on the other line those times the phone rang and Grandmother's eyes would dart over Rosemary and she'd disappear around the corner, the coiled phone cord stretching tight. Her voice hushed.

On the way back inside the house, Rosemary trailed her hand over the intricate ironwork trellis. In the summer months, her grandmother insisted it supported an award-winning purple clematis. But in the cool almost-spring weather, it remained bare, with no promise of life.

Rosemary paused and glanced down the street to a little white house with yellow shutters. The cottage looked so similar to her grandparents' home. But there was something different about that place. A faraway and foggy memory she'd tried and failed to unearth.

She entered through the back door into a bright and sunny kitchen.

"Rosemary? Is that you?" Her grandmother tottered into the room.

"Yes, ma'am. Would you like me to put on the tea?"

The elderly woman glanced at the watch that hung on her necklace. "Indeed. It is that time." She glanced to Rosemary's dirt-stained hands and jeans. "Why don't you freshen up a bit and meet me in the dining room."

Rosemary climbed the stairs and entered what her grandparents said was her mother's old room. She couldn't tell by looking that it had ever belonged to anyone. It was nicely decorated in floral patterns and filmy curtains but retained an absolute lack of personal touches. A catalog photo room. Not the type of place someone could call theirs.

She switched out of her jeans into a tea-length skirt and blouse her old-fashioned grandmother would find more acceptable for afternoon tea.

She met her in the dining room.

"Well, that's much better, dear. But do remove that twig from your hair."

Rosemary dislodged the offending foliage. "How's Momma?"

Grandmother's rose-patterned teacup paused halfway to her lips. "Whatever do you mean?"

"I know you've spoken with her."

"If you are concerned about her well-being, you ought to go back home and see for yourself. She's sick about the way you left."

Rosemary shook her head. "I would only make it worse. She's not sick about me. She's sick about losing the love of her life."

Grandmother's teacup returned to its saucer. Tea splashed over the rim. "Love of her life?" Her brow arched and her voice raised an octave.

Rosemary tipped her head. "Of course. He was her husband."

Grandmother frowned. "You're a child. You don't know a thing about love or husbands and wives."

Heat pricked the back of Rosemary's eyes, and she choked on her tea as her throat convulsed. "Sometimes I'd sneak out of bed late at night when I couldn't sleep. I'd sit on the floor and peer around the corner into the kitchen. They'd stand side by side at the sink with the radio on. She'd wash and he'd dry." She bit the inside of her cheek, attempting to make her mind focus on that instead of the pain in her heart. "At some point along the way, a certain song would come on, and he'd take her soapy hands in his and they'd dance slow circles in the kitchen. She'd rest her head on his shoulders with her eyes closed, and it was like every worry melted away. Maybe I am a child, but if that's not what love looks like, then I don't want it."

As Rosemary spoke, the life-hardened lines in her grandmother's face relaxed. "Well, I'm sorry for her then, if she really had come to love him."

Rosemary gaped. *Come to love him*?

"Close your mouth. There's no flies to be caught in this house."

She snapped her mouth shut. "Why would she have married Daddy if she hadn't loved him?"

"People marry for a lot of reasons, none

of which I plan on discussing with you. Come now and let's drink our tea before it's so cold that we ought to just add ice to it and drink it with dinner."

Rosemary studied the woman in front of her as she sipped her tepid tea. There were traces of her mother, that no-nonsense way of speaking. But her mother was freer. Gentler with others, even though sometimes it seemed she was harder on Rosemary than the rest of the world. Was Daddy the one to credit for cultivating the sweeter qualities her mother possessed?

Even though her grandmother seemed reluctant to talk about her daughter, maybe she could help Rosemary solve another puzzle. "Have you always lived here?"

"Since the day I married your grandfather."

"And the little white house down the street. The one with the yellow shutters. Who lives there?"

"A young family with two little boys."

"And before that?"

"Another young family before they outgrew it. It's funny now, how people outgrow houses like clothes. It wasn't that way in my day."

Rosemary shook her head. "It's the strangest thing. I feel like I know it."

Grandmother's crepe-paper face paled, and she stared into her teacup. "That can't be so. The last time your mother brought you to visit me, you couldn't have been more than two. Must be some house back in your neck of the woods that looks similar, making you think that one stands out."

Grandmother was wrong. There were more memories struggling to surface. Sights and smells from the interior of the house. Beige shag carpet. Apple pie. And a dog. There had been a little hound dog there who laid his head on her lap and looked up at her with his droopy eyes. A living version of the figurine Momma gave her all those years ago. The one Daddy did his best to mend.

"I understand why you needed to get away, Rosemary. But I think it's time to go back to your mother."

Cool sweat broke out on Rosemary's forehead. "No, Grandmother, you didn't hear the way she —"

"I know better than most that words spoken out of fear and hurt can be the start of lifelong rifts between a mother and daughter." She stared into the leaves floating in the tea dregs, and then she fixed her gaze on Rosemary. Pain swam in her wrinkle-framed eyes. "You think more time apart will make this better, that it's what she wants. But time doesn't magically heal wounds all by itself. Sometimes hurt leaves a gaping place, and the only thing for it is to stitch it back together and learn to live with the scars."

Jessamine had chosen to return to school that morning, despite the fact that Glory Ann wasn't ready for life to fall into a routine. A routine meant accepting that this was their new normal. A life without Clarence.

Glory Ann had squeezed her youngest daughter tight and reminded Jessamine that if she needed to come home before the end of the day, she understood. She could call the moment it got to be too much. Her daughter had extracted herself from her embrace and with a resolute set to her shoulders, swung her pink backpack on her back and hurried to the waiting bus. Leaving Glory Ann alone. Waiting for Rosemary to come back home.

When Jessamine had told her where Rosemary had gone, Glory Ann refused to believe her mother's home, of all places, was where Rosemary had chosen to seek asylum. Thankfully her mother had called straightaway, informing Glory Ann of Rosemary's safe arrival. Glory Ann could only pray her mother refrained from speaking too much about the past. And that she was kind and loving, at least in the sparse way her mother knew.

Surely she wouldn't spill the truth, not when she had shunned her own daughter and granddaughter for years in efforts to bury the secret. This was not the time for Rosemary to discover that Clarence hadn't been her biological father.

Glory Ann sat in the kitchen, warm mug clasped between her hands, staring at the place Clarence always occupied at the round table for four.

What would Clarence do if it had been he who outlived her? He'd get up and go to the store. He'd serve the community. He'd "keep on keepin' on," as he used to say. He'd face the hard things head-on.

Glory Ann tidied the kitchen and then traded her bathrobe for her slacks and an Old Depot T-shirt. Palms sweating, Glory Ann tried not to think about what she'd face as she drove toward the store. The broken front glass that needed to be replaced. The food that spoiled while the store was closed. The . . . the blood staining the wood-planked floors.

Tremors shook her body as images from

that night played in her mind. Images the officer tried to shield her from, but she insisted on surveying, knowing her imagination would substitute reality with something far worse.

She should turn the car around. Board the place up. There would never be a day she'd be ready to face Old Depot without Clarence's steady strength by her side.

More images played in her mind. Clarence taking her hand that first day she walked through the door. Uncertain and sure all at the same time when he told her father he'd marry her. His quiet strength as he worked beside her. Not saying a word about the chill she sent his way or her halfhearted efforts. Or the childish way she willfully stocked items in incorrect places for weeks on end as Rosemary grew inside of her.

Years later she asked him why he'd been so kind to the woman who waged a passive war against him, and he'd said he'd known from the start that it wasn't really him she was fighting, but a war on foreign soil that neither of them could win. So he might as well be an instrument of peace in all of it.

Taking the last turn, Glory Ann then recited the prayer Clarence had so dearly loved — no — lived.

Lord, make me an instrument of your
  peace,
Where there is hatred, let me sow love;
Where there is injury, pardon;
Where there is doubt, faith;
Where there is despair, hope;
Where there is darkness, light;
Where there is sadness, joy.

The road blurred before her eyes, and she clutched the steering wheel, pulling off the side of the road. The words continued to whisper up from her soul, squeezing past the tightness in her throat, strangled by the sobs breaking through.

O Divine Master,
Grant that I may not so much seek
To be consoled as to console;
To be understood as to understand;
To be loved as to love.
For it is in giving that we receive;
It is in pardoning that we are pardoned;
And it is in dying that we are born to
  eternal life.

When her bone-rattling sobs subsided, Glory Ann straightened and sucked in a breath. Courage. She'd borrow Clarence's courage. He'd poured his heart and soul into this store to support their family. To serve his community. Glory Ann would carry on that legacy. She'd be a poor substitute, but she'd give it all she had. To be an instrument of peace for this community. For her daughters.

When she pulled into the parking lot of Old Depot, a shock wave shot through her. A crew of men worked together to fit the front window with a new pane of glass. The parking spaces were full.

When Glory Ann stood from her car, a slight feminine figure, clad in a green apron, appeared in the doorframe of the store. The stance uncertain. Yet sure. So much like Clarence.

Each took a halting step toward the other. Rosemary lifted a hand to shield her eyes from the sun, her stance lopsided.

The question in her posture so clear: Was she wanted? Loved?

Glory Ann hurried to her daughter and pulled her into her arms, stifling a sob. "I'm so glad you're home." She leaned back from the embrace, studying her face. "When did you get back? Why didn't you come home first?"

Rosemary yanked her gaze away. "I needed to be here. Do something. I-I let him d-down. And —"

Glory Ann shook her head. "I shouldn't

have said what I said. You're just a girl. One who is growing up and learning how to make your own choices. You couldn't have known the consequences. No one could have known. Please forgive me."

27

Present Day

Sarah followed the sound of rapid chopping. Her mother stood at the kitchen counter with her back to her, her favorite hen-print apron tied around her waist. Her arm pumping up and down, chopping with the deftness and speed of a professional chef.

"Mom?"

Her mother spun with her knife raised. "Sarah Lynne Anderson, you scared the daylights out of me!"

A corner of Sarah's mouth lifted at the use of her maiden name. "Sorry."

Her mother heaved a sigh that drooped her shoulders as she lowered the knife. "Me too."

"Can I explain? About the house?" She didn't want this anger between them. How well Sarah knew the brevity of life. There were so many things she should have said to Aaron. She didn't want to repeat her mistake, wasting the time she was allotted on this earth with anger between her and her mother.

"Sarah, I know you think I'm overbearing, but I'm trying to help you. I just know you'll regret settling for Brighton."

Sarah sat on one of the kitchen chairs. "There's nothing for me back in Kenilworth. I didn't have a job I loved. Sure, I served on a few charity organization boards, but it was just to fill empty time. An empty house. Empty hours. It's enough to make anybody lose their mind."

"It won't always be like that. You can't just shut away a part of your life and go on living."

"Isn't that what you did? With your dad? You've never talked about him." She didn't even keep his picture on the wall.

Her mother stiffened and she turned away, laying the knife down. She gripped the quartz countertop as if it kept her upright. "You don't know a thing about that. It doesn't compare at all."

"Doesn't it though? You lecture me about running away from my pain, but you won't even tell me about my own grandfather. It makes no sense."

"It's complicated."

"Grief is complicated. Don't oversimplify

mine and I won't oversimplify yours." She understood on some level why Mom was so tight-lipped. There were things about her relationship with Aaron she'd never share. About feeling love-starved and lonely. Her mother would never understand why she'd been planning to leave him that night.

Mom spent weeks on end never even seeing Dad, and Sarah had never once heard her complain.

Mom looked over her shoulder, one hand propped on her hip. "Fair enough. But can I say one more thing about selling the house?"

Sarah chewed her lip, bracing herself for her mother's words. She wanted to be able to hear her, not fight with her. She lifted a silent prayer asking for wisdom.

Mom stepped closer. "Grief is so consuming, especially in those early days. And what seems like a good idea at the moment might not look that way down the road. I just don't want you making an emotional decision and regretting it later. You chose that life in Chicago for a reason. It might not seem like it now, but you're going to want that back."

Air stuck in Sarah's lungs, making her chest grow tight and her pulse pound in her ears. She'd never want that life back. But maybe there was something she could say that would make her mother pull her closer. "I'm pregnant." The moment the words broke free she wanted to call them back.

Her mother stilled. "What did you say?"

Heat rose in Sarah's body, along with her nerves, dampening the fabric underneath her arms. "When I went to the doctor, I found out that was why my appetite has been so off."

"It's Aaron's?" Her mother's voice went up an octave.

Sarah grimaced and shook her head. "Of course it's Aaron's."

Her mother wrinkled her nose and shrugged. "You never know. People have secrets."

How much of those words were true about her mother? She couldn't fathom Rosemary Anderson having earth-shattering secrets in her life. But that locked trunk in the attic begged to differ. She glanced to the hook on the wall where Mom kept her keys.

Her mother walked to Sarah and bent to wrap her arms around her. "I know it's got to be scary thinking about raising this child alone. No wonder you're so insistent on moving back here. But, honey, you're going to be okay. I'll help you any way that I can, but please don't limit yourself just because you are afraid of the way your life is changing. Moving back here is not your only option."

But it was the only option she wanted. Sarah rested her head against her mother. "Thanks, Mom. I just really could use your support. Even if you don't agree with all my decisions. I need you in my corner."

Her mother straightened and wiped her eyes. "I can't wait to tell the whole town that I'm a grandmother."

"About that. I'm still adjusting to the idea myself, so if we could keep it under wraps for a little while longer?"

"Sure. Sure. It's your news to share. But you better tell me the instant I'm free to spill the beans. I've got a baby shower to plan."

Sarah stood from the table and helped her mother finish chopping vegetables for the soup. Maybe Mom would never be open to telling Sarah more about her grandfather, but maybe the start was getting her to open up to other areas of her life.

"Did you and Dad always only want one child?" Sarah had never minded being an only child, but sometimes she wouldn't have minded her mom's life management obsession to have had a little room to spread out among siblings.

Her mother glanced sideways. "I wanted to make sure I could give you my whole heart, Sarah." The ache lacing her tone perked Sarah's ears.

She put her arm around her mom. "I've never doubted, not for one minute, that you loved me." She smiled. "It was fun, telling my friends that my mom insisted that I was her favorite child. They'd look at me horrified that I said such a thing, until I told them I was your one and only."

Her mother glanced her way and gave what was probably intended to be a smile but came off more like a grimace. "When did I ever say that? About you being my favorite because you were an only child."

Sarah shook her head. "I meant it as a joke, just to see people's expressions when I said it."

"Oh." The single syllable was quiet.

Did Mom open up to anyone? Dad? Cathy? Or did she live isolated on some island inside her head?

Her mother went back to chopping potatoes with that same rapid-fire precision as before. Then she gasped. Her fingers splayed, dropping the knife with a clatter onto the cutting board. She clasped her cutting hand against her chest with the other.

Sarah grabbed a towel. "You cut yourself?

Here. Put some pressure on it."

Mom shook her head. Her eyes were wide. Her chest rising and falling in short, rapid breaths.

"Are you in pain? What do you need? Tell me what's wrong."

Her mother gave her a tight smile that did nothing to hide the worry in her eyes. "Just a little cramp." She kneaded her hand. "Would you mind finishing the vegetables? Just one more potato to go."

Before Sarah had a chance to answer, her mother disappeared from the room. She finished chopping the last potato and heated garlic and olive oil in the soup pot. As the garlic began to sizzle, fragrancing the air, she eyed the junk drawer beside the stove that had been taunting her ever since Mom's arrival had cut short Sarah's daylong search for the key. The catchall seemed as good a place as any for a key to a forgotten trunk.

She added the rest of the vegetables, sautéing them before she added the liquid ingredients to the soup. While everything cooked, she shuffled through the extra batteries, paper clips, sticky notes, screwdrivers. Various owner's manuals. Sarah laughed to herself. Who actually kept those things when you could look up everything you needed online?

She dug all the way to the back of the drawer, past stubby pencils and a multitude of Old Depot Grocery ink pens. Her fingertips found a lump in the paisley drawer liner. She lifted the edge, shifting the drawer's contents to reveal a skeleton key.

28

Present Day

The next morning, Sarah wandered to the kitchen, where her mom pulled a pan of biscuits from the oven. She placed the pan on a trivet and eyed Sarah's robe and messy bun. "Are you not coming to the store this morning?"

Sarah feigned a yawn and stretched. "I didn't sleep very well last night." Partially true considering all the time she spent imagining what Mom possibly kept in a locked trunk at the back of the attic. Her mind had run the gamut from childhood diaries to wild imaginings of her mother's secret life. Murder clues. Evidence her mother had gone into witness protection as a child. Not a helpful activity for warding off vivid pregnancy-induced dreams.

"I'm glad you're getting some rest. I've been trying to tell you to take it easy." She flicked a glance at Sarah's stomach that now had a bit of a curve to it, easily disguised by clothes unless you knew what you were looking for. "Now, maybe you'll listen to me."

Sarah shook her head and smiled as she sat. The shaft of the skeleton key in the hidden pocket of her yoga pants bit into her thigh.

"Have you told your dad yet?"

"No. Nan knows . . . well, has suspicions roused by her little gossip ring that I've yet to confirm. I thought I'd tell Dad the next time he's in. It feels like something I need to tell him in person."

"You know he's going to be over the moon. He loves kids."

Sarah leaned forward and propped her elbows on the table, resting her chin on top of her folded hands. "Really?"

"Oh yeah. He was an absolute fool around you as a baby. Crawling around on the floor, growling like a lion, pretending like he was going to gobble you up. You loved every second. He'll probably be trying to do it again with your little one, even with his bum knee giving him fits."

"Speaking of fits, how's your hand?"

The smile lines on her mother's face disappeared. "Fine. Just a little cramp, like I said."

Maybe, but it hadn't escaped Sarah's notice that Mom had eaten her entire meal left-handed instead of right.

Mom passed her a saucer with a perfect cathead biscuit in the center. "I noticed that you ate this more than everything else I'd been putting on the table."

Sarah smiled and cut the top off the biscuit, releasing curls of steam. She spread a thin layer of butter that melted into the crevices.

"Would you like some preserves? These are from the pear tree by the store."

Sarah accepted the jar. Pear wasn't her favorite, but it tasted like home.

"You'll probably be feeling better before you know it. Those food aversions will fade, and you'll probably feel like eating everything in sight. At least that's how I was when I was pregnant with you. Your grandmother threatened to put locks on the ice cream coolers more than once."

Sarah smiled, imagining a younger version of her mother sneaking through the aisles, spoon in one hand, the other resting on her burgeoning middle.

This pregnancy was not something Sarah had ever imagined she'd want, but in some strange way carrying Aaron's child was changing the way she thought about her marriage. Though she and Aaron had lost so many opportunities to love each other well, she still had the chance to love their child. And that gradually growing love was somehow healing.

Mom glanced at her watch. "I'd better go. I'm not in the mood to hear Momma's fussing if I'm late." She walked to the sink and grabbed a rag and dish soap.

Thank goodness. Sarah would've crept up to the attic last night if her mother wouldn't have thought a burglar was up there. "You cooked," she said. "I'll take care of the dishes."

"Sarah, it's fine. You need your rest."

"I said I was dragging a little this morning, not that I needed to be put on bed rest. I can handle a couple of plates, cups, and pans."

Sarah watched her mom pull out of the drive from the gap in the butter-yellow living room curtains. She paced the floor, letting minutes slip by, making sure her mom hadn't forgotten anything that would cause her to reappear while Sarah snooped through her life.

She shrugged out of her robe covering her yoga pants and T-shirt and pulled down the hideaway attic stairs. Armed with an LED camp lantern and the key, Sarah prepared to face whatever ghosts Mom kept interred.

The piercing bright light illuminated the dark space, casting long swaying shadows as Sarah crossed the small attic.

She'd known from the moment she spied the trunk pushed off by itself that the locked box couldn't be Dad's. Bo Anderson wasn't the type to keep things locked away, always forthcoming with answers to any questions Sarah had. Unless, of course, her questions crossed the carefully maintained borders between Dad's past and Mom's. At which point he'd say, "That sounds like a question for your mother." Then Sarah and her dad would exchange looks, knowing just how well that would go. Pieces of her parents' histories left incomplete, like a book with the middle chapters ripped out.

Sarah squared her shoulders and fit the key into the lock. It turned easily, and the hinged lid opened without a creak.

Sarah crouched, peering inside. There were little pink journals. Childhood artwork done in crayon. Little stick figure families with rainbows and houses. Sometimes pictures of the store. Mom always drew herself with a dark, drab crayon. Her sister and Nan were always vibrant pinks and greens on the opposite of the page from Rosemary and her dad, who always held little Rosemary's hand and was drawn taller than the buildings or the trees or any other structure.

Had distance always existed between the two women Sarah loved most in the world?

Mom and Nan bickered, but she'd always known Nan loved Mom. She'd see them arguing one minute, and then in another minute, she'd catch Nan looking at her daughter with pride and love shining in her eyes, watching Mom work with a customer or handle a delivery.

Sarah lifted away the layer of crayon drawings and sat cross-legged on the floor, flipping through journals. Most were Mom's childhood logs of ordinary days in a rural town. Stories about so-and-so's goats getting loose and being found standing on top of a neighbor's car. Records of store gossip she'd heard while, no doubt, dusting bottom shelves just as Sarah had done to earn allowance money.

She came to a page that made her pause. There were only three words. The letters bold and jagged, like the one who penned them ground the graphite into the paper. *I HATE HER.*

Who? Nan? Aunt Jessie? And why? It was obvious from the other journals and drawings that she and her sister fought. That young Rosemary often saw their family split into sides. Whether that was an accurate portrayal or a child's skewed perspective, Sarah couldn't be certain. But one thing she was sure about, the words on the page chilled her heart.

It was as though, even after all this time, the page still bore the weight of the hand that had scratched those words into the paper.

A few pages later, she found her answer.

Dear Diary,
This morning when I came to the table, the little porcelain dog was there. He wasn't like before. Little chips where it used to be cool and smooth. Cracks filled with glue. Momma wanted to throw away the pieces that night, but Daddy fixed him the best he could. I wish I could go back. I would have hidden him where he could be safe, not put him on display on that little shelf. Don't they know Jessamine broke him on purpose? She didn't get in trouble, not even a little bit. I don't really hate her though. I wish we could be friends, but she makes it so hard.

Rosemary Clearwater

Sarah's mind flashed back to the ugly

porcelain dog she'd found tucked behind all the chicken figurines lining the tops of Mom's cabinets.

Sarah lifted away more journals. Beneath she found an 8x10 photograph of a man she only recognized from her grandmother's walls. Her granddad Clarence. There was something about his gentle expression that told her he was the type of person people wanted to know.

She found another yellowed photo. This one was loose, free from any frame. It had to have been taken inside Old Depot. Granddad Clarence wore a green apron and there was a curly-haired blonde girl on his shoulders. The child's head was thrown back as if in midlaughter. Her tiny frame certainly made him look like the giant figure little Rosemary had immortalized in crayon.

Why wouldn't her mother want this image on display? The obvious love and joy on both of their faces made Sarah smile just looking at it. There were a few more. Some from Christmas, Granddad Clarence wearing a misshapen sweater that Sarah could only guess little Rosemary knit herself.

Underneath the photos she unearthed a crumpled manila folder packed full. She unwound the string, a figure-eight wrap between the two white buttons. The envelope was stuffed with newspaper clippings. Sarah carefully slid them free and spread them out on the floor.

Stories about an arrest and trial. A robbery turned homicide. Sarah's eyes widened. She'd known Granddad Clarence had died unexpectedly in an accident of some sort, but she hadn't realized his life had come to such a violent end. At the store, of all places.

She was surrounded by headlines about the robbery that had taken her grandfather's life. Stories about the man who'd broken into the store to steal cold medicine and other supplies to make crystal meth. Sarah shuddered at the details that even the town of Brighton had chosen to forget. No one spoke about this piece of her family history. At least, not in Sarah's presence. And Mom had it all preserved in black-and-white newsprint. Why?

The other articles were a tribute to the man her grandfather was. Honoring the way he'd helped the community. Bringing groceries to the elderly in bad weather. Extending credit to families in hard times. Testimonies of how his generosity had touched so many lives. Other stories talked of his integrity and wisdom.

That drug addict took away her chance to

meet Granddad Clarence, but in some ways her mother had been just as guilty. Robbing Sarah of knowing someone who had been so precious to her mother. Why? Grief? Because it hurt too much to remember?

She continued reading and froze when she read the last article.

> My friend Clarence Clearwater and I were having a late-night dinner, talking over improvements to the town. We drove by his store after a couple of other local business owners came in the diner talking about an odd fellow wandering around town, looking in windows. Clarence jumped up and I, of course, followed.
>
> He drove, taking curves on two wheels. I begged him to tell me what was going on. Why he'd taken out of the diner like that.
>
> When we stopped in front of the store, we saw a shadow moving inside the darkened store. He jumped out of his car and ran for the front door. I called out for him to wait. To call the police. That the store wasn't worth risking his life.
>
> He looked back at me and said, "My daughter is in there."
>
> Those were the last words he ever said to me.

Sarah pressed her hand to her chest as if applying counterpressure to the ache could diminish the pain.

She kept digging through the trunk until she scraped the wooden bottom. Tucked flat against the side was an envelope, blackened on one of the edges, addressed to Glory Ann Clearwater.

29

June 1986

Rosemary sat in the cramped office, running through the numbers — again — with the same result. They were short of what they'd expected to sell, for some reason. Which meant food wasted, product lost, and profits not made. She sighed and rubbed her grainy eyes.

Things had been rough at the store since Dad died three years ago. Not just because their family kept trying to walk forward despite the gaping hole in its middle with two daughters who'd graduated high school and had to step into their adult lives without their father's presence.

The recession hit. They almost lost the store. Dad had always been the one to take care of the books. Mom was a whiz with the customers, but she made a mess of the numbers in the best of times.

Now bookkeeping and orders were Rosemary's domain. Things had been on an upswing for a while, but the drought had produce prices going through the roof. Just like with the recession, it left people gravitating toward dried goods and canned meat.

If she lowered the produce prices, the store wouldn't profit. If she ordered less to compensate for the lack of sales, her farming neighbors would suffer. The only solution was to lower the prices just the right amount so that the farmers still made something and she didn't bankrupt Old Depot. It's what her dad would have done.

Rosemary sighed and pushed away from the desk. Jessamine had managed to finally make her escape. After the Chernobyl disaster, she'd run off and joined Greenpeace. She was off crusading to save the world, while Rosemary was simply trying to keep one country grocery store afloat.

Outside of the office, the store hummed with life. Mothers pushing carts with squirmy, plump babies on their hips. Mom ran the register while Bo bagged groceries, occasionally loading the bags into cars for half-dollar tips. How she loved to tease him about the way he jingled when he walked. All the elderly ladies in town were half in love with him.

When she passed by, Bo nodded and gave

her a small smile. She touched the blue thread tied around her left ring finger.

Bo tied the thread there after church last Sunday while they sat on a picnic blanket by Eagle Creek. When he finished tying the knot, he gave her a small smile and said, "You don't have to answer. Just think about it, will ya?"

The strangest almost proposal she'd ever heard of, and she hadn't been afraid to tell him so. But she hadn't taken it off either.

The bells clanked against the glass as Rosemary exited the store. The sun was warm and comforting after sitting in that dim office. Bo was a good guy. But she was young yet. There was time. There was more life to see and experience before she settled down.

When exactly she'd venture out and taste and see this fuzzy unformed ideal of life, she wasn't sure.

Rosemary sat on the bench on the front walk and lifted her hand to wave as Ms. Paulette approached the store.

"How's your sister, dear?"

"Oh, just fine, I imagine. We don't hear from her too often lately."

"I don't know what I think about all that environmentalism hype."

Rosemary shrugged in answer. It was

important to Jessamine. And she agreed that people should do a better job caring for this world, but she wouldn't mind if taking care of their little home front was a little higher on Jessamine's value scale, giving Rosemary her own chance to discover life outside of Brighton. But Momma needed her now. And that might not ever change.

A hot breeze licked at her cheek, tugging tendrils of hair free from her ponytail. She bounced her knee.

Despite the fact that Bo said he wasn't in a hurry, he'd want an answer soon. Bo was safe, which was in his favor in Rosemary's opinion. If Lynyrd Skynyrd needed a muse for their song "Simple Man," Bo fit the bill. But whenever she looked in his eyes, she could hear Jessamine's voice needling at her. *He's a small-town country boy. Don't you want somebody who'll challenge you? Push you outside your comfort zone? Someone who wants more than all this?*

Problem was, Rosemary was caught somewhere in between. Between relishing life in Brighton and the idea of raising a family in a little house with a picket fence and feeling like there was more out there. That nagging sense that she was always two steps behind.

The familiar white jeep with its red and blue stripe bounced into the lot. Two o'clock on the dot, just like always.

The mailman pulled alongside her and mopped his forehead before digging in the bin beside him. Mr. Clark's wild, bushy gray hair always made her think of him as a long-lost cousin of Albert Einstein.

"Afternoon, Rosemary! Fine day, isn't it?"

"Yes, sir," Rosemary said, looking over her shoulder to hide her grin. Rain, sleet, snow, or blazing hot, he always said the same thing.

"Here you go. Have a good one. Tell Glory Ann I said hey."

She waved as he drove away then walked back to the store, flipping through the mail. The old bachelor was probably sore at her for intercepting him before he put the mail in Momma's hands. Daddy had been gone for three years. Whenever people thought they were out of earshot, they'd whisper that Momma was young yet and ought to remarry. But Mr. Clark? He was about twenty years too old for her. Besides, Momma had loved Daddy so much her heart didn't have room for anyone else.

Rosemary went back to the office to sort through the bills. Stuck in the middle was a letter envelope. Addressed to Momma, no return address. Since it had come to the store it was most likely a thank-you letter from one of the local farmers who supplied produce. She slid her finger beneath the seal and pulled out a piece of notebook paper. It was a letter written to Momma, dated June 25, 1986.

Rosemary's hands tightened on this letter full of longing and regret. Who was Jimmy? Who was this version of Glory Ann he spoke of? The Glory Ann Rosemary knew loved one man with her whole heart. This Jimmy spoke of mistakes. Of a relationship gone too far. Of lost years.

Momma had been unfaithful? Air lodged in Rosemary's throat. The last letter this Jimmy said he'd written was five years ago. Her father had been in the prime of his life then. Whatever this thing was between Momma and this man, it had happened while Daddy was alive.

The band around her chest tightened. Apparently, the same woman who'd railed at Rosemary about honesty the night after her father's funeral had secrets of her own. Big secrets.

One thing she knew for sure and certain, she would not allow this stranger to swoop in and try to take her father's place.

Rosemary restuffed the envelope and hurried back to the office. She struck a match, watching the flame flare and settle. With a shaking hand she held the match to the edge of the envelope. Just as the corner of the paper blackened, she blew it out and sank into the desk chair, chest heaving. Destroying this letter meant never learning the truth when she'd finally worked up the courage to hear it. But confronting her mother about the contents could bring this interloper into their lives.

30

August 1986

Glory Ann waved over Carson, the new butcher she'd hired last week, who'd just arrived for his afternoon shift. The last one had retired with his wife to Florida. Quite a change from the years he'd spent working in a refrigerated room where he trimmed and packed meat at the request of the store's patrons. She grinned. Maybe the gruff man would finally thaw out a little.

Carson, the new fellow, was young and eager for work. He'd be a good fit for the place.

"Yes, ma'am. You needed something?"

Glory Ann pulled an envelope from her apron pocket. "I just got another letter from Jessie. You remember her from school, don't you? Here she is on a Georgia beach, helping with conservation efforts." She passed a photo into his large hands. "She's so busy, you know. She's got that job at the research company that she volunteered with, and she's decided to go to college, after all. I'd always imagined my girls staying close to home, but my Jessamine was born with wings. I guess I always knew that."

Glory Ann glanced up. Carson's face stretched in a smile, but his eyes were as glazed as the donuts in the bakery case. She scrunched her nose. "Goodness. Sorry about the rambling. I get carried away when I brag about my girls."

From the register came a huff. Rosemary's back was turned to her as she rang up Cora Smith's groceries.

Glory Ann hurried to Cora. "Cora, look, I just got another letter from Jessamine." She would understand. Her son had gone away to college and had a new life in some big city she couldn't remember the name of.

She and Cora swapped stories about their far-flung children and all their exciting adventures. Cora smiled. "John keeps trying to get me to come for a visit, but even the thought of driving on those busy highways breaks me out in hives."

Glory Ann smiled politely, working hard to keep the corners of her mouth from trembling. Jessie had never asked her to come for a visit, but that was probably just because she knew how hard it would be for her to get away from the store.

She glanced at Rosemary, whose face was stony. Glory Ann sighed, a fruitless attempt to shove the weight off her chest. One daughter lived a thousand miles away, and somehow the one across the counter from her felt even more distant these days.

After their falling out after Clarence's death, she'd thought they'd made their peace. But a couple of months ago, something shifted, bringing a glacial chill between them. When Glory Ann asked her what was bothering her, Rosemary denied anything to be amiss.

Cora said her goodbyes and their new stock boy, Morrow, scurried to the front of the store to help her load her groceries. Glory Ann chuckled. Everybody knew Cora was a good tipper.

Glory Ann stepped closer to her daughter. "I love you, Rosemary."

Rosemary froze and lifted her eyes. Her lips twitched, and she pushed a heavy breath from her chest. "I know you do. I love you too."

Rosemary's gaze went over Glory Ann's shoulder when a quiet rumble filled the air. "The dairy delivery is here. I'm going to go out back and settle up if you'll take over the register. Send Joey or Morrow back to help me get everything stocked."

Glory Ann turned and saw the other reason for her sudden retreat. Bo Anderson, having just emerged from his car, stood speaking to a customer, most likely chatting about the nice weather they'd been having. Why Rosemary wouldn't give that boy an answer she'd never understand. Either give him a no and let him go or make the leap and say yes. Why was that lovesick boy still hanging around on a maybe, anyway? Couples these days, they didn't have a clue the way things used to be.

Rosemary carefully rocked the two-wheeled hand truck side-to-side, attempting to work it over the hump of the doorsill without upsetting the too-tall tower of milk crates she'd stacked in her aggravated state.

At least back here she'd escaped all Momma's prattling. Momma touted Jessie's accomplishments like she was some sort of hometown hero. Did the daughter who stayed behind get any credit?

But then again, she'd always played second fiddle to her sister, so why should it be any different now? Thoughts of the secret letter Rosemary had stuffed in the bottom of her keepsake trunk pricked at her mind.

Daddy had always been in Rosemary's

corner. Maybe it was because he knew what it was like to be someone's second choice too. How could Momma have claimed to love Daddy and receive a letter like that? A letter that hinted at an improper relationship with some man who wasn't her husband.

Why did Mom love the ones who didn't stay by her side more than the people who were actually there for her?

"Joey?" She called for the young stock boy whom she'd left filling the milk cooler with the last load she'd brought in. Nothing. He probably had his Walkman clipped to his hip, metal blasting in his headphones, even though she'd told him not to bring it to work anymore.

Her efforts to ease the wheels over the doorsill were useless. She yanked. The tower swayed to the left, and she braced herself for the sound of milk jugs bursting on the concrete floor of the stockroom. Out of her peripherals, two hands appeared, stopping the sliding crate.

Bo's quiet laugh filled her ears. "Fill the hand truck too high again?"

She stepped back to give him room to work. Her ears burned and she shrugged as Bo guided her haul over the hump. "Did you come to escape my mom fawning all over Jessie's latest accomplishments too?"

He gave her a small smile and shook his head. "Just to give you a hand. May I?"

"You won't catch me arguing. You know Mom was getting on my nerves if I volunteered to deal with the dairy order to escape."

Bo released a low, quiet laugh.

Rosemary fixed a haughty expression on her face and flicked her wrist, putting on mock airs. "Oh, don't even pretend like you wouldn't be falling head over heels for Jessamine just like everybody else if she was around."

He rolled his eyes skyward. "Ya think so, huh?"

"Who doesn't? Nobody even notices that I have brought this store back to life on more than one occasion. But you don't see me getting standing ovations for that."

Bo nudged her shoulder with a tender smile. "I don't care what you say. If Jessie were here, I'd still be trailing after you like a lovesick pup."

"Why?"

"Because I like you. Because you are dedicated and loyal. Because you are strong, and you don't fall apart when things get tough. Because you're you. So if you thinking you're second choice to Jessamine is what's holding you back from giving me a real answer, rest assured, it's always been you, Rosemary, ever since you chased down my car and demanded I give that stolen ice back. Maybe you feel invisible, but I see you, Rosemary Clearwater."

Rosemary's pulse pounded at the heartfelt outpouring of words from the backward boy who tied a string around her finger instead of asking her outright.

"So, if you just don't see us ever getting married, I need to know. I said take your time, but good grief, woman, it's been two months. Put me out of my misery and reject me. I'll take it on the chin. But if you're just scared that I'm not sincere, then put your mind at rest."

He straightened the hand truck to upright and bent on one knee. "Tell me once and for all, Rosemary Clearwater. Will you be my wife?"

She hid her trembling lips behind her hand and nodded.

He moved to pull the blue string she still wore around her finger, now faded to gray.

"Leave it. I don't need a different ring."

"You need something that will last as long as we will, and that string just won't do." He pulled a ring box from his pocket and popped it open. A round diamond solitaire nestled in the velvet.

She laughed. "Did you actually plan this? To propose to me in the storeroom of this shabby old store?"

He grinned. "I tried to the other day when we were laid back looking up at the stars, but you changed the subject to this week's delivery schedule. So I thought you were dropping hints."

She punched his shoulder. "I oughta tell you no just for that."

He slid the ring on her finger. "Nah. Rosemary, this place seems just right."

Bo stood and placed a hand on her cheek. "What's that sad look in your eye?"

There was no way she was answering that. She leaned in, finding his lips with hers, losing herself in the kiss. Turning off all her thoughts and worries. At least for the moment.

Out-of-tune whistling reached her ears. She and Bo broke off their kiss as Joey appeared through the doorway, bopping his head to whatever music blared in his ears. He removed his headphones. "I finished stocking the last load, what's taking so long?" Completely oblivious to Bo and Rosemary wrapped in an embrace.

Bo cleared his throat and stepped from Rosemary. "Joey, we've got it covered back here. I saw Ms. Mable come in a little bit ago. If you hurry, she might still be here. She gives almost as good tips as Ms. Cora."

Joey perked and smiled. "Hey, thanks. You sure you don't mind?"

Bo grinned wide. "I've got more important business to attend to. You enjoy that extra half dollar."

Rosemary hid her own smile behind her hand as the skinny kid scurried off.

Bo wrapped his arms around her. "Now, where were we?"

"About to get this milk in the cooler before it all ruins." She tried and failed to sound no-nonsense.

He touched his forehead to hers. "The milk can wait one more minute, I think."

31

Present

Sarah walked through the wooded area of the community park. The raucous cheers from the town's Little League fields competed with the buzz filling her mind.

Her waking and sleeping had become consumed with the letter she'd found in the bottom of Mom's trunk. So full of love and heartache. Who was Jimmy? And why did Mom have this letter that wasn't addressed to her buried in her trunk?

Had Nan even seen it?

"Sarah!"

She paused, searching for the voice calling out her name. Libby sat on a blanket with little Caroline on her lap. She was waving Sarah over. The twins rolled a ball to each other while an older child kept watch. Sarah left the path and cut across the grass.

"Hey, girl. Out for a walk?" Libby motioned to the older girl standing beside the twins. "This is my oldest, Cheyanne. Chris is playing ball tonight and Ben is coaching. I hate to miss him playing, but the littles needed a quick run around."

"Hi, Cheyanne." Sarah lifted her hand in a small wave at the girl who had the gangly look of a preteen who'd just gone through a growth spurt.

Cheyanne smiled shyly and waved back.

Libby put the baby down to let her crawl and walked to Sarah. "I meant to ask you the other day how long you were planning to stay in town."

Sarah bit her lip. "Don't bring it up with my momma, but I'm making it a permanent arrangement."

Libby's eyes went wide. "Really? I figured this little old town was boring after all you've seen. Your momma was always flashing around pictures of places you've been. Everything from that temple thing in Thailand with all that gold and the Taj Mahal to Big Ben and the Eiffel Tower. Honey, I got more of a geography lesson from your momma than I ever did in school." Libby grinned. "She's proud as a peacock about you."

Sarah grimaced. "Please tell me she's not still going on about that." It had been years since those college summers with Aaron's family.

"She's always telling us something about — Charlie, Chance, stop that right now."

Sarah's head swiveled to the twins who were tugging the ball between them.

"Caroline, no!" Cheyanne cried out, hovering over the baby, who'd crawled off the blanket. Cheyanne attempted to pry a rock from Caroline's fist that the baby seemed determined to shove in her mouth. "Momma! Caroline's eatin' rocks again."

Sarah went to Cheyanne's aid while Libby settled the squabble between the boys. When Cheyanne slipped the rock free from the baby's hand, Sarah swooped Caroline up and twirled her in a circle to distract her.

Libby walked over to her after she settled the mild disagreement between her boys. She shrugged with a sheepish smile. "Sorry." She took Caroline out of Sarah's arms. "Just to give you fair warning, this kind of interruption-filled conversation is par for the course being friends with a mom."

Libby might think she was a mess, but Sarah saw experience and calm despite intermittent chaos. The kind of person she wanted to navigate this new phase of life with. Sarah wound a strand of hair around her finger, watching the light reflect in her gold strands, as she summoned courage. "Actually, I'm about to join the club in about six months." She shrugged. "Think you could show me the ropes? I-I'm a little out of my depth with all this." She let out a shaky laugh and placed a hand on her stomach.

Libby gasped and then pulled Sarah into a hug, squishing poor Caroline between them. "You're pregnant? Oh, Sarah, you're gonna be an amazing momma."

Something about the way Libby said those words made Sarah believe her just a little bit, and a smile found its way to her lips. "You really think so?"

Libby stepped back from the embrace and flicked her wrist. "Girl, you've got this. And I'm here to stop you from buying all those senseless things everybody tells you that you need." A crease appeared between her eyebrows. "I'm sure this was never how you imagined having your first baby, but this little one is going to be a beautiful thing in your life, I just know it." She squeezed Sarah's shoulder.

Sarah sat down on the blanket beside Libby, watching her kids play. Libby quizzed her on all her pregnancy symptoms, things Sarah had tried to ignore. Libby pulled out her phone, punched in Sarah's due date and read all about the baby's development so far. As Libby gushed over each little change Sarah had been experiencing, Sarah couldn't help the wide grin taking over her face. There really was a little person growing in there. A little person who'd have their own hopes. Dreams. And she knew in that moment, she'd do anything in her power to help her child reach them.

Libby stood and started packing toys in her oversized bag. "Well, we better get back to Chris's game and catch the ending of it. I'm glad you told me about the baby, Sarah. Call me anytime you are tempted to freak out about bringing a new life into this crazy ol' world. I've got your back."

Sarah stood and helped Libby pack her things away.

"We're going out for pizza after the game. You should join us."

Sarah dug in her purse for her phone to check the time, her fingers brushing the letter that had brought her to the park in the first place.

"I'd better not. I told Nan I'd close up so that she can meet up with a couple of her friends this evening."

Sarah watched Libby and her children walk to the ball fields before finding a nearby park bench.

She pulled out the letter to read it again.

June 25, 1986

Dear Glory Ann,

It's been five years since the letter I sent to your parents. I could only assume your lack of response meant that you had no interest in seeing me again. I can't say I blame you. It was selfish, inserting myself into your life all over again.

And maybe it's wrong — this throbbing ache in my heart that sneaks up on me sometimes in the quiet watches of the night, dreaming of this life that should have been mine. The stack of if-onlys I carry in my heart are taller than the water tower in Humboldt.

I'm sorry. I shouldn't say these things. As brief as it was, we had a beautiful romance, Glory Ann. I know we made a mistake, took our relationship to a place it shouldn't have gone. Maybe it's not right, but the truth is, the memory of you in my arms kept me going so many days when I'd done my best to snuff out what was left of my miserable life.

I'd like to see you. Just to say hello. I know that it can't be anything more than that. But, in full disclosure, I hope it doesn't shock you to know that I've never stopped loving you.

Always,
Jimmy

"Mrs. Clearwater?" The produce delivery driver holding the clipboard shifted his feet.

"Yes, Warren?" Glory Ann had known this was coming. At least Rosemary wasn't there to crow "I told you so."

Their fresh food orders had been lighter and lighter over the past several months. Dry goods weren't as much of a problem. If they didn't sell, they had a long shelf life. But fruits and vegetables wouldn't keep, and their orders had matched their dwindling sales.

"Boss said that if we have orders dipping under a certain amount, we're going to have to stop delivering. It's nothing personal. It's just costing us more than we're making."

This was like times before when the economy was bad and people bought canned and dried goods only, but this time their lack of sales had nothing to do with the economy and instead was a lack of demand. They could get in-season stock from local farmers, but with a limited produce section, people would be even less motivated to shop there.

She patted Warren on the shoulder. "Thank you for telling me. I'll miss you stopping in." She handed him the sack lunch she always made up for him as a thank-you.

Maybe Rosemary could think something up. Some way to overcome this new setback like all the times before. She could if she wanted to. Glory Ann was sure of it.

After Warren drove away, Glory Ann wandered back into the empty store, the wood creaking beneath her feet. The only trouble was, she could no longer discern the message of those old floors. Was the two-beat creak urging her to hang on or let go?

Pain throbbed in her chest. They'd bulldoze it in a heartbeat. This place where her children had grown into women. Where she'd watched her granddaughter play. This place that had kept a community fed in good times and lean times. Dependable and true, so much like the man who took this wasted place — this abandoned train depot — and made it into a place where people nourished their families.

She walked into the office and slumped into the desk chair. And if she and Rosemary didn't have the store pushing them together, what would they have left when it was gone?

Lord, what should I do? I can't keep going like this. But I can't help feeling like I'm giving up.

She sighed. If there was some way Clarence could look down from heaven and see the state of things, she sure hoped she didn't disappoint him.

The front bells chimed, and Rosemary came through the door.

"Rosemary?"

Her daughter lifted her head. The streak of silver in her blonde hair catching in the sunlight. Weariness creased the corners of her eyes. "What is it, Mom?"

"We need to talk."

Rosemary heaved a breath. "Yes. Yes, we do. But what I'm about to tell you, you have to promise me you won't tell Sarah."

32

March 1987

Rosemary sat on the living room couch admiring the sparkle of her ring — the way the incandescent-light lamp refracted in the many facets. This was the life she wanted. Maybe Momma wanted the people who left her. Rosemary would be different. She'd treasure the people who stayed.

Bo entered the room with two glasses of cola. "Popcorn is popping. When's your mom getting home? Think she'll want to join us?"

"Depends on the movie. What'd you get?"

"*Platoon.* I know war movies aren't exactly your favorite, but you said tonight was my choice. I lived through *Sixteen Candles* last week."

"Momma's not a big fan of war movies either, but she might join later."

He sat beside her, scooted close, and wriggled his eyebrows. "Then we better get the smooching done now."

She gave him a sly smile and bounced up from her seat. "I just heard the microwave beep. Nothing worse than soggy popcorn."

Rosemary scurried for the kitchen and Bo chased after her. "Come back here!"

Her sock feet skated when she reached the linoleum, and he grasped her arm to keep her from falling. He pulled her close with a roguish grin. "Caught ya."

She gave him a doe-eyed innocent smile, then poked him in his ribs. He jerked to cover his ticklish side, letting go of her. "You rat!"

Almost doubling over with laughter, she retrieved the popcorn from the microwave. "Eating popcorn while it's fresh and hot is a serious matter."

"Noted, Mrs. Anderson."

She scowled, a struggle considering the way her face wanted to stretch into a smile. "Not Mrs. Anderson yet."

"Speaking of which, isn't it about time to set a date?" He knelt on one knee in front of her with big puppy dog eyes and hands clasped under his chin while she poured popcorn into a big glass bowl. "Please, please, pretty please, let's not drag this engagement out any longer."

She popped a hot, buttery kernel into her

mouth. "Not my fault you waited so long to properly propose. A 'Hey, think about it, will ya?' was not a proposal, Bo Anderson."

Rosemary grabbed his hand and tugged it until he stood.

"So, I have a lot to learn," he said. "I'm a willing student. I'll shop for flowers and invitations with you. Menus. Cakes. The whole works."

"We should elope."

His eyes went wide. "Now?"

"No, you goof. When we have everything in order a little. Where we're going to live and all that."

He slapped his hand over his heart. "Oh, okay. You scared me a little bit. I thought the real Rosemary had been abducted by aliens or something."

"Well, I think you're not the real Bo. Groveling on one knee. Committing to flower shopping."

"Ever since you told me yes, I've had my head in the clouds."

She brushed a kiss to his cheek. "Don't change. Promise we can live with our heads in the clouds from now 'til forever."

They settled on the burnt orange couch, popcorn bowl between them.

Not long into the movie, Rosemary found herself staring either at her lap or into the popcorn bowl. After a brutal scene, Bo glanced at her, brow furrowed. "I'm sorry. I didn't realize this movie was so . . . so dark. We can turn it off."

An explosion sounded from the television and Rosemary flinched. "Do you think this is what Vietnam was really like?"

"Turn that movie off this instant."

Rosemary and Bo turned in their seats. Momma stood rigid. Face blanched white. Hands curled in shaking fists, clamped to her sides.

"Th-that . . . that language is filthy. I" — she drew a shaky breath — "I don't want to hear words like that in my house. Ever again." She stalked from the room, and her bedroom door shut with a thud.

Bo looked at Rosemary with knit brows. "I'm so sorry."

Glory Ann sat on her bed, folded in half with her arms around her middle, trying to find her breath. Those images burned into her mind. The gore. The hatred. The darkness.

There had been so little information about what happened to Jimmy in Vietnam.

She scrubbed her hands over her face, trying to erase what she'd seen on her television screen. That man, blinded by shrapnel. The merciless way his enemy unloaded his gun, while his fellow human being was so defenseless.

It wasn't fair that the last image the boy who used to write her poems about springtime and the unfolding of flowers had of this world was so full of cruelty and hate. He couldn't have become like those soldiers portrayed on the screen. Could he? Or was that the real horror of war? The way it altered everybody beyond recognition, stealing people's souls and everything that made them who they were.

Shoulders shaking with sobs she tried to muffle, Glory Ann prayed for God to take these thoughts and images from her mind. She prayed for the men who'd survived the nightmare to come home to be fathers and husbands.

How? How could they find normal after that? Love when they'd been baptized in hate. It had been almost twenty-two years since she'd heard the news of Jimmy's death, and the images of war still sent her running to her room to escape it. How much worse it must be for those who actually lived it.

A light tap sounded on her door.

Glory Ann swiped at her face and took a few deep breaths. "Come in."

Rosemary opened the door slowly. "I'm really sorry. Bo is too. He didn't realize that movie was so rough when he picked it from the video store."

Glory Ann's mouth opened, filled with a sudden urge to explain that she hadn't been entirely truthful, that it wasn't the foul language that had affected her so much. But then she clamped her lips tight. Jimmy was gone. Telling Rosemary about him wouldn't fix anything.

"Please, watch the ratings on what you bring home. Garbage in, garbage out. You know that's always been the house motto."

"Yes, ma'am."

"Is Bo still here?"

"No, he went ahead and left."

"I didn't mean to ruin your time together. I just wanted that movie turned off."

Rosemary wavered by the door. "You're looking a little pale. Can I bring you some tea or something?"

"I think I'm going to go on to bed. It's just been a really long day."

"Okay." Rosemary backed toward the door. "I love you, Mom."

"I love you too." Why did their "I love yous" always come out like that? Like a reassurance rather than a declaration?

Alone again, she went to her closet and

pulled out the hatbox she'd tucked way in the back. On her bed she laid out Jimmy's high school picture. His high school ring. The tiny packet of wildflower seeds that he'd given her the last day they'd been together. "When I get back, we'll plant them on that little plot right over there," he'd said as he pointed across to the other side of the cornfield. "My grandfather said that it's ours if we want it."

She ran her fingers over the edge of the seed packet. *I wonder if they'd grow after all this time.*

She tucked everything back in the box, pushing away her foolish notions and the ache burning in her chest.

33

Present Day

Sarah stepped onto the wide lawn in the center of town where the members of Brighton Community Church congregated for their yearly homecoming picnic. Nan and Mom stood shoulder to shoulder, rearranging congregant contributions at the long folding tables that nearly sagged with the number of casserole dishes covering every square inch. Sarah brought her pair of two-liters to the drink station and did a quick scan of the crowd.

Libby stood with Caroline on her hip, talking to another mother. Small children tumbled at their feet. A few other women, younger than Sarah, stood nearby with toddlers and babies in their arms. Libby, who must have sensed Sarah observing, smiled and waved her over.

Sarah crossed the lawn to the small group of women, trying to shake off the sensation that she intruded on a world she didn't yet belong to.

"Sarah, this is Jessica. Pastor Gary is her daddy. She graces us with her presence every now and then when she comes to visit."

"Hi, Sarah. I'd shake your hand, but mine are a little full at the moment."

Sarah dropped her gaze to the ground, feeling even more like an interloper when she realized Jessica had a nursing baby beneath the shawl she wore. Sarah offered a smile, hopefully succeeding in covering her mild embarrassment. "It's good to meet you, Jessica."

Jessica brought the baby from beneath her shawl, simultaneously shifting to adjust her wardrobe beneath the covering. Sarah tried not to stare, but she was a little taken aback by how smoothly this woman nourished her child in the midst of carrying on a conversation. She bit her lip to hold back a grin. If it was her in the same position, she'd probably have unintentionally flashed half the picnic goers.

"Oh, excuse me, ladies. I believe I'm being summoned." Jessica headed off in the direction of a small voice calling for his mother.

Sarah shook her head. "I don't know how

in the world you and Jessica do all this."

Libby laughed. "Caring for a newborn might feel like dancing with two left feet for a little bit, but you'll get the hang of it. You don't have to have motherhood all figured out going into it."

"Afternoon, ladies."

Sarah turned. Clay tipped his battered hat and offered a wide grin that crinkled the corners of his eyes.

"Where should I put this?" He held up a bowl of berries, a bright rainbow of colors. No doubt all fresh-picked from his farm that morning.

Sarah pointed to the table. "Nan and Mom are traffic control. They'll be able to help you out."

"Come back and sit with us after you drop your bowl off." Libby grinned and nudged Sarah after he'd walked away. "He's a good-lookin' fella, ain't he?"

Sarah tugged her gaze away from Clay's tall form bent to listen to Nan and wiped away the beginnings of an involuntary smile that softened the corners of her mouth. She sat beside Libby, and Caroline squirmed until Libby let her go. "I hadn't noticed." Sarah's cheeks grew warm. "But I believe you're taken, Libby Lou." Caroline crawled into Sarah's lap, and Sarah busied herself with making silly faces at the baby.

Libby laughed. "I'm just commenting on God's creation. Not a thing in the world wrong with that."

"Wrong with what?" Clay's deeper voice made Sarah start. He sat down beside them on the grass. Caroline squealed and traded Sarah's lap for Clay's.

"Admiring the beauty around us." Libby shrugged and leaned back on her elbows and stared up at the cotton candy clouds floating by.

Caroline tugged the hat from Clay's head and clumsily plopped it on her own head, covering her entire face. Clay laughed softly, adjusted the hat so that Caroline could see, and then he looked into Sarah's eyes. She never knew the color blue could hold so much warmth.

"Surely you don't take offense to admiring beauty, Sarah. Some things are so beautiful you can't help but take notice."

"I —" She blinked and cleared her throat and leaned back on her elbows to match Libby's posture. What would he say, if he knew he was the subject she and Libby discussed? "I love it when the clouds are fluffy like this. Do you remember when we used to sit back for hours and see which shapes we could find, Lib? Small-town entertainment at its finest."

Libby nudged Sarah's shoulder with her own, and then her face lit. And that spelled trouble. Throughout childhood Libby was always getting her into some mild scrape or another. Like the time she convinced Sarah to rescue a newborn kitten that turned out to be a baby opossum. She leaned close to Libby's ear and spoke in a hissed whisper. "Why does it feel like you are up to something? I don't care how handsome you think —"

Clay cleared his throat. "Excuse me, ladies. I didn't mean to interrupt a private conversation. My apologies."

Libby sat up and grinned pertly. "Not at all. Sarah here was just lamenting to me about having to go back to Chicago to close up her house all by herself. I really wanted to be able to go and help her, but with all the little ones, I just can't make the trip."

Sarah narrowed her eyes at Libby and shook her head. "Wait a minute now, I would've never asked you —"

"Your mom and grandma can't go with you?" Clay asked.

Sarah was going to strangle Libby. She'd expressed her worries about going back to the house to her friend a few days ago, just to vent. She never imagined Libby would use it to . . . do whatever it was she was up to. "I can't stomach listening to Mom trying to talk me out of selling my house for the entire eight-hour drive. And I can't take Nan from the store. But I've got this. It won't be much."

Libby sent a meaningful look Clay's direction. "You said yourself that you were a little worried about handling some of the bigger items on your own. Clay, somethin' you need to know about Sarah, Glory Ann and Rosemary have nothing on this girl's stubbornness. She got a double portion from both of them."

Sarah glared at Libby, hoping her friend could feel the daggers she shot her direction. "No. I . . . I'll be just fine. I'm leaving most everything at the house other than a few personal items. I can hire extra hands if I need them."

"I could come with you." Clay looked at her earnestly. "I don't have anything pressing going on at the moment. I've had this high school kid helping me out around my place all summer. I think he'd like the challenge of keeping an eye on everything for me for a day or two."

She choked on her sip of water. "No. I . . . uh . . . That's not necessary. It's —"

Clay lifted an eyebrow. "Just the other day,

I heard you say that one of your favorite things about small-town life is the way neighbors help each other out. That a moving company tried to make it here once and they had to close because the people here were so accustomed to taking care of each other's needs."

"That's completely different."

"Only thing different is a few extra miles. This is what friends are for. You said so yourself." He flashed a full grin.

Libby chortled.

Why did it feel like Libby and Clay had prearranged this conversation? "A few extra miles, my foot." She laughed at herself using one of Nan's signature phrases. "Did you miss the part where I said eight-hour drive?"

"A good chance to get to know my new friend better."

This was insane. Sure, Sarah and Clay had had several good conversations at the store whenever he came in. And she'd already embarrassingly blabbed all her worst moments at his house after he'd rescued her on his tractor. Things she hadn't even mentioned to Nan and Mom. But spending eight hours, one way, in the car together? Letting someone into the home she'd shared with Aaron? "No. I don't think it's a good idea." She stood. "I'm going to see if Nan and Mom need any help." She hurried in the direction of the tables.

"Sarah! Hey, wait up."

She flinched at the sound of Clay's voice, but paused, turning to see him jog to meet her.

"I didn't mean to upset you."

"You didn't. It's just that I've started feeling like I'm a charity case with you. And that's the last thing I want."

"Did I do something to make you feel that way? Because that's not how I feel at all. I've been through some things, and I've learned firsthand the importance of letting people in when all you want to do is hide. So to me, offering to come with you isn't charity. It's friendship. And I know ours is pretty new, but at least think about it. Let me know if you change your mind." He gave her shoulder a soft squeeze before turning away.

She shifted her feet as she watched him walk away. Maybe he was right. He knew more than Mom and Nan about her complicated feelings about Aaron. Maybe she didn't have to face this alone.

34

June 1987

Rosemary sat ramrod straight, her shoulder brushing the passenger door, as she stared out the front windshield of Bo's pickup. The same truck she'd ridden in the night he'd brought the news about Daddy. She gripped the handles of the duffel sitting in her lap.

Bo glanced sideways. "You sure you don't want to put your bag in the back? We've got quite a ways to go. Might as well get comfortable."

"No. I'm fine." She kept her eyes focused forward. If she looked at him, saw the concern for her in his eyes, the firm line she'd made with her mouth would crumble, and all her carefully constrained emotions would break loose.

The truck slowed and rumbled onto the shoulder and stopped. Bo killed the engine. Rosemary stared at the faded nylon fibers of the duffel bag handle, at the way some of the tiny blue threads had snapped and curled away from the others.

"Rosemary." His voice was quiet and steady.

There was a line of dirt under one of her fingernails. She picked at it until her clear-polish manicure was perfect again.

"Sweetheart, look at me." His hand reached across the bench seat, having to stretch to find hers on the far side of the cab.

She lifted her chin and met his eyes when he gave her hand a gentle squeeze.

"We don't have to do this. I can turn around right now. Or, in another few hours, when we get inside the Gatlinburg city limits. Even when you're standing by my side at the front of that chapel, you can change your mind."

She chewed her bottom lip, trying to ground the emotions that swirled and swelled in her chest.

He gave her hand another squeeze. "Even . . . even if that means you're changin' your mind about me. I sure hope not, but this is supposed to be the happiest day of our lives, and you look the opposite of that." His green-gray eyes pulled away from hers and stared out the windshield.

He was right. She should be curled next

to him, dreaming of their future, adrenaline coursing through her veins because they'd dared to elope.

The sense of adventure she'd been craving was hers. Why did it leave her feeling sick in the pit of her stomach, flooded with the distinct foreboding that something terrible was about to happen? "I-I want to marry you, Bo."

"Do you want me to turn the truck around?"

Did she want the wedding and all that went with it? She tried to picture it. Walking down the aisle of the church. The space her dad was supposed to occupy at her elbow, a throbbing void. Surrounded by people who knew her story, who'd pity her. Who'd whisper behind her back about how he'd died trying to keep her safe but she hadn't even been where she was supposed to be. No, she did not want heartache coloring her wedding day. Bo deserved better than that. A day that was about them, not her grief. "No. I want to do this."

Surely Momma would understand. From the limited things Momma had said about her own wedding, it had been a humble affair. Momma and Daddy hadn't even had wedding photos done.

Rosemary released her bag and let it slide

to the floorboard between her feet. She scooted closer to her fiancé, letting her head rest on his shoulder. "Just pre-wedding jitters, I guess." She tried to insert levity into the moment. "Besides, I can't pass up the chance to finally drop my hideous middle name, and let Clearwater take its place."

He leaned his head to rest his on top of hers. "It's okay to be happy. You know that, don't you? Your dad would want you to be happy."

She didn't doubt that. But at the same time, chasing after her own desires made her stomach knot and her forehead break out in a cold sweat.

Hours later, feeling more than a little rumpled, they arrived at a little wedding chapel nestled in the foothills of the Smoky Mountains. A wizened minister met them in the office of the storybook chapel. After making sure both she and Bo understood the gravity of their decision, he asked them about the particulars of the ceremony. What song she'd like played as she walked down the aisle.

Rosemary squeezed Bo's hand. "I don't want to walk down the aisle. I'd rather just start the ceremony standing at the front, by each other's side the whole time."

■ ■ ■ ■

Sitting at the register, Glory Ann ran her finger over the rough edge of the torn-off note. It made sense now, why Rosemary had ignored the wedding magazines Glory Ann had slid beneath her nose at the breakfast table over the past several months.

The important thing was that her daughter was marrying a good man. A man that she loved. Their relationship was of the quieter sort, not unlike hers and Clarence's, although she and Clarence had said "I do" long before love had bloomed.

But Glory Ann would have liked to have been there on Rosemary's special day. To plan the sort of wedding she'd envisioned for herself before loss doused her fairy-tale dreams. A mother was supposed to be there on her daughter's wedding day. Glory Ann scrubbed her face, trying to relieve the prickles behind her eyes.

Once Clarence had tried to get Glory Ann to renew their vows when she'd let slip about the scrapbook she'd started as a girl for her someday wedding. But she'd laughed her loss off as silly dreams of pretty things, and the renewal ceremony had never happened. With two daughters she'd thought she'd have two weddings to plan.

Holding Rosemary's note, those hopes for a someday wedding slipped out of reach again, and she couldn't help but blame herself. If she'd found some way to traverse the rift between them, maybe Rosemary wouldn't have eloped. She sighed. Maybe Jessie would let her be there for her if she ever decided she'd like to marry.

Mae Anderson burst through the front door. "Glory Ann. Do you know what those fool kids of ours have gone and done?"

The bustle of the store went whisper-quiet in an instant.

Glory Ann pursed her lips and lifted her note.

Mae cracked a smile and stamped her feet in a happy little dance. "Finally! Took them long enough." She hurried forward and wrapped Glory Ann in a tight hug. "You okay about it?"

Glory Ann nodded, not trusting herself to speak.

"They better have us a whole passel grandbabies to make up for cutting us of the wedding festivities."

Glory Ann released a choked laug sniffed back her tears. "Not too soo Let 'em find their way first."

Mae clapped her hands. "My,

see it now. Three or four of 'em runnin' up and down the aisles, raising Cain. Just like Rosemary and Jessamine used to do."

A pang throbbed in her chest. Stored-away memories she'd like to uncork and live all over again surfaced. "They did no such thing. They were angels." Glory Ann smirked. "Most of the time."

She was so thankful Rosemary hadn't been afflicted with the same wanderlust as Jessie. Maybe she would have a whole bunch of babies and one of them would love Old Depot like she did. Then generation after generation would run the place. Clarence's legacy of love going on forever.

35

Present Day

Why, oh why had she said yes? Sarah glanced at the man in her passenger seat, who gazed out the window. Clay's knee jittered up and down.

She'd told him no that day at the picnic. But the more she thought it over in the following days, this stranger who claimed himself as her friend made the idea of walking back into that house more bearable.

So at six this morning, before the sun had the chance to crest the horizon, she'd picked him up from his farm with a thermos full of coffee for him and a water bottle for her in the cupholders between them.

They'd had long stretches of light conversation and easy silences, but in the past hour, he'd grown restless in the passenger seat. Did he regret boxing himself up on this endless drive?

Clay paused Sarah's latest memoir, an audiobook of a soldier's journey to reintegrate with civilian life after being in a war zone. "Can I ask you a question?" He looked a little pale.

Her mind flashed to that photograph on his mantel. She should've been more sensitive in her book choice. Just because it was next on her to-be-read pile didn't mean she couldn't have skipped it. "Are you okay?"

He shook his head like he was trying to clear it. "It's fine. If we could switch to something a little more lighthearted for a bit, I'd be grateful."

"I'm so sorry. I wish you would've said something sooner."

He shrugged and offered a lopsided smile. "Really, I'm okay. I've come a long way since the guy who first came back from Afghanistan. When I first moved to Brighton, I had a half-cocked plan for some serious self-destruction, thinking that out there alone on my uncle's farm the only person I'd be hurting was me. But that was before your grandmother got ahold of me and set me straight. Somehow or another I came into Old Depot planning to buy out all the beer in the store and I left with a Bible and a *Farmers' Almanac* instead."

Sarah laughed. "That sounds like Nan."

"She's a real good lady. I wish there was

something I could do to keep her store from going under."

Sarah stared out the windshield at the crystal-clear horizon. "Selling my house could help. At least for a while." Mom was right though. Money would run out eventually. "Nan loves that place." She chewed her bottom lip. "So do I. That store was my playground growing up. Nan said that ever since I was old enough to walk, I insisted on wearing a green apron and playing store." She traced her fingers over the stitching on the steering wheel.

"Maybe it sounds strange, but when I was little, I used to imagine that the creaking wood floors could talk. That they knew all the stories of the people who walked them. My mom doesn't really talk about her childhood, and I guess there's a part of me that feels like I'm missing out on who and what has shaped the person she is. I have this fear she'll never open up or, like Aaron, there'll be an accident and she'll never get the chance to tell me and that it'll get lost and forgotten. But if I believe the store holds the stories, that if I could just understand their secret language, those wood floors could tell me everything."

Sarah shook her head and laughed. "Dumb, I know. I don't know why I'm telling you all this."

"It's not dumb. I think it's why you love biographies and memoirs so much. And even those goofy reality shows. Because you are drawn to the way the stories of the past help you make sense of the present."

There was some truth to that. It's why a letter that didn't belong to her was hitchhiking in her purse.

She took her eyes from the road for a moment. Clay studied her. "Glory Ann has always talked a lot about you. Said you almost never came home to visit."

She squirmed under his scrutiny. "It's complicated." Actually, it wasn't all that complicated, but when she looked back at the girl who left Brighton and the one who returned, she liked the second one a whole lot better. Even if that second one was broken and confused and a little lost. "Somehow I guess I convinced myself that Brighton was too small. That my little girl dreams were childish."

"And now?"

"Now I can see everything that I want slipping away and it feels like there's nothing I can do to stop it. I can't come back to Kenilworth, and I'm not sure what there is for me in Brighton. Or anywhere, for that matter."

Sarah merged onto I-94, her eyes lingering on the familiar skyline of the Windy City in her rearview.

"Take that first step that feels right and see what happens next," said Clay. "I think that's how God works in our lives a lot of times. He doesn't give us the whole picture. He gives us that one step. We just have to have the courage to take it and trust that when we do, it will become clear where to put our next foot."

She had taken that one step. Going back to Brighton, even if it had been more of a desperate leap than a prayerful decision. Now with the store maybe closing, there seemed to be no place for her next foot to land.

After another half hour, they pulled up in front of the house. Clay let out a low whistle. "Shoo-wee, girl. That's some house you got there."

She jerked her gaze away. Some people might take pride in owning property like hers, but in front of Clay she felt exposed by this oversized house. Big, expensive, and empty.

"Good bones," the realtor had said when she'd guided Sarah and Aaron through the vaulted rooms and up the curved staircase three years ago. But what did bones matter when there was no heart, no soul? No life.

In a few weeks, some other realtor would cite the same quote to another well-off couple eager to fill the vacancy in the coveted neighborhood. Maybe, unlike Sarah and Aaron, they'd fill it with more than unmet expectations.

"I'm going to leave most of the furniture and sell it with the house if the buyer wants it. Nothing in here will fit life in Brighton. I just need to get my personal items and paperwork out."

Clay followed behind her up the walk.

She unlocked the heavy door and it swung inward with a groan.

Sitting on the floor, like a waiting accuser, was the bag she'd packed after those anniversary candles melted down to nothing and the food had grown ice-cold waiting for Aaron to come back home. That night, she'd marched down the stairs full of self-righteous anger with her getaway bag over her shoulder when the doorbell chimed.

When she opened the door, the police officer on her front step removed his hat. "Are you Sarah Ashby, wife of Aaron Ashby?"

Sarah clutched the bag's strap. "Yes . . . yes I am."

"There's been an accident. Your husband sustained severe injuries and he didn't . . ."

The officer shook his head.

Her getaway bag had dropped from her hands.

Two months later it was still there waiting for her to pick it back up. All the ghosts she'd left behind patiently waiting for her return.

She looked over her shoulder at Clay, fighting to hide the trembling jarring her frame. "I n-need a minute." She handed him her car keys. "Can you find something for dinner or just drive around for a little while. Anything you want."

She needed a moment alone with her haunted house.

Sarah watched Clay drive away. She'd lost her mind, bringing this stranger into this private world she and her husband had shared. Although shared seemed the wrong choice of words.

It was more like the place she'd become stuck, always orbiting Aaron's life, never knowing how to break through the atmosphere.

And that was what had driven her to pack her bag that night. Not because he'd left their anniversary dinner for a work emergency, and not even because she was tired of his promises that it wouldn't always be like this. But because she'd stopped believing him. Though Aaron's father had cut himself out of Aaron's life years ago, he was the reason Aaron couldn't let a single thing fail. And that was a void she could never fill.

Sarah walked through the foyer, her footsteps echoing in the empty space. She peered around the corner. Shattered bits of crystal glittered on the floor where the light came through the gap in the drapes. She wrapped her arms around her middle and went back the way she came. She ran her hand over the cherry handrail of the curved staircase and sank onto the polished step, gripping her knees.

Sitting there she was consumed by memories of the days that passed like entire weeks after Aaron died. The well-meaning people who lined up at the funeral home to offer condolences that stung rather than comforted. Why had she allowed Aaron to pawn their marriage in order to buy a someday that never came?

She'd thought she would be safe to sort through her conflicting emotions in private after the funeral, but that was when the food started arriving.

Every day like clockwork.

Apparently Aaron's office had set up a meal train. A little insensitive, if you asked

Sarah — delivering huge casserole dishes to a newly widowed woman who ate alone. Every day, for two weeks, someone had shown up with enough food to feed a family. Until one day she'd snapped.

She rubbed out the tension in her forehead. At least she'd waited until Aaron's secretary had left before she totally lost it.

Sarah stood and went to the closet to grab a broom and dustpan. She opened the heavy drapes wide to let the late afternoon light spill into the dining room. The remains of the candelabra she'd shattered lit up in the sunlight, casting a million glittering rainbows on the deep mahogany floors.

She swept the bits into her dustpan. That candelabra might be fractured now. Worthless. But the crystal remained crystal whether a glowing candelabra or in pieces as fine as a grain of sand.

After all the bits of crystal had been swept away, she faced the refrigerator full of old food. She wrinkled her nose. Unlike crystal, that did not remain unchanged in composition with the passage of time.

Two hours and a lot of prayer and elbow grease later, there was a light tap at the door. "Hello? Sarah, can I come in?"

Clay. She'd momentarily forgotten anything existed beyond the house and the tasks at hand. She released a sigh and with it a bit of weight she'd been carrying on her shoulders since the day she'd left. It wasn't that Old Depot hadn't helped her heal over the past months, but something about cleaning up the messes she'd left behind filled her with peace she had yet to attain.

"Come in." She went to meet Clay in the foyer.

He entered with paper bags from a local Tex-Mex eatery, his gaze taking in the entryway. "Are you getting hungry yet?"

Her mouth watered. "Surprisingly, I'm starved." She thumbed toward the direction of her patio. "Would you care if we sat out back? I could use some fresh air."

He gave a single nod and followed her outside. She couldn't help the flood of gratitude that washed over her at his . . . his acceptance of her situation. He didn't ask the wrong questions. Didn't try to fill the awkward silences with platitudes. All he'd offered was a helping hand if she needed it. And that was enough.

Once outside they settled across from each other on the wrought iron patio furniture. She waited for him to breach the silence, to ask the dreaded "are you okay" question after she'd practically shoved him out the door when they'd first arrived, but it never came. He passed her a box of street tacos with a crooked grin. "Have you changed your mind about me coming with you?"

She stared at her food as she unwrapped the tacos from their foil, trying to come up with an answer to a question she'd asked herself more than a few times. "No. No, I'm glad you came. I've tried keeping this part of my life that I'm not so proud of sectioned away like it never existed and that left me feeling even worse. Mom and Nan, they've never really been great at talking about hard things in life. I used to see that as strength, but I'm starting to realize that maybe that's not so great."

She shrugged. "And I've already blurted out enough uncomfortable things about my life that me breaking down like some crazy person all over again might not phase you too bad. I know we haven't known each other long, but so far you've been a pretty great friend to have in my corner." She hoped this declaration of friendship sent a clear enough message of where she was at. He was definitely the type of man she could see herself loving someday when the jagged edges of her complicated feelings for Aaron had healed and softened. She shoved away this strange turn of thought.

Clay gave a succinct nod, bit into his burrito, and chewed, looking past her. "I'm glad you felt comfortable bringing me here."

She gave him half a grin. "Well, I don't know about comfortable."

"You know what I mean. I'm glad it was me. Your Nan was that person when I first moved to Brighton."

She released a breath. His being here was about his gratitude to Nan. Not any ill-fated attraction to her. She picked at the edge of her tortilla, remembering his face as he'd listened to the audiobook about soldiers trying to go on with their lives after having seen combat.

She didn't even want to imagine the things he'd experienced. No doubt about it, this man knew a thing or two about being made whole after life had broken him. "Is that what helped you, growing corn and potatoes? Maybe I ought to give it a try if things don't pan out with Old Depot."

He shrugged. "It's healing, I guess, bringing life to things after you've spent so much time as an instrument of destruction."

The next morning, Sarah sat on the edge of the bed in the master bedroom with the house phone clutched in her hands. There were at least ten messages from her husband's lawyer, asking her to call. Messages from weeks ago.

Dealing with the lawyer and the assets he alluded to on the phone brought complications she didn't want to consider.

She chewed her bottom lip and dialed.

"The law offices of Howard and Shrub." The woman's voice came through the line crisp as a starched shirt.

"This is Sarah A-Ashby. I'm returning Matthias Howard's call."

"He'll be so pleased you're returning his calls. He became quite concerned when he wasn't able to reach you."

Sarah resisted the urge to explain herself and let the silence thrum in her ear.

"Please hold just a moment while I connect you."

"Thanks." Sarah let out the breath she'd been holding.

The elevator music in her ear ceased a moment later. "Sarah, it's good to hear from you." Matthias's voice was filled with warmth and familiarity though he had been Aaron's college friend, not hers. "We have a lot to discuss."

Sarah listened, wide-eyed, as Matthias told her about Aaron's investments and the way he'd set up his company so that a board would continue to run it in the event of his death or incapacity to continue as CEO.

Sarah would continue to receive benefits and quarterly checks, and as long as the company continued to do well, she wouldn't have to worry about financially providing for herself or her child. Her chest clenched at the sum Matthias quoted that she would receive from insurance.

After rattling off the intricate details, Matthias's voice softened back into the familiar tone he'd greeted her with. "It was really important to Aaron that I made sure you could maintain your current standard of living. He wanted everything ironclad so that if anything ever happened to him, you wouldn't have to worry about anything."

Her pulse throbbed in her ears at his words. She was grateful. She couldn't deny it. But every word Matthias spoke confirmed just how much Aaron misunderstood what she wanted from her life with him.

"All that's left is you coming by to sign a few things. Or I can fax it to you."

"I'll come by."

Aaron had always been attracted by the grand things in life. Like the night they'd stood in awe of the Colosseum in Rome, lit by moonlight. He saw the grandeur of architecture of ancient civilizations while Sarah's heart had been swept away by a child standing in the arched entryway offering her father a flower.

She scoffed. That was her problem with Aaron, wasn't it? That she'd never felt she could compete with the glamour of the wonders of the world. Not when deep down she was still that little girl with scabby knees stocking the aisles of her dear old store.

And like her grandmother and mother, she'd been afflicted with the belief that she just needed to persevere when times were hard. Which was true, but sometimes you needed to use the voice God gave you too.

36

August 1989

Glory Ann locked up the store and slid into her car's front seat. Bo and Rosemary had gotten home this morning with their little bundle of joy. Sarah Lynne Anderson.

A grin spread across her face so wide her cheeks cramped.

The workday had flown by, buoyed by the congratulations of every customer who clanked their way through those front doors. But that was no replacement for how she really wanted to spend her day. Oh, she couldn't wait to get her hands on that baby. She'd held Sarah a little while at the hospital when she visited, but not near long enough.

This was Glory Ann's golden opportunity to love her daughter well.

After she'd parked in Bo and Rosemary's driveway, she picked up the big cardboard box she'd placed in the back seat. A dinner that only needed heating up, paper towels, paper plates, milk, bread, bananas, a jar of peanut butter. Plus a few baby items people had dropped off when they came to shop.

Glory Ann set the box on the front stoop and tapped lightly on the door, hoping Bo would hear her. She didn't want to risk waking Rosemary and the baby if they were getting a nap in. Those early days were simultaneously exhausting and effervescent all at the same time. Glory Ann had had Clarence at her side. Never her own mother.

Glory Ann winced at the pain jabbing her heart. But that had been Mother's choice. At least they'd made amends enough over the years that her mother had gladly accepted Glory Ann's presence at her bedside a few months back. Mother had squeezed Glory Ann's hand one last time and asked for her forgiveness, a desperation in her eyes that Glory Ann didn't understand. She'd already forgiven her for the way Mother had so easily removed herself from her life, and she'd told her so years ago. Maybe in the last moments lingering guilt still plagued her.

The oddest thing about it was that she could almost have sworn Mother whispered Jimmy's name with her last breath. For a moment Glory Ann had wondered if her mother in that moment could see through the veil between this life and the next and caught a glimpse of the boy Glory Ann had so dearly loved.

She shook away those painful remembrances and tapped softly on the door again. She would be there for Rosemary — be available to answer all her questions about motherhood. Babysit. Teach her all the little tips and tricks she'd picked up in her years of experience. They might always struggle to connect, but she would never give up on being there for her daughter, no matter how messy or uncomfortable things got.

A moment later, Bo opened the door. "Hello, Glory Ann. Here to see the baby?" His bone-weary eyes were full of light.

"I'm glad you heard me. I didn't want to wake Rosemary and Sarah if they were resting."

"I wish Rosemary would rest. Here, let me take that big ol' box for you. Come on in."

When Glory Ann stepped inside, she registered the bang and clang of pots and pans coming from deeper in the cottage-style house. "Is she cooking? For heaven's sake, she doesn't need to be up doing that. She should be cuddling that baby."

Bo lifted his hands in a gesture of surrender. "I tried tellin' her, but you know how she gets."

Boy, did she.

Glory Ann walked into the kitchen. Rosemary was setting pots on the stove and pulling items from the pantry one-armed, while the other arm cradled a tiny babe who was working up a fuss. "Rosemary, what in the world are you doing? Take that sweet baby and go feed her. That's a hungry cry."

Rosemary turned. Her hair was a little disheveled and her coloring pale. Eyes a little wild. "I can take care of my family, Momma."

"Of course you can. But you're still recovering. I brought dinner so you and Bo would have extra time resting, 'cause I'm willing to bet you won't be getting a whole lotta sleep if little Sarah is anything like you were."

Rosemary shifted her feet and grimaced, as if letting her mother have run of her kitchen was more than she could bear. Or maybe it was the idea of being still for a moment and letting others do for her what she thought was her responsibility that scared her more. When Rosemary passed by, Glory Ann's arms practically ached with how bad she wanted to hold Sarah. There would be time enough for that later though. Right now, she'd better help as much as she could while Rosemary was occupied with feeding her little one.

Glory Ann heated food, wiped counters, took out the trash. After finishing in the kitchen, she slipped into the living room. Bo had his feet up, snoring. She straightened around him, finishing up the half-folded pile of laundry on the couch.

When she was done with the laundry, she fixed a tray and walked back to the bedroom. She tapped lightly on the door. She nudged it open to find Rosemary, still upright, dozing on the bed while gently rocking Sarah's bedside cradle in her sleep.

Glory Ann walked to her. "Rosemary," she whispered.

Rosemary started. "I'm coming. I was just getting Sarah to sleep."

"You sit right there and have some of this pot roast. You need sustenance and rest."

"I . . ."

"I know you don't take well to me bossing you around, but listen to me this time, will you?"

Rosemary offered her a lopsided smile. "That food smells good."

"I know I'm intruding on you, so I'll go. But can I give you a little advice?"

"As long as I don't have to promise to take it." Rosemary grinned sleepily.

"Laundry and dishes will always be there, but that little baby girl will grow in the blink of an eye. If you need a hand around here, I want you to know that I'm here for you. I know you're tough enough to handle all this on your own. Just know that you don't have to."

Glory Ann let herself out of the house after kissing her daughter on the forehead. Maybe there would be another day she could sit and snuggle that sweet newborn, but today, if only today, she was able to serve her daughter who was so bent on not needing anything from her.

37

Present Day

Glory Ann stared at the desk in front of her, flanked by Mable and Paulette, her little circle of strength. She traced her fingers over the decades-old pencil indentations in the soft pine, then rested her head on her folded arms. "How in the world am I going to break the news to Sarah?"

Mable put a hand on her shoulder. "Sarah will understand."

Glory Ann jolted as the shrill ring of the rotary phone sounded beside her. "Old Depot Grocery, this is Glory Ann. How may I help you?"

"Nan?" Sarah's voice came through the line, lighter than Glory Ann had heard her since she'd been back in Brighton. Maybe Rosemary was right and Chicago was where Sarah belonged.

"Hello, dear. I'm so glad to hear you made it safe and sound. Are you well? Has Clay been a good help?"

Paulette and Mable, who sat in the chairs opposite the desk, leaned in.

"I'm good. Great, actually."

"I have some news." They both spoke at once, but each with contrasting tones. Glory Ann's tinged by defeat. Sarah's victorious.

"Nan, is everything okay?"

Glory Ann squared her shoulders and sat tall in her chair. "I've decided to sell Old Depot. The store is no longer profitable. Delivery companies are canceling on us because our orders are so small that it's a waste of time to deliver. So either our delivery charges go way up or we lose the ability to have decent variety. We have several coolers on the fritz. The Band-Aid solutions my repairmen have implemented to delay the inevitable are no longer working. They'll need total replacement. Maintaining the store has become an untenable situation. It's time to let go."

"That's why I called, Nan. I can buy out Mom's portion and invest new money into all the repairs needed. Pour some investment into marketing. I can save Old Depot."

Glory Ann sighed.

"As soon as I get back, I can show you all the spreadsheets I put together that show the funds available and the estimated costs to do some updates and pay off accrued debts. There's still plenty left over to keep things running even if we're not able to overcome the recent deficit in sales."

Nan stood and paced behind the desk as far as the phone cord allowed, her chin trembling. "Sarah, I appreciate what you're trying to do here, but I cannot accept this." She cleared her throat to try to rid herself of the tremor in her voice. Paulette's and Mable's gazes followed her stride like the eyes on those Felix the Cat clocks. She ceased her pacing.

Silence stretched though the phone line.

"Please, Nan. This is what I want. I want Granddad Clarence's legacy to live on."

Glory Ann swallowed, clearing away the lump forming in her throat. She squared her shoulders and stood tall. "You need that money. For you. For your future."

"This is the future I want."

"I cannot take your money and spend it on this store. The store would devour your investment in a slow burn with nothing to show for it. Your mother is right. The more I think and pray, the more I know that it's not what your grandfather would've done. He loved this store, but not for the pride of owning it. It was a tool he used to make sure that I and your mother and aunt had a good life. And Old Depot has done that.

"When I was a young woman, it became like a haven for me, giving me a purpose when I felt like life had left me empty-handed. When your granddad passed, his hard work lived on, and this store provided an income long after he was gone. But the store was never here for the sake of having. You are about to be a mother. You have your child's future ahead of you and planning the wisest way to provide for your new little family."

"But, Nan, I *want* to spend my money in this way. I want my child to grow up there. I don't care if my money goes to the store only to preserve this place so he or she gets to experience it too."

"Sweetie, I hear you. But it is time to let go. Aaron would want this money used to make sure his baby never has to want for anything. There will be college and all sorts of things in the future. That's what that money is meant for, not this dried-up old place full of nothing but memories. Invest your money in your new life."

"I thought you said you needed this place?" The energy in Sarah's voice ebbed.

"It's true, it feels like losing Clarence all over again in some ways. We had so, so many memories here. I married that man in the office I'm sitting in right now."

"What?"

Glory Ann smiled. "Sure did. Kinda a long story as to why. But this place is where I met, married, and fell in love with him. The order in which it happened hardly matters anymore."

"I thought I had done it. I thought I'd saved the store."

How she hated the ache in Sarah's tone. "It will all turn out okay. You'll see."

Glory Ann sank into the desk chair as she ended the call. All this time, she'd been racking her brain to come up with a way to scrape by. And then her granddaughter had laid everything the store needed and more out in front of her. Somehow that was exactly what she needed to let go.

"You did the right thing." Paulette reached across the desk and squeezed her hand.

Mable nodded in agreement. "It's time you retired like the two of us. Just think of how much trouble the Poker Night Prayer and Sewing Circle can stir up in this little town when you've got more time on your hands."

Glory Ann gave them a shaky smile. Moments before they'd been arguing up a storm with her, telling her it would be a mistake to close the store. Now that her decision was final, they only offered support. Good friends like that didn't come along every day.

This store had served its purpose. And the sale of it would do the same. She'd be financially cared for so that Rosemary didn't have that weight on her shoulders. Rosemary would have extra money saved so that she didn't have additional worry about possible medical bills and any remodeling that her home might need to accommodate her health struggles. And Rosemary could stop fretting that Sarah was throwing away her life just to ease Glory Ann's loss.

The good old store would come through for them one more time. Just in a different way.

Sarah placed her phone back down on the side table, her shoulders sagging. What was she supposed to do with Aaron's money if not to save Old Depot? She didn't want it. This house. This life.

She walked to the master bathroom. Her bare toes curled against the chill of the marble floor as she approached the ornate vanity. She stared at the reflection before her. Who was this woman? Without life with Aaron. Without the store. Just Sarah. Granddaughter. Daughter. Widow. Mother-to-be.

The reflection staring back at her squared her shoulders. She was a Clearwater girl. And Clearwater girls were strong. Resilient. And they didn't back down. But what did that mean in this scenario? Clay's words from the drive rang in her ears.

Sarah gripped the edge of the white marble vanity and lifted a silent prayer. *If you'll give me that one next step, Lord. I'll take it.*

Silence thrummed in her ears and she heaved out a breath and straightened. Maybe no answer would come, but at least this time, likely for the first time in her life, she was really listening. Not for the grating voice inside her head always nudging with *shoulds* and *ought tos* that had driven her before. Sometimes the imagined voice of her mother. Sometimes her own. Even Aaron's on occasion. This time it was only that still small voice she sought.

Sarah wandered out of the master bedroom, tracing her hand over the cherry railing that separated the upper floor from the foyer below, surveying the closed doors to all the empty rooms.

She placed her hand over the curve of her lower belly. "I'll do better for you. When you grow up and become an aggravating teenager and we butt heads or distance comes between us, I'll fight my way through it to you. I won't let it stew and fester like I did with your father. Or the way it seems to have happened with Mom and Nan. I'll air the hidden things so that when you grow up there will be no secret letters from unknown lovers to find or parts of your history you're left wondering about."

Sarah swiped the moisture from her cheeks. Maybe this was her one next step. Maybe she was the one who was supposed to press through to the things no one would say. To give oxygen and light to the things shut away in the dark corners of her family's attic.

"Sarah, is everything okay?" Clay's voice wound its way to her. She'd told him she was going to give Nan a quick call while he loaded a few things she'd decided to keep. She glanced at her watch. She'd been up there for almost forty-five minutes.

She descended the stairs, calling out to him. "Yeah, I'm fine, just doing some thinking."

He met her at the bottom of the stairs. "What did Glory Ann say? Was she over the moon? I wish I could have seen her face when you told her Old Depot was safe."

Sarah sat on the step and shook her head. "She told me no."

Clay jerked his head back. "You're kidding?"

"She's convinced it is time to let go."

"And you? What do you think?"

Sarah shook her head. "I . . . Something in me hasn't let go of the store yet. This sense that there is still more work to be done there. But I don't know what. I've prayed, but no answer on that front. Not yet." She bit the inside of her cheek. "But I think I might know that one next step I'm supposed to take." She went to her bag and pulled out the yellowed envelope. "This might sound strange, but I think my next step is to find out what this letter means."

Clay took it from her hands. She watched his eyes tracking over the words. He lowered the paper. "What is this?"

"That's what I want to find out. My mother had this buried in a trunk, and I don't know why she'd have something so personal to Nan hidden away like this. There are things my family just doesn't talk about, and that's not a part of my heritage that I want to pass on. I want the secrets to stop with me. I'm going to find out who Jimmy is."

38

May 1991

Rosemary spread out a blanket in the park. The late spring air was a little hot and thick for her liking, but it beat taking in another meal stuck inside the walls of Old Depot. Bo ambled alongside her, their almost two-year-old daughter perched in one arm and a white takeout bag from the deli in the other.

Bo set Sarah down and lay back on the tattered blanket. Shadows from the maple leaves mottled his handsome face. Rosemary smiled at her husband while keeping one eye trained watchfully on Sarah, who squatted in the grass, plucking handfuls of the stuff. Any minute those tight-clenched fists were going to fly to her mouth.

Rosemary sighed, and stretched out the crick in her neck, still feeling the effects of stocking night. Balancing her work at the store was getting harder now with Sarah on the move, always underfoot. Especially with the latest trick the little stinker had discovered — how to climb out of her playpen. Mom had tried to get Rosemary to go home, but it hadn't felt right abandoning her on the busiest night of the week. Rosemary had managed, but it felt like a wrestling match between the two roles in her life all night long.

Bo propped himself up on one elbow. "I'm thinking about taking a new job."

"Sarah, no!" Rosemary hurried to her daughter, swept her into her arms, and began plucking blades of grass from her berry-red lips. Bo's words echoed inside her head. They'd worked side by side in that store for years. It was a little stressful sometimes, both of them depending on that place for their income, but there weren't a whole lot of options in Brighton. Did he intend for them to move?

Her heart did funny things in her chest, two separate sets of emotions firing off at the same time. She owed it to her mother to stay, but if Bo needed to move for work, then Momma would have to understand.

Rosemary sat on the blanket with Sarah wriggling to get out of her arms.

"Sweetheart, did you hear me?"

Rosemary blinked, refocusing on the man

beside her. "What new job? Where?"

"That's the thing that makes this so great. We wouldn't have to move."

"Oh."

"Yeah, the delivery driver was talking to me last night. The hauling company he works for is hiring. I just need to get some training and a license to drive the big rigs."

"Sarah, come back here." Sarah toddled across the field as fast as her tiny legs could go, slowing a bit at her mother's voice but continuing to approach that invisible boundary Rosemary deemed *too far.* Rosemary stood. "Sarah Lynne, you heard me." At least Rosemary would never have to worry about Sarah becoming stuck living here. She was a born adventurer. This time Sarah stopped, but her pudgy toddler legs remained rooted to the spot.

"Rosemary, what do you think?"

"Let me grab her." Her mind seemed to sigh in exhaustion in this tug-of-war on her attention. If only she could have one minute to let her brain breathe.

"I'll get her." Somehow Bo transformed Sarah's small defiance into a game. Rosemary watched him scoop her up and spin her around. The air filled with her shrieks and giggles and "Again! Again!"

Rosemary scrubbed her hands over her

face, massaging the tension away. She laid out their sandwiches and chips tucked in the bag. Maybe lunch would distract Sarah long enough so that she and Bo could get in a real conversation. She couldn't bear to leave this topic tabled until their daughter's bedtime.

Bo came back with Sarah, red-cheeked and with tiny beads of sweat on the bridge of her upturned nose.

"Okay, you little stinker. Let's eat lunch." Rosemary drew her sweat-sticky daughter into her lap and bowed her head as Bo prayed the blessing over their lunch, his deep, calm voice filling the air. Still, her thoughts raced.

How long would he be gone? How long could she go without his calm steadiness that always had a way of settling her worries?

When his prayer concluded, she handed him a sandwich.

"The pay is really good, Rosemary. Especially if I do the long over-road hauls."

"How long will you be gone?"

"A couple weeks on the road and then I get a week home. A whole week."

"That's a lot of time gone, Bo. A lot of time you won't be around Sarah." *And me.*

Bo took a bite of sandwich. Sarah pulled

hers apart, eating the turkey separate from the cheese and bread. Rosemary picked at her crust.

"I know it will be different. But it's good pay. I'll be able to put money back in savings for once. There are opportunities for growth in the company. Health insurance. A lot of things we don't have right now." He nudged her. "Maybe we'd get to a point where we'd even feel like we could afford to give Sarah a little brother or sister."

Rosemary bit her lip. Finances were always her excuse when Bo asked about adding to their family in the near future. But money had nothing to do with her hesitation.

Rosemary pushed her thoughts about family planning away. "You really want to do this?"

"I think it could take a lot of strain off our finances. I mean, I know things are okay. But I see the worry it puts on you, the stretch of balancing the books at the store and all that time in the back of your mind also thinking about what the profit margins mean for our own household. I need to do more, Rosemary. It was fine working there when I was fresh out of high school." He nudged her again. "With my wife and mother-in-law as co-owners of the establishment, there isn't a whole lot of room for upward mobility unless I stage some sort of coup."

Rosemary smirked. "Oh, so this is all about your male pride. I knew it's been eating you alive — working for two women. Me being your *boss.*"

Bo growled and playfully tackled her. She shrieked in laughter as his fingers prodded the places between her ribs. "Bo, stop it."

Sarah jumped into the mix, making it a dog pile. "Bo, stop it," she mimicked with her toddler lisp.

Rosemary and Bo dissolved into laughter and pulled Sarah between them. Rosemary plucked a piece of lettuce from Sarah's hair as they all sat up.

Bo put his hand on her arm. "I like working for you and your mother, but I would feel better if we had more than one source for our income."

She refrained from offering her unformed and divided opinion while she busied herself with gathering trash and the hodgepodge remnants of her two-year-old's lunch. Bo rose from his place beside her and played with Sarah, stomping about like a great roaring giant while Sarah giggled, darting in and out of trees. Bo knew her well enough to realize that her busy hands meant she was in no mood to talk.

After another moment or two of watching their game, she glanced at her watch. "We'd better go. Momma will be wondering where we've gotten off to."

On the walk back to Old Depot, she looped her arm through Bo's and rested her head on his shoulder. "You should do it. See where this new opportunity takes you."

He grinned and tugged her tight against his side, Rosemary tucked close in one arm and Sarah hoisted in the other. She'd like to feel whatever emotion played across his face in that moment.

They entered through the back of the store. Bo went to the deli counter to relieve the morning shift person. Sarah played in a little nook under his feet that was stocked with toys and books. Her own little hide-away.

Rosemary breezed to the front, forcing away the weight that had settled on her shoulders. This was a good thing. Bo was right. She was always concerned about their family finances when she balanced the store's books. And he was always worn thin working extra jobs here and there to try and tuck meager amounts into savings.

Her mother had her head bent, phone receiver to her ear. A small queue was building up at the checkout line. Rosemary grabbed her apron, slipped it over her neck, and tied it at the waist, stepping in front of where her mother stood at the register to take over ringing up items.

Rosemary pasted her smile in place and politely conversed with a new woman in town. They'd moved into the old Smith farm out of the big city, wanting to make a go of small-town life. One by one Rosemary talked with the customers coming through the line. Ringing up orders on the ancient cash register. Catching up. Inquiring about family members. Offering to remember in prayer those who came through the line downtrodden and burdened. Sometimes working the register felt more like five-minute therapy sessions than ringing up groceries.

"I'm so glad you're back," Mom said over Rosemary's shoulder.

Rosemary handed a final bag to Ms. Mable and then faced her mother.

"Paulette is down in her back again, and her husband has taken a bad turn. He's got the cancer, you know. I'm going to collect some groceries for them, and Mable and I are going to run 'em over to her house. You can hold down the fort here, can't you?"

"Of course, Momma." Rosemary would always be there to hold down the fort. At this store. At home now too. She sighed, chiding herself for the way the cord of muscles had tightened along her spine. She had too much to be thankful for to entertain such useless emotions.

39

Present Day

Sarah's stomach dropped at the sight of the neon orange signs plastered on the windows and doors of Old Depot. Their bright hue attracted attention when all she wanted to do was pretend this wasn't happening.

But Nan needed her to be strong. That was one thing she could do. The bells clanked against the glass at her entrance.

Nan lifted her head from where she braced herself at the register. She attempted a smile that failed to produce anything more than the stretching of her thin lips.

"Hi, Nan. How can I help?"

Nan shook her head. "Not much to do. People trickling in and out to purchase at sale prices. We've got a buyer coming to pick up some of the freezers and coolers, but that's not until next week so that we can hopefully sell some more of the merchandise before then." She sighed. "Honey, your time would probably be best spent somewhere besides here. You've got your whole life ahead of you to plan. Endless possibilities. And this place is just another ending."

Sarah wasn't quite sure "endless possibilities" was an accurate description of her current situation. But that one next step she'd determined to take echoed inside her head.

She toyed with the ends of her blonde hair. "Have you ever been in love with anyone besides Granddad Clarence? You were still pretty young when he passed. Was there ever a time when you considered getting remarried?"

Nan tilted her head and then walked to Sarah, wrapping her in a hug. "Honey, just because you are about to have a baby, don't rush into anything. Give your heart time to heal from losing Aaron. You're not alone. You've got me and your parents by your side. Now, if you're already ready to move on, I'm not judging. Just don't feel pressured by life circumstances. Times have changed and thank goodness for that."

Sarah laughed nervously. How had her question gone so far off course? "No. No, I'm not looking for love, Nan, not now. But you've lost a husband. You know what that's like." Nan's natural conclusion seemed an innocuous course to take the conversation.

"I was just wondering if you'd ever fallen in love again. Or if there had ever been anyone before Granddad . . ." She added on that last bit quietly and left it dangling. She wasn't sure what kind of relationship Nan had had with Jimmy or where it fit into the time line of her life.

Nan smiled softly. "There was this boy once. I was such a fool for him. We would have married, too, if the war hadn't taken him." Her gaze traveled the room while she spoke, like old memories played before her eyes. "It near about laid me flat, him dying. Loss is a funny thing. On the one hand, even after all this time I find myself yearning for what could have been. And on the other, I wouldn't trade the life I've lived for all the gold and silver in the world."

Sarah chewed her lip. "What was his name?"

Nan gave a tender smile. "Jimmy. Jimmy Woodston. He was a farmer. Or at least that's what he wanted to be if this old world had given him the choice. He was my first love."

Sarah's heart thudded in her chest. The name scrawled at the bottom of the letter, years and years after the end of the Vietnam War, was imprinted on her mind. What were the odds Nan had loved two separate men with the same name? Because the Jimmy in her letter sounded very much alive and very much in love in 1986. "You've never mentioned him before."

Nan lifted her shoulders and let them fall. "Your granddad knew about him, but he's about the only person I shared that part of my life with."

Sarah's heart pounded. "Not even with Mom?"

Was it her imagination or did Nan go a little paler at her words?

"No." The word came out a whisper.

Why did she believe Jimmy to be dead?

Sarah tightened her fists until her nails bit into her palms, keeping herself from blurting out the whole thing. She needed to tread carefully. Do a little research and find out exactly who this Jimmy guy was and what had really happened between them.

Sarah twirled her hair around her finger. "Do you, ah . . . still . . . I don't know . . . love him?"

Nan blinked. "Jimmy?"

Sarah nodded.

Nan's face softened. "I was blessed to have two people I loved who both shaped my world for the better. I appreciate the person Jimmy was. I mourn the ways that something as ugly as war took such a beautiful soul. So, I guess you could say that I still love the person he was."

"If you could talk to him again, what would you say?" Sarah's pulse throbbed in her ears.

Nan's mouth opened and then closed. Moisture gathered in her eyes. She shook her head and scrubbed her hands over her face. "I'm sorry, I —"

The front bells chimed and a mother with three children came in the door.

Nan took a deep breath. "I'm going to go entertain Elsie's brood while she gets some shopping done." She turned her back to Sarah and emitted a loud sniffle.

Sarah's hands trembled, rocked by the weight of the knowledge she held.

Nan looked over her shoulder, locking eyes with her. "To move forward with your life, you don't have to forget the good Aaron brought to it. He'll always be a part of you." She turned and stepped to Sarah, placing a gentle hand on her belly. "Especially now."

Yes, especially now she wanted to set them all free from the secrets they kept.

After Sarah climbed in her car and left, Glory Ann herded all three kids to the front register and had them in a huddle as she taught them how to play jacks. Elsie had visibly relaxed when Glory Ann offered to keep her children entertained. How well she remembered the treasure of being able to fully concentrate on a simple task.

Elsie's middle child, a little boy named Dover, crouched in front of the jacks, bouncy ball in hand, tongue poked out the side of his mouth in concentration.

Glory Ann soaked in every detail, from the colors in the children's clothes to the sound of their laughter and the lingering smell of the pine-scented cleaner she used on the floors every night. Anything to distract her from the words that had almost slipped free at Sarah's last question.

"If you could talk to him again, what would you say?"

I'd tell him he had a daughter.

Words locked tightly away, but she'd almost spilled the truth talking to Sarah about Jimmy. It did her heart good saying his name out loud. She never dared speak of him to anyone but Clarence. And Clarence had been gone for nearly forty years. If Rosemary found out she'd kept that from her all these years — that Clarence wasn't her biological father — Rosemary would never forgive her. What purpose would it serve, inflicting that sort of pain on her daughter? Jimmy was gone.

Elsie's oldest child, a willowy nine-year-old girl, jumped to her feet and cheered, the apparent victor in the game. Dover's bottom lip poked out. The youngest, a toddling boy, watched the whole display with his thumb poked in his mouth and a jack gripped in his other hand.

Glory Ann patted Dover's shoulder. "It's okay not to win because life isn't about winning and losing. It's about learning, pushing yourself to play the game better and better. So buck up and challenge that sister of yours to a rematch."

His sister smiled and nodded and laid out the jacks. "C'mon, Dover. Let's give it another go."

Glory Ann stepped back to the register while they played another round.

Rosemary breezed in the door. "Afternoon, Momma."

"Have you told Sarah the truth about what's going on with your health yet?" The words had burst forth before she thought them through. The cord of muscle between her shoulder blades tightened. She was one to talk about telling the truth.

She'd never forget the day Sarah came into the store chanting a little rhyme she'd learned at school. *Secrets, secrets are no fun. Secrets, secrets hurt someone.* How

many people had been hurt by the secret Glory Ann's mother had urged her to keep? But what if those secrets stopped? Would everything really fall apart?

Rosemary walked close and spoke in a hushed whisper. "I told you. I'm not telling her about my diagnosis until she gets herself settled. Out of my house and living her own life."

"Have you ever thought that God may be using this change in Sarah's life to bless you?"

Rosemary scoffed. "Please tell me you're not suggesting God widowed Sarah so she'd be available to babysit me."

Glory Ann winced and shook her head. "I'm saying that Sarah could have done anything in the world when Aaron died, and she chose to come back home. Instead of pushing her away, embrace the blessing of having your daughter close, that she *wants* to be here."

Rosemary's jaw clenched, and her mouth worked like she was fishing for words, but none would bite.

Elsie came through the line, forcing the words between Glory Ann and Rosemary to remain unspoken. Two archers who'd shot arrows, but they'd supernaturally suspended in the air. The intended targets just waiting

for them to fall.

Glory Ann smiled and helped Elsie out to her car with the kids.

After all the groceries were loaded and the children buckled in, Elsie smiled gently and placed a hand on Glory Ann's shoulder. "I'm going to miss this place, Glory Ann. I'll never forget that time you delivered my groceries when all the littles were down with the flu. You don't get love and service like that just anywhere."

Elsie wrapped her in a hug. "Brighton won't be the same with Old Depot gone." She sniffled and climbed in her car and drove away.

Though Elsie's words warmed her, Glory Ann couldn't help but think that if that were true there wouldn't be gaudy closeout signs plastered all over the front of her store.

She trudged back inside.

Rosemary paced. The store was empty. No need to whisper now. Glory Ann's daughter rounded on her. "I refuse to be that selfish. It would not be fair to my daughter to trap her here in this town. Maybe right now it feels like a novel idea, moving back home where it feels safe. But sooner or later the shine will wear off."

Glory Ann's eyebrows shot high. "And if one day she decides this isn't the life she

wants, she can go. What's stopping her?"

Rosemary flung her arms out at her side. "Life. Obligation. My health is going to go downhill, not get better. She'll get so tangled up helping me that she'll lose sight of everything. Life in this town will coil its way around her. Deep down she'll want to go but feel like she can't."

Glory Ann's heart twisted in her chest. She took a slow breath, refusing to let the crush of Rosemary's words infiltrate her tone. "I'm sorry that I was so blind to just how miserable this place made you. At least with Old Depot gone, you can stop using it as an excuse." She shouldered past her daughter before the tide of emotion pulled her into waters too deep to navigate. Maybe the truth didn't set you free. Maybe it just caused pain.

40

Present Day

Sarah sat in the corner booth of the diner, tucked into the one spot she could get decent reception in the building. People came in and out. Food sizzled on the grill. But all of it existed outside of Sarah's focus as she scrolled through her Google search for Jimmy Woodston.

Nan said he'd died in Vietnam. Had he been missing in action and presumed dead? But that wouldn't explain why he never came back to her. It didn't sound like they'd had a falling out after he returned. It sounded like she didn't know he'd returned at all.

What possible motive would Mom have for keeping that letter from Nan? She should just ask Mom what she knew about Jimmy and face her wrath for snooping through her private things.

She chewed her bottom lip, thumb hovering over the call button.

Sarah started as a male form slipped into the booth seat across from her. She tried to ignore the automatic smile that bloomed on her lips at Clay's sudden presence.

"Hiya, stranger." Clay slipped a laminated menu from its perch in the napkin holder. "Mind if I join you?"

Sarah offered a small smile. "Suit yourself."

"How are things with the Old Depot? I saw the signs, passing by."

Sarah lifted her shoulders and let them fall. "Nan's trying to be strong, but I see her struggle to hold back tears when no one is looking."

Clay peered over the menu. "Do you have any plans now that the store's closing?"

She drummed her fingers on the table. "I have a few ideas I've been mulling over, but nothing feels quite right. I still feel so connected to the store, but I don't know . . . I've been to college, graduated with a business degree, served on a multitude of boards for hospitals and charitable organizations, and somehow I still don't know what I'm good at."

She looked to her left and her right to make sure no one was within earshot.

"I'm actually working on something that

I'm hoping could help get Nan's mind off losing the store."

"A new project to show her that there is more than one way to serve the community than running the store?"

Heat rushed to Sarah's face. "Not exactly." She laughed softly. "Your idea sounds better."

He grinned. "What's your idea?"

"Um. You remember that letter I showed you? I poked around, asking Nan questions, and come to find out she thinks Jimmy died in Vietnam. But that letter was from 1986."

"Whoa." Clay sat back against the booth.

"If you saw the way she talked about this man . . . tears came to her eyes, even though he hasn't been a part of her life for almost sixty years."

Clay sucked in air through his teeth. "Why would your mother keep that from Glory Ann?"

"I don't know. It's crazy, thinking about opening up this whole can of worms. I don't even know if this Jimmy guy is still alive, or if he's the sort of man she needs in her life, but after all this time, if she can say that a part of her still mourns him, it's not fair not to at least do some digging."

"Have you found anything?"

"He doesn't exist on social media. Now

I'm trying to do some general Google searches and see if that brings anything up. No luck yet." Sarah resumed scrolling through the populated results. Her heart dropped. "Here's an obituary from last year."

She clicked on the link and read, her knee jittering. She stilled. "Not him. This guy was only in his midthirties."

Clay leaned his elbows on the table, angling so he could see her screen. "What do you know about him?"

"He fought in Vietnam. Nan said he was only there for a short while before they got a report that he had been killed in action. She said he wanted to be a farmer, that he had dreams of coming back and working on his grandfather's farm. But I already checked the public records from Nan's hometown. There isn't anyone with the Woodston name who owns land. It looks like there was a farm, but it was sold and split into parcels in the late sixties."

She scrubbed a hand over her face. "I even looked up stories about soldiers who were thought to be dead and turned up alive years later. But no sign of him."

"Have you looked to find his name in the military records?"

"Not yet. I wasn't really sure where to start."

Clay held out his hand. "May I?"

Sarah handed him the phone. He brought up a search page for Vietnam casualties. He typed in the limited information held on Jimmy, but his name did not pop up. They tried variations of his first name, James and Jim. Still his name didn't appear.

Sarah pointed to another search link. "Vietnam War Casualties Returned Alive."

Clay filled in Jimmy's name.

A short list filled the screen. There at the very bottom was the name James McCoy Woodston.

They exchanged looks.

Sarah sat back against the booth, shaking her head. "He really is alive. Or at least was."

They continued their search, huddled around her phone until the battery drained. She pulled out her charger and plugged it in under the booth. "I guess I better leave a big tip since we've taken over this table all afternoon and I've only bought an order of fries," she said, glancing at the cook who worked the grill loaded down with hamburger patties and eyed her and Clay.

"Let me go order us some food." Clay stood. "What do you like on your burger?"

Sarah's head shot up. "Oh no. I can't ask

you to do that. Besides, I've already roped you in to this enough."

"Too late. I'm all in now. I've got to meet this mystery man who stole Glory Ann's heart all those years ago." Clay leaned his hip against the table and crossed one ankle over the other like a casual cowboy. All he needed was that ugly hat of his.

Her stomach growled. She'd gone far too long without eating. "Cheddar, mustard, and extra pickles, no onions. If you're sure you don't mind."

He nodded and went to the register to order. It wasn't until he was walking back that the implications of letting him pay for her meal hit her. This was a mistake. They'd already spent a lot of time together on that car trip. Sharing far more of her life and pain in her past than she'd intended. Did this further blur the lines of friendship beyond what was wise?

She dug in her purse to pay him back, but was only able to scrounge up four wrinkled one-dollar bills. If she was going to live in this little town, she'd better get used to carrying cash again. She was pretty sure Clay had never used Venmo in his life.

When he sat she held out the crumpled bills. "Sorry, I just realized this is all the cash I have on me."

He waved her hand away with his nose wrinkled. "Put that away. It's on me."

Ugh. This was so awkward, but she had to say something. "Clay, I want to be up front with you. I'm not looking for a relationship. I'm not comfortable with you paying for my meal. I just . . . I don't want to give you the wrong idea."

Clay gave a quick nod. "A friend can buy a friend a meal."

She ducked her head and dug back into research while they waited for their food to arrive.

A few minutes later a waiter arrived carrying a tray laden with two burgers, two large fries, and two milkshakes swirled with a tower of whipped cream each.

Her mouth instantly watered. She was hungrier than she'd realized. "I love you."

The waiter's eyes darted between her and Clay, and it hit her then what she'd said.

Clay just laughed. "Are you talking to me or the food?"

Cheeks hot, she said, "The food, of course. Although the way to my heart is definitely through my stomach."

He nodded with a sly smile. "Duly noted."

She focused on stuffing her face with French fries and bites of the enormous burger to prove she only had eyes for the meal in front of her.

The uncomfortable moment passed — at least, uncomfortable for Sarah. Clay didn't seem the least bit fazed.

Following leads on his own phone, he scrolled while he ate, occasionally glancing up at her. There was a softness in his expression that made her broken heart do funny things in her chest. Aerobics it hadn't healed enough to perform again. Yet.

Clay stilled. "I think I found Glory Ann's Jimmy."

Sarah dropped her burger on her plate and scrambled for a napkin to wipe away the mustard that had dripped onto her fingers. She reached for the phone Clay extended.

He propped his elbows on the table as she scanned the article. "This article is about a James Woodston who lives in Memphis, Tennessee," he said. "This guy founded an organization that helps people start community gardens. It's his mission to help eliminate food deserts and change the landscape of a city through horticulture."

Sarah stared at the picture of the man featured in the article. He was tall and thin with a thick head of wavy white hair. His eyes were a striking blue.

"Well, he's a farmer of sorts. So I guess

that fits. What should I do? Should I call him? Find out if it's really him."

Clay shrugged. "Is that the kind of conversation you have over the phone? 'Hi, my grandmother used to date you, but she thinks you're dead. Were you just going to extreme lengths to ghost her, or what?' "

Sarah choked on her sip of milkshake. "Yeah. I have no idea how I'd start that conversation. With him or my mom and her buried letter."

Clay scrubbed a hand along his jaw. "Do you want to meet him? I'll drive you."

Sarah opened her mouth and closed it. "That's crazy . . . isn't it?"

"Maybe. But can you imagine if this was all some weird misunderstanding and you were able to reunite your grandmother with her first love?"

41

October 1997

Glory Ann smiled as Sarah skipped through the opened door that Kevin, one of the new high school boys she'd hired to bag groceries, held open for her. He gave a slight bend at the waist as if little Sarah was the grand duchess of Old Depot Grocery.

Rosemary trailed behind her, a slight stoop to her shoulders. It wasn't easy on her, Bo being on the road all the time, not that she would admit it. "Did Sarah have a good day at school?"

Rosemary's smile seemed pasted. "She did. Chattered nonstop all the way here about her new teacher."

"It's Carson's girl, isn't it? I know he and Lydia are happy she decided to move back after college."

"Mmhmm." Rosemary was looking past her to where Sarah stood speaking to one of the customers. Her hands pantomiming whatever story she shared.

"Rosemary?"

"Huh?" She blinked as if Glory Ann's words had called her back from another world.

"Sweetie, why don't you take the rest of the afternoon off. Leave Sarah here. She can help me around the store. With the high school crew coming in there will be plenty of help."

"The bookkeeping —"

"Can wait."

"Sarah has a birthday party later this evening."

"All the more reason to take a few minutes and breathe before being surrounded by a pack of giggly eight-year-olds. Go to the park and take a walk. Better yet, go home and get a nap."

"I don't know . . ." Rosemary worried her bottom lip between her teeth.

"I do know. Now, scoot. Your momma's got this covered." She wished Rosemary understood that it was okay to be at rest. That was part of the blessing of being so close, that they could share each other's burdens. But Rosemary always insisted on trying to carry both of theirs.

After Rosemary drove away, Glory Ann slipped back to the office and retrieved the brightly wrapped package she'd tucked away earlier that morning. She poked her head around an aisle and watched her pigtailed granddaughter chattering with the teenage girl working the register, trying to copy the older girl's stance and mannerisms.

"Say-rah." Glory Ann called out the girl's name in singsong.

Sarah spun with a wide grin and a sparkle in her eyes. "Yes, Glory Nan?"

"I've got a surprise for you."

Sarah scurried her direction.

Glory Ann presented her with the package.

"But, Nan, it's not even my birthday."

"Oh, this is just something small. You've been such a big help around here, I wanted to give you a little gift."

Sarah gently took the package from her hands with a gap-toothed grin. Carefully peeling away the paper, she let out a little squeal of delight when she revealed the kelly green fabric embroidered with her name. "My very own store apron?"

"Yes. You've been helping out quite a bit around here and it was high time you looked like an official member of the team." The truth was, Glory Ann had caught her trying to wear one of the adult-sized versions on their last stocking day, and Sarah had tripped all over the too-long hem.

Beaming, Sarah slipped the apron over her head and tied it around her waist. Once it was secure, she flung her arms around Glory Ann's middle and squeezed tight. "Thank you, thank you, thank you!"

"Of course, dear. Now let's get to business. I need some help restocking a few things that we're running low on. Can you help me out?"

Sarah gave her a little salute. "At your service, boss."

Glory Ann grinned and shook her head as she and her granddaughter hurried to the back. How sweet it was, getting to share this place with Sarah, even more so because Sarah loved being there so much. She only wished Clarence could have lived to see her. It was so much like watching their own girls. The way she'd skip through the aisles or play hide-and-seek with the children who came in with their mothers.

Rosemary worried all the time that Sarah spent too much time there. Life at Old Depot had been a good enough raising for Rosemary and Jessamine. They'd both grown into strong, well-rounded young women. At eight, Sarah was already at ease conversing with both young and old. And she was learning a thing or two about work ethic. Clarence would have been so proud.

Glory Ann read off a list of items that needed to be refilled on the shelves. Sarah went straight for the heaviest item, a box of canned green beans. She stood with it, swaying under the weight. Glory Ann hurried forward to lift away the burden.

"I'll grab this. Why don't you grab that box of potato chips we need? It's huge." But far lighter.

"I wanted to do the cans."

"Sure thing. Let me carry the green beans to their spot and I'll let you stock them. The pintos too."

Rosemary hurried through the front door of Old Depot. It had taken her a little longer than she'd expected at her walk-in appointment at the salon, and she'd barely had enough time to grab a birthday gift. If she didn't hurry Sarah back out the door, she would miss out on the festivities.

The lines were long and the aisles full. Kids clung to their momma's legs while their mothers chatted with neighbors next to full shopping carts.

Katie and Kevin, her latest hires, seemed to handle the rush just fine. The two high schoolers had dubbed themselves the K

Team. Cute. Mom was probably rooting for another grocery store romance. She was always trying to match people up. She should probably mind her own business and stay out of people's love lives. Get her own, maybe.

Rosemary stiffened at the thought. Maybe Momma should stay out of relationships altogether if she couldn't be faithful.

"Hey, Katie? Have you seen Sarah?"

Katie shifted her attention from the register where she was ringing up a large order. "I think they're on aisle four, stocking canned goods."

Rosemary hurried to the aisle, weaving around shoppers. Sarah sat on the floor next to where Mom crouched. Both of their heads were bent in earnest conversation. Genuine happiness softened her mother's features. A little of the guilt for leaving her daughter in Momma's care dissolved.

"Sarah, we need to go. The party starts in just a few minutes."

Sarah's head popped up, and she stood. "Momma, Momma, look what Nan made for me!" She did a little twirl, showing off the kid-sized apron.

Rosemary's chest clenched. It should be cute, her daughter dressed up in this miniature version of the store uniform. Instead, she wrestled the urge to remove the thing tied around her daughter's neck. "How nice. Now let's get going."

"I want to stay here with Nan." Sarah propped her little hands on her hips. That glint lit her eyes, so much like her grandmother's.

"We already told Hannah you were coming to her party. It would be rude not to go."

"But I'm having fun here. With Nan. This is better than a dumb girly party."

Rosemary's eyes widened at the foot stomp that accompanied her daughter's words.

"Sarah Lynne Anderson, take off that apron and get your feet walking toward the front door this minute. Not another word. You will not live your life shut up in this grocery store. I won't allow it."

At Rosemary's words, Momma stood. That softness that had graced her face moments before vanished. She placed her hands on Sarah's shoulders. "Come here, dear. I'll hang up your apron for the next time." Then Momma leveled a hard stare in Rosemary's direction and stalked past her. But it wasn't anger in her eyes. It mirrored Sarah's little face.

Rosemary straightened her shoulders.

"Come on, young lady. You heard me. Now scoot!" She swept her hand toward the front door. Always delicately balanced between strong-willed and obedient, Sarah walked past with rigid shoulders. Whether Rosemary had allowed her to stay or forced her to go to the party, she was sure she was somehow letting her daughter down.

42

Present Day

Three days later, Sarah climbed into Clay's truck with two piping hot biscuits left over from breakfast.

"Did you ask your mom about Jimmy?" he asked when she shut the door behind her.

Sarah shook her head. "I couldn't. I don't want to confront her about it until I talk to him myself. Make sure he's the same guy. See if he knows why Nan still believes that he died in Vietnam. If this guy is messed up and crazy, I don't want to involve Mom and Nan. They have enough going on."

He nodded with his head cocked to the side. "Fair enough. Where does she think you're going right now?"

She offered a sly smile. "I gave some vague answer about getting some loose ends tied up. She might've assumed it was about my life in Chicago, and I didn't happen to correct her."

He laughed. "Well, I think I figured out what you're good at."

Sarah tilted her head. "What?"

"Snooping through long-lost family secrets and stirring up general trouble."

She smacked him on the shoulder. "You, hush."

Miles passed with stretches of silence punctured by scattershot conversation. Which oddly enough wasn't as uncomfortable as it should have been. She didn't feel the pressure to fill the quiet in Clay's presence. Maybe because the two of them weren't trying to *be* anything other than two people curious about a decades-old secret.

With Aaron, she'd carried the weight of their relational health on her shoulders like a backpack loaded down with too many books, always feeling the pressure to keep the conversations going.

She shook away the fact that she'd thought of Clay and Aaron in the same thought stream. Aaron had been her husband. Clay was a nice guy who cared about Nan. Of course, things were different with him. Zero expectations.

Heat crept into her face, remembering her mother's words this morning when Clay pulled up.

"You two have been spending a lot of time together."

"What are you talking about?"

"It's a small town, Sarah. People talk. The diner. The park. The long car trips."

"I don't see how it's anyone's business . . ."

Her mom shrugged. "Personally, I think Clay is a nice young man. But don't you think it's a little soon?"

She'd skirted out the door rather than face the rest of her questioning. It wasn't too soon, because whatever this was with Clay was strictly platonic. Mom just wanted to make sure she wasn't getting tied down with some country boy with no aspirations.

Like that time in high school when she forbade Sarah to date Tyler Andrews. For the longest time she imagined that there was some secret feud between their families, but it turned out that Mom just didn't think he was good enough for her. Sarah had seen him just last week with his wife and twin daughters at the park. He must have been on his lunch break because he was wearing his grease-stained overalls while he pushed his girls in the swings.

Nobody in that little bunch of people was wearing designer clothes and the girls' outfits were worn and mismatched, but she couldn't shake just how happy they all looked. And this strange feeling that crept over Sarah that she'd been cheated out of something.

She shook off the thought. Sarah had made her choices. And like Clay had said, there was still breath in her lungs. And that meant there was still time to take a chance on something new.

Clay glanced her way. "Do you need to stop for anything before we get there?"

"We're only fifteen minutes outside of Memphis. I'll be fine until then." She gazed out the passenger window, scrunching her nose. He was probably having flashbacks to the ridiculous number of bathroom breaks she'd needed on the Illinois trip.

Clay tilted his head. "Don't you think it's weird that this Jimmy guy lives less than an hour away from your grandmother all these years later?"

Sarah toyed with the ends of her hair. "I know. It's like he wanted to stay close, but something held him back from coming closer. I wonder what the real story is."

"How did he act when you called and asked to meet him?"

"He sounded normal enough. Soft-spoken. Humble. Of course, I didn't tell him that I thought he was my grandmother's long-lost love, only that I worked at a small-town grocery and I was eager to learn more about his mission to decrease food deserts in America."

Clay's eyebrows arched. "So you're going to make this guy break down his life's work for you when all you want to know is if he literally ghosted your grandmother over fifty years ago?"

"I *am* interested." Her voice raised an octave in self-defense. "I think what he is trying to do for lower-income families is admirable. Just because I also want to see if a little epic matchmaking is possible doesn't mean that's the only reason I'm interested in what he does. Although, it seems like Nan and Jimmy already have one thing in common — care for their community. Maybe love and common values are enough to conquer time, distance, separation, war, and a false report of death."

Clay raised an eyebrow. "Somebody has started to sound like a bit of a romantic over the past few days."

She wanted to believe in love, that it could endure all those things, especially now, with this ridiculous plan she had in her mind to glowingly reunite two long-lost loves. Forgetting so easily the lies that must have been told. The secret her mother must have kept.

And a dozen other potential land mines that would cause her fairy-tale imaginings to implode.

In Memphis, Clay parked his truck along the street, and they walked side by side to the barbecue joint where they were supposed to meet Jimmy for lunch before he took them on a tour of the community gardens and the mobile farmer's markets his organization ran. The windows of the restaurant sported signs that read BEST BARBECUE IN MEMPHIS. More than a few places they'd passed seemed to make the same claim, but in Jimmy's email he'd insisted that Barb's Que was the true blue-ribbon best.

Just outside the front door, Sarah recognized the tall, slim, white-haired figure from the article. He turned. She sucked in a breath at the expression in his eyes. A quality that the photograph had been ill-equipped to capture. There was something so familiar in this stranger's gaze. Something she couldn't quite put a name to. Her nerve endings felt raw. Every sound louder, her heart thumped hard in her chest.

She stuck out her hand. "Hi, I'm Sarah . . ." Her voice dropped off, searching for which last name to give. How long would this identity crisis last? To lay claim to her deceased husband's name felt like a lie, but going by Anderson didn't feel quite right either.

Jimmy's hand was large and calloused. A hand accustomed to hard labor.

Clay took his turn introducing himself, then Jimmy showed them into the restaurant. The people who worked there knew him by name and waved him back to what they called his table.

Behind her menu, Sarah's mind raced. Maybe she wouldn't bring up Nan today. Instead, she'd get to know this guy a little and decide for herself if the story could possibly match up. And then one day, a door would magically open in their conversation, and she'd step gracefully through and tell him she thought that her grandmother could still be in love with him.

A round of sweet teas in front of them, they lowered their menus and waited for the waitress to return.

Jimmy offered a friendly smile. "So, your email mentioned that you had some questions for me. Now, I don't run much of the day-to-day operations anymore, I leave that to some young up-and-comers, but I definitely have an inside scoop on all the inner workings. What would you like to know?"

The truth burst out of her. "Do you know Glory Ann Clearwater?"

A pert waitress strolled up the moment the words left Sarah's lips. "Hi, y'all. So what'll it be?"

White-faced, Jimmy stood. "Ex-excuse me." He hurried away.

43

Present Day

Sarah winced and glanced at Clay. "Do you think he'll come back?"

Clay peered over her head to look out the windows. "No sign of him. You really know how to go for the jugular, don't ya?"

Sarah propped her head in her hand. "I don't know what came over me."

"Maybe he'll come back after he's had a chance to calm down." He shrugged. "At least we know one thing for sure."

"What's that?"

"We found the right Jimmy."

Just then the waitress reappeared, having pulled up short in her offer to take their order after witnessing Jimmy's sudden retreat. "Do you want to wait for your dinin' companion to return, or would you like me to go ahead and get your order in?"

Clay ordered barbecue nachos as an appetizer, stalling for time.

"I can't believe Nan thinks he's dead. After all this time. I bet he doesn't know that *she* doesn't know that he's alive. Mom intercepted that letter for some reason. What would possess her to do something so horrible?"

"Whoa, take a breath." Clay laughed behind the tea he'd been about to sip. "Maybe if he doesn't come back you can send an email and catch him up. Since you've already . . . um . . . broken the ice." He smirked.

Ten minutes later, Jimmy reappeared, fidgeting with his hands. He sat and opened his mouth to speak.

The waitress reappeared, ready smile on her face. "Sir, what would you like?"

Curse this woman's eagerness to help.

"J-just my tea for now is fine." He lifted the cup in his shaking hand.

The waitress disappeared into the kitchen.

Jimmy cleared his throat. "I'm sorry, who did you say you are? How do you know Glory Ann?"

Sarah folded her hands in her lap, clasping them tight. Her knee jittered up and down. "I'm her granddaughter. I . . . I found a letter hidden in my mother's private things. I asked my nan about you, but she said you died in Vietnam."

She glanced at Clay for reassurance that she didn't sound like a chattering lunatic.

"I suppose that is the easiest way to explain me." The crease between Jimmy's brows deepened. "I sent her parents a letter. I told them there had been a mistake, that I had not died in Vietnam as my parents and everyone else believed. I didn't want to give Glory Ann a heart attack, seeing as how I was coming back from the dead sixteen years after my funeral, so they were supposed to help me break the news. She was supposed to write or call if she wanted to see me, but I never heard from her."

Sarah dug in her bag for the letter she found. "This letter?"

Jimmy clutched it, making the brittle paper crinkle in his hands. She watched the rapid back and forth dart of his eyes as he scanned the letter. He shook his head. "I sent this one five years later. I'd never heard from her, and I decided she didn't want to hear from me. I didn't want to interrupt her life, you see. But I was just missing her one day, and I wrote her another letter. It wasn't fair of me to insert myself into her life again, she'd moved on so beautifully, after all, but I felt like there was so much left unsaid between us."

Sarah leaned forward in her seat. "Like?"

A corner of Jimmy's mouth twitched at her eagerness. The waitress reappeared to bring the appetizer, once again putting an unbearable pause on their conversation.

After the waitress left with their dinner orders, Jimmy propped his elbows on the table, his fingers moving in a slow but agitated wringing of his hands. "What has Glory Ann told you?"

"That you were her first love. That even to this day she misses you."

Jimmy grimaced and expelled a heavy breath. "Why would she never call? I know she's happily married. That war took from us what should have been ours, but it was never my intention to come between her and her husband. I hope she understood that. Maybe she's angry I waited so long to tell her that I was alive?"

"That's what I'm trying to tell you," Sarah said. "She doesn't know you're alive. I don't know why her parents wouldn't have told her about your letter, and I have no idea why my mother would have opened, much less hidden, a letter addressed to Nan. However it happened, Nan said she still mourns you."

"Maybe your mother was concerned I would interfere in her family."

"That's just the thing, my grandfather

passed away in 1983. You didn't write the letter she hid until 1986. She'd have had no reason to be concerned that you'd be trying to break up her parents' marriage."

Jimmy stilled. "Her husband passed away?" His shoulders sagged. "She lost two men who were supposed to be there for her. Take care of her."

At this Sarah couldn't help but grin. "I don't know what Nan was like when you knew her, but the Nan I know sure doesn't need any man to take care of her." She reached across the table and squeezed Jimmy's tough hand. "But I do think she'd like to see you again. One thing I don't understand, though, is why it took you so long to reach out to her."

Jimmy looked from Sarah to Clay and back, a misery in his expression that tore at Sarah's heart. "I should have died over there. I really should have. I hadn't been there more than a couple days when we ran into some heavy fire. A buddy of mine was hit real bad. I dragged him into cover, and I draped my jacket over him. But he was gone. I knew there wasn't anything I could do for him. I moved away from him for just a moment to get a better line of sight and an explosion went off. I couldn't hear. I couldn't see. Next thing I knew I was in a prisoner camp."

Sarah's eyes widened. "Oh . . . wow." That explained why everyone thought he'd died.

"I was there until '72. Seven years as a prisoner of war. It wasn't until I was released that I learned about the mistaken identity. It was a bit of a mess trying to sort that out, to prove I was who I said I was. When I looked in the mirror, I saw a man who really did look like something that should be dead. I asked that my family not be alerted. It was going to be a bad enough shock for them to realize that I had been alive all those years, but even worse seeing what I had become. I decided I would try to find my way back to that same boy that left for war all those years ago before contacting them, but I found it impossible." Jimmy shut his eyes tight, and his voice cracked over his next words.

"Every night I'd sit huddled with my back to the wall, trying to keep sleep from claiming me, until exhaustion would take me anyway, only to be shaken back awake by the demons haunting my dreams."

Sarah glanced at Clay who nodded at Jimmy's words, staring at his own clasped hands, sharing in a pain she could never comprehend.

"I tried for a while — to rehabilitate

myself," Jimmy continued. "Instead I fell into the bottle and when that didn't work, anything I could inject, snort, or swallow to make my living nightmare stop for a little while. One time, when I almost killed myself with the stuff I put in my body, I dried out in a rehab facility. That helped for a little bit, and during that time, I tried looking up my parents. It wasn't easy. Asking around my old hometown, claiming I was a long-lost family friend. I discovered they'd moved across country. And that Glory Ann had married mere weeks after my death notice. That was a shock I wasn't expecting." He let out a soft laugh that was more like a sigh. "Not that I thought she'd have waited for me, but for her to marry so soon? Then I learned that my parents died in a terrible accident five months after I had gotten back stateside. Five months I could have had with them if I hadn't been so afraid to reach out." He clenched and released his shaking hands. "I thought I was doing them a favor, but I was just stealing time. That whole experience sent me into another tailspin, and I fell right back into my addiction."

The ache in Jimmy's words, pain that was clearly raw and fresh after all this time, caused moisture to well in Sarah's eyes.

"I'm not proud of the wasted years of my

life, but back then I just couldn't see a way forward. I'd lost all the parts of this life that had mattered. My parents. Glory Ann. . . . I crashed a friend's car into a telephone pole, high on something that I couldn't even remember what it was, and I ended up in court-ordered rehab.

"One day I was praying, asking God why He'd let this happen. Why all these years had been stolen from my life. I had been a good person who just wanted to make the world a better place, but I'd become so tainted by darkness I couldn't feel the warmth of the sun anymore. And while I was praying, it was like this calm came over me. Even though it was dead silent during that dark night, it was like I heard the words, 'It's not too late.'

"From that day, it was different. I'm not saying I didn't still struggle, but whenever darkness came for me, those words buried in my soul would sing louder. *It's not too late.*"

Sarah glanced at Clay again. Jimmy's words were such a clear echo to what he had said to her on his front porch after she'd confessed the mess her marriage had been. He offered her a tight smile and nod in reply.

Jimmy twisted his napkin. "After I had

gotten healthy, I sent that letter to her parents. I just wanted to make sure she was okay. That the ugliness of war hadn't left her as scarred as it had me.

"I didn't blame her for not responding. I imagined she was more than a little angry finding out I'd let her believe I was dead for so long. But you see, Sarah, I couldn't have come back to her like I was. After that I tried to move on. To find love. But those relationships never lasted. One lonely day I penned the letter you have now. I've finally resigned myself to the fact that I'm better off on my own."

Sarah stood. "But you should come back now. She still loves you. I know she does."

Jimmy's eyes grew moist. "It's been almost sixty years." He blinked. "We could've been married almost sixty years if I had never been drafted." His voice went breathy, but then he shook his head. "But I don't think this is a good idea. For me or Glory Ann."

Sarah gripped the edge of the table where she stood. "I don't agree. She won't admit it, but she's lost seeing the store she loved closing. Seeing you again could be exactly what she needs. To see the way that you've found ways to impact your community, that she still has the ability to start fresh even now."

Clay put a hand on hers. No doubt to remind her where she was. Other restaurant patrons had stopped their meals to listen to her overloud voice laced with desperation.

Jimmy laughed under his breath as Sarah took her seat again. "I think the only thing I'd do is raise her blood pressure. Letting her go decades believing I was dead and then showing up."

"It's not your fault. She'll see that. Her parents didn't tell her for some reason, and my mother hid the second letter."

"Your mother must have had her reasons too."

"What she did was wrong."

"Maybe she knows something we don't." Jimmy pulled his gaze from her and shook his head. "Please don't tell Glory Ann about me. I know you're curious about how all this came to be, but I want her to hear it from me if she hears it at all. This isn't some fairy tale. It's my life and it's not pretty."

"Of course."

Jimmy, Sarah, and Clay finished their meal and left the restaurant with more than a few curious stares following them out. Sarah gave Jimmy a parting hug. "No matter what you decide about Nan, I'd like to stay in touch."

He nodded once, a small smile on his

weathered face. “I will, Sarah. I’m glad you found me. If nothing else, at least I know she wasn’t silent because she didn’t want to see me.”

44

Present Day

Glory Ann turned the lock and flipped over the open sign. Motions she'd performed for almost sixty years. She stared out over the empty parking lot, her mind wandering through the memories. Watching infants turn into children and then teens, and then coming to shop with their own children in tow. Generations of families this place had served.

She heaved a breath and turned to the bare shelves. Almost bare. The community food pantry was going to come by tomorrow to pick up the rest of it.

Rosemary appeared from the office, dusting off her hands, though Glory Ann knew she'd been on the phone, not doing manual labor. "I just got off a call with the potential buyer. They've made quite the offer."

Glory Ann raised her eyebrows and crossed her arms over her chest. "You must be pleased."

"Mother, don't take that tone with me. I know you're not happy about it, but we agreed it's for the best."

"You don't have to be so excited about it though." Glory Ann sighed.

"Mom, you know I'm not. I'm just relieved."

Glory Ann sank onto the stool behind the checkout counter. "I don't understand why you stayed if you hated it so much. Why couldn't you have been like Jessamine and —"

"Why couldn't you have appreciated what I did?" Rosemary threw up her hands and let them fall at her sides. She paced the space in front of the door. "It was always Jessamine this and Jessamine that. Like she was some kind of hero, out saving the world. No matter how hard I worked here, serving, going half crazy trying to keep this store afloat for you, it was always Jessamine that you were bragging about."

"I only meant —"

"I know what you meant."

Glory Ann stood and blocked Rosemary's pacing path. She gripped her shoulders. "Stop it. Stop it right now. I am sick and tired of you feeling sorry for yourself. What I meant was that Jessamine lived her own life on her own terms and she's happy. You're not. Maybe I did flash around Jessie's pictures and latest updates all the time, but that was only because it was all I had. She wasn't here. You were. I got to see you every day. Work alongside you, even if we didn't always see eye to eye. If you think I took that for granted, you're wrong. If I made you feel less than her, I'm sorry." She let her hands fall from her daughter's shoulders.

"You've been a rock. But, Rosemary, I feel like you've been trying to pay penance when you never needed to. Your father worked hard at this store to make sure that we could all have the lives we wanted, and if this isn't what you wanted, you should have left." Glory Ann's heart throbbed in her chest. All the times she'd been at a loss of what to say to her hurting daughter crashing over her. "That would be the way to honor him, not this bitterness tainting your life. Living like you're trying to earn your keep. I know that your illness was a big motivator in wanting to sell the store. But it was more than that. It was like it was the only way you could be free. But you've always been free."

"You're the one who doesn't understand." Rosemary looked away, staring through the front glass.

"Maybe not. But you should know this. Sarah wanted this store as much as I did. She always has. But you made her believe it wasn't enough. Pushing her to chase things she never wanted. All because you were afraid she would be as unhappy as you are. Instilling in her a belief that her dreams were too small."

Rosemary jerked her head back like she'd been slapped. "I never told her —"

"You didn't have to. All she had to do was listen to you for a minute, always telling her that she wasn't stuck here like you were." Glory Ann ran her hand over the corner of the checkout counter, the sharp edge worn smooth over the years. "I said no to Sarah's offer for you, Rosemary. Because the store closing would be the only way you'd see the door to your life has always been open."

"I was trying to help her."

"At some point you have to let her live her own life. And you need to start living yours. It's not too late. I know you're worried about your diagnosis limiting your life, but it doesn't have to entrap you any more than the store did. Your life is still full of possibilities. It always was."

Rosemary's blue eyes filled, and she looked away with a sniffle.

"What? What's going on in your head right now?"

"It stopped being my life the night Daddy died."

Glory Ann stilled. "Is that why you hated it here?"

Rosemary shook her head. Her voice came out on the crest of a wail. "I killed him. I killed the person who provided for our family. When I wanted to sell the store, all I wanted to do was make sure you'd be taken care of when I couldn't do it anymore."

Glory Ann pulled her into a hug. Her middle-aged daughter who was taller than her by a head. What she would give to be her shelter like an unshakable sequoia tree. Like her Clarence. "Oh, honey. That was never supposed to be your burden. You didn't break into the store. You didn't fire the gun. And you weren't your father who rushed headlong into a dangerous situation. It was a terrible thing, your father's death, but it wasn't your fault. Do you hear me?"

Rosemary's shoulders shook in silent sobs.

Glory Ann pulled her tighter to her chest. "All I *ever* wanted was for you to have a good life. A life you could be proud of."

Their embrace lasted but a moment longer, and then Rosemary stepped back and swiped away the tears. She blinked hard and that vulnerable little girl in her eyes was shuttered away. "It's okay," she said as she turned.

But it wasn't okay.

She watched as Rosemary headed toward the back door, her fingertips grazing the ends of the shelves she passed.

As she walked, the familiar squeak of the floorboards under her feet seemed to call Rosemary out as the worst kind of traitor.

Today's call from an investment company up north had been a real victory.

But it didn't feel like it.

Rosemary exited the back of the store and sank into the driver's seat of her car. She rested her head against the steering wheel, mind reeling from all the words that had passed between her and her mother.

She hadn't meant to blurt all that out about Jessie. Bare that part of herself she worked so hard to hide.

She dialed her sister's number.

Jessamine picked up on the third ring. "Hey, sis."

"I just accepted an offer on the store. Mom finally consented."

"Wow. How's she taking it?"

"Okay, I guess. You know how she is about Old Depot. If she had her way she'd be buried in that place, I think."

The other end of the line stayed silent, and it hit Rosemary then, what she'd said. There were days not long after Daddy died, she'd catch her mother standing in the place he'd been shot, and Rosemary had feared Momma would curl up in that same spot and die of heartache right there.

Rosemary huffed as if she could puff away her careless words. "Then we got in this sort of argument about how I've ruined Sarah's life and how you were the favorite child, even though I was the one who devoted my life to sticking by her side."

Jessie's bold laugh burst through the line. "You two are a real pair, you know that? For once you ought to lighten up and stop trying so hard to be the best daughter."

Rosemary rolled her eyes. "Easy for you to say. You never had to work at it."

"I never was trying to be the best anything. *Or* please anyone. I was just me. I got jealous of you sometimes too, you know. Mom and Dad bragged all the time about how responsible you were. Forget the fact that you had Dad wrapped around your little finger." There was no ire in Jessie's voice, only a gentleness. "Mom told me what the doctor said. It makes sense now why you were so ready to sell."

"I —" But her words were cut away by the thickness building in her throat.

"You're going to be okay."

"I know. From everything my doctors say, late-onset MS is rarely fatal. It's hard, though, having no idea how bad it will get. I could stay the same for years or I could be in a wheelchair within months. I don't —"

"Rosemary, I know that you've never been a big fan of uncertainty. I'm not trying to be insensitive when I say this, but what if this helps you set yourself free from always needing to be the dependable one? What if you could just be, sis? Take each day as it came without trying to plan for all the ways life could possibly go wrong."

Rosemary shook her head with a soft smile tugging her lips. "Only you could find the sunny side in being diagnosed with a chronic, life-altering disease."

"Let your daughter be there for you. I know you're scared she's going to get tied down or lose out on whatever mystical thing you think lies beyond Brighton, Tennessee. But, sis, there's not some magical place where everybody is automatically happy and fulfilled in life. In all my wanderlust ways, I've figured out that happiness doesn't come from the 'big break' or 'buying the big house' or the 'big whatever.' It comes from the everyday choice to embrace the beauty in the little things. And Brighton taught me that. Not some grand adventure."

45

Present Day

Sarah was determined to make Nan's final days at Old Depot Grocery as memorable as possible. Aunt Jessie showing up yesterday was definitely a good start.

She balanced a huge tray of cupcakes and nudged her way through the back door of the store where Mom was hanging streamers in sweeping loops along the edges of the walls.

Clay walked to her and took the cupcakes from her arms. Sarah stared at the scene in front of her. No more aisles. No more register. The coolers and freezers were gone. She visualized new walls going up, dividing the large open room. It could work, these daydreams she'd been toying with.

She followed Clay, those old floors creaking beneath her feet. "Mom, will you do me a favor?" Her mother turned with a bit of streamer clamped between her lips while she twisted another piece and Sarah had to stifle a laugh. "Please come down off that ladder and let Clay do that for you."

"I'm perfectly capable —"

"I know you are." But what if she got another spasm in her leg like she had yesterday. A spasm that caused her to stumble walking down a flat sidewalk. After that episode, Mom had finally confessed her health issues and why she'd been withholding them from her.

"Sarah, are you sure that boy knows how to hang streamers without them looking like tangled spaghetti noodles?" She stepped back onto the wooden floor. "This needs a woman's touch."

"Ms. Rosemary," Clay said, clearly listening in, "I can't claim to have a woman's touch, but I'll do my best to do your streamers justice. I'll coax them into shape like I do the little pole bean shoots that come up in my garden." He winked and took her place on the stepladder.

Mom whispered to Sarah as they walked to the front of the store. "Nan is right, you better watch that boy. He could charm a tiger out of its stripes with those eyes and those dimples."

"Mom . . ." Sarah hissed. "We're friends." She glanced at Clay, who busily hung streamers as though he hadn't heard a word.

Mom grinned. "You never know, you might change your mind when the timing is right."

Sarah willed her cheeks to stay free of a betraying blush. Was Mom actually supportive of her falling for someone like Clay? "Anyway . . . I have some more cupcakes out in the car. Want to give me a hand with those?"

At the car, Sarah handed Mom a tray of cupcakes. Arms loaded, Mom's mouth worked like she was looking for words but was unable to land on anything sufficient.

"Mom?"

"Sarah, I'm sorry."

"Um?" Sarah shifted her feet, uncertain how to respond to the abruptness of her mother's declaration.

"I never meant to push you away. I just wanted you to be happy."

Sarah looked over the adjacent field, the maple's branches waving in the soft breeze. "I made my own choices. I chose not to come back here after college. I chose to marry Aaron and embrace the life he had. That was on me. You didn't force me."

"But would you have chosen those things without my pushing? What if I let you be all those times you wanted to work on the store instead of going to piano or ballet? Those times you'd rather have tailed your grandmother around the store instead of going to birthday parties. What if your whole life I hadn't lived in fear of you becoming me and I just let you find your way?"

She shook her head. "What-ifs won't get us anywhere, Momma. We can't change the past. But we can choose a new tomorrow." Sarah forced a smile. She'd finally found her path forward. Her mother would not approve. At all. "Let's get the rest of this inside before the party starts."

A few hours later, Old Depot Grocery shone from floor to ceiling. The food table was bursting with the things Sarah and Rosemary had baked the night before, accompanied by other dishes brought in by friends of the family. True to his word, Clay had done Rosemary's streamers justice.

People began to fill the store. Some newer families, some Sarah had known her entire life. Aunt Jessie should be there any minute with the extra drinks and snacks they decided were needed with the volume of people who'd come out to celebrate.

The surprise set in motion, Sarah left to pick up Nan from the nursing home where Sarah had dropped her off earlier that morning. Nan had been visiting with some of the elderly members of the community every week without fail for as long as Sarah could remember.

She had once asked Nan why she went so often when she didn't have any family members there. The gravity in Nan's voice when she responded was so heavy it made Sarah's heart do a stutter step in her chest.

"Because people need to know they are not forgotten."

Sarah always wondered if the sadness in her tone came from experience or out of a fear of what her future might look like. She couldn't conceive of a version of Nan's life where she wasn't surrounded by people who adored her.

When she drove up to the curb of the nursing home, Nan stood gripping her cow-print pocketbook in her hands. She shook her head as she slipped into the passenger seat. "You're late. I could have driven myself over here. I don't know why you were so fired up to play chauffeur."

"I'm sorry, Nan. It wasn't that I didn't have the time. I just . . ."

"Pregnancy brain? I remember how it was." Nan clicked her tongue, and a faraway look took over her face. "One time, when I was pregnant with your aunt Jessie, I had closed up shop and was on my way to the bank to make the day's deposit. I got caught up talking to somebody — I can't remember who now. But I do remember that I drove off with a bag of cash on top of my car. You can imagine my panic when I parked at the bank and all that money was nowhere to be found."

Sarah's eyes widened. "Did you get the money back?"

Nan laughed behind her wrinkled hand. "Your granddaddy Clarence must have spied it on the car as I was driving out. The way I heard it, he took off after my car, running and waving his arms. But my tired self was so focused on getting to that bank and then getting home so I could put my swollen feet up I was oblivious to it all. I don't know how far he ran, trying to keep up with my car, but I guess that bank bag finally slipped off. Thankfully Clarence found it before someone else did. Had somebody else found it, I guess they'd be crediting God for dropping down manna from heaven."

Sarah smiled wide. "I could listen to you tell those old stories all day long. I bet I don't know the half of them."

Nan scoffed. "You've got that right."

Sarah drove past the turnoff to Nan's house.

"Honey? You just passed my road."

"Sorry, Nan. I meant to tell you that I needed to do something at Old Depot. I'll be quick. Promise."

Sarah stopped in front of the store. Nan stared at the banner spanning the storefront. GOODBYE, OLD DEPOT. A STAPLE OF BRIGHTON, TN, FOR 56 YEARS.

Nan's eyes lit up. "Well, I'll be."

"Come on inside, Nan. You're the guest of honor."

The little shindig was everything Sarah hoped it would be. Even more people had arrived since she left to get Nan. People snacked on finger sandwiches and sipped lemonade and told stories about days gone by, flipping through the scrapbook Sarah had put together for the occasion. Some stories Sarah had lived herself. Others from before her time.

After a little too long in the thick of it, Sarah stepped outside for a little air and watched the party continue on through the front glass.

"Penny for your thoughts?"

She spun to face Clay, and her heart did a funny little jolt in her chest that had nothing to do with being startled. "Just getting some air." She sighed. "This place really was a staple in this community, and I know its job isn't finished yet."

She leaned close and confessed to him what she had done. His eyes went wide, and his gaze shot to Nan and Momma. Clay put a hand on her shoulder. The weight of his touch loaning her confidence. "A whole new way for community to thrive in this place. A new way for it to grow."

46

Present Day

Rosemary watched the last of the party guests say their goodbyes and trickle out the door. It had been a long, emotional day, and Rosemary was ready to slink away from it all. Maybe have a good cry while she was at it.

"How are you holding up?" Cathy sidled up to her.

Rosemary took a deep breath, trying to ease away the emotion weighing her chest. "I'm okay. Not entirely sure what I'm going to do with myself once everything is finalized here."

"I could use some extra help at the travel agency. You know I've been trying to steal you away from Old Depot for years. You oughta finally let me."

Rosemary laughed. "That's rich. A travel agent who has never been anywhere."

Cathy squeezed her upper arm. "It's not

too late to change that, you know."

"Did you know Sarah's pregnant? She sold her house. Took up all the roots she put down in Chicago. And I don't know what she's going to do. I need to be here for her."

"Sarah is a big girl, Rosemary." Cathy draped an arm over her shoulder. "You raised her well. She'll find her way, stumbles and all. You don't have to hold her hand to be there for her."

Cathy bid her farewell and gathered up a bag of trash to take with her on the way out. Rosemary grabbed a broom and swept, her mind playing over the thousands of times she performed this same task. Those late nights with the radio blaring. Those old floors, creaking under her feet, always talking back.

Louder when Daddy used to scoop her up and spin her around to the music. Quieter when she and Jessamine used to sneak down the aisles to escape out back before Momma caught them and put them to work. Plaintive when loaded shopping carts rolled down the length of them. It was a sound that had filled so much of her life, that she was pretty sure on her deathbed, if she thought hard enough, the sound would still echo in her memory.

She paused and pinched the bridge of her nose. They'd make a whole new sound when a bulldozer tore through them, reducing them to splinters. Her chest tightened. She'd never hear the sound of her grandchild's feet pitter-pattering across those floors. But that was what she'd wanted, wasn't it?

"Ms. Rosemary, here's a chair. Why don't you let me finish that up for you?" Clay scooted a chair close to her and reached for the broom.

"No. I need to do this."

He tipped his hat and put the chair away. "Yes, ma'am." Clay busied himself with another task and Rosemary resumed her sweeping. It was a funny thing. Working so hard to make the place shine when in a week or so the new owners would reduce it to rubble. Their whole lives scraped up and shoveled into a dumpster. Hauled off, load by load.

Rosemary huffed and swiped at her face. Why had she gone all sentimental now?

She turned, looking for Jessamine. Her sister washed the front glass door. Rosemary smiled, seeing a little girl version of her sister wiping down the glass while perched on a stepladder. "You always fought me over that chore, Jessie. You'd stand there watching the world beyond the front door of the store, just itching to escape."

Jessamine stopped wiping and faced her. "Is that what you thought?" she asked. "I liked washing the windows because at night, when it's dark outside and light inside, it turns the glass into a mirror. I'd wash and wash trying to get all the streaks out. The whole time, watching Momma counting money at the register. You stocking shelves and mopping floors. Daddy here and there, doing whatever needed doing to keep things going. And my own face. I could see all of us when I washed those windows, working together to make this place shine."

She sighed. "Sometimes when I lie down at night, I still can see it all. My little world reflected back at me. I didn't leave here because Brighton and Old Depot weren't enough, Rosemary. After Dad died, that little world reflected back at me was missing something that could never be returned."

A wave of emotion crashed over Rosemary, forcing her sweeping to cease. She stared at her feet, the air going out of the room. She stood on the place her father fell. The strength went out of her legs, and she sank to sit on the floor. "I'm sorry."

Whether she spoke to Jessie or Daddy or

herself she wasn't sure. She ran her fingers over the floorboards. The wood that had been bleached and scoured and restained in an attempt to match the flooring in the rest of the store.

What a sound those floors must have made when that great man fell.

Jessamine sat beside her. It wasn't until she swiped her thumb across Rosemary's cheek that Rosemary registered the moisture dripping from her chin. Clay, who'd been stacking folding chairs they'd borrowed from the church, slipped quietly out the front door.

"Whether you had been there or not, Daddy would've barreled through that door. You think it would have been better if both of you had died?"

For whatever reason, it felt like the time to admit the truth. "Yeah, I do. He ran to save someone who should've been there. If I *had* been there, I could've called the police when that man was slinking around outside the store. Maybe they would've gotten there before Daddy did. Maybe he never had to die. Maybe it was supposed to be me."

"Oh, Rosemary. Think about what you're saying. I know you feel like his death had no purpose. But Dad's life mission was loving Mom and us girls. That's how he lived.

And that's how he died. Loving us. If he could talk to you, he'd say that the day he died was just another ordinary day, doing what he was put on this earth to do." Jessie brushed a stray hair off Rosemary's cheek.

"When I left Brighton, I wanted to do something that would've made Dad proud. For me that meant chasing dreams and taking chances. It meant seeing the world, because his death showed me how fleeting life really is. And maybe you're mad I left and you stayed, but it was my way of connecting with Dad. He might not have been a world traveler, but he seized every opportunity every day. He lived life to the fullest." She squeezed her sister's shoulder. "It's time to forgive yourself, Rosemary. Let yourself live that full life Daddy wanted for you."

Rosemary swiped at her eyes.

"Pull his pictures out. Hang them on the wall. Let it hurt. And let it finally heal. Tell your daughter about the amazing man that her grandfather was.

"I don't think you'll ever find that 'full life' you've been craving until you accept the life you have. Mistakes. Heartache. Grief. All of it. Then you've got to decide if you're ready to let God have these burdens you've heaped upon your own shoulders, or if you'll keep on carrying that pain and regret, miserable under the weight of it."

47

Present Day

"Thank you, Sarah. It was a perfect last day." Nan's eyes were bright and shining in the light from the setting sun coming through the large glass front of the store.

Libby walked to Sarah and pulled her in a half hug, little Caroline blinking sleepily in her arms. "You did a great job pulling this together. We're gonna get out of your hair and give you all some time." She motioned to where her husband herded the rest of their brood into their minivan. "Did Clay cut out of here already?" She nudged Sarah and whispered in her ear, "He couldn't keep his eyes off you all day today."

Sarah shook her head, sending Libby a playful glare. Clay was probably just trying to process her new plans for her future. Especially after she'd asked him to consider partnering with her. "Stop trying to play matchmaker, Libby Lou. What will be, will be." She patted her friend's arm. "Thanks again for coming. Are we still on for our lunch date next week?"

"Ben promised that I get a full kid-free afternoon. I won't know how to have a real conversation without all the interruptions."

Sarah chuckled as Libby joined the rest of her family, doubtful that Libby would ever suffer from a lack of things to say.

Her smile deepened when Dad pulled into the lot. A little late, but he'd made it. He'd worked at Old Depot too. It was only fitting that he be there for its last day.

After the guests trickled out, Sarah and Jessamine laid red gingham blankets on the floor, making an indoor picnic. Nan had mentioned that on late nights, after a long night of stocking, she and Granddad Clarence would throw out a blanket and indulge in a midnight snack of lemon cookies and Glory Ann's syrupy-sweet tea while young Rosemary and Jessamine slept. They'd talk for an hour, enjoying the quiet after the rush before lifting their sleeping daughters and driving home.

Nan settled on one of the blankets. "We were dead on our feet on stock nights. But it was a satisfying exhaustion. The kind when you knew you'd worked hard and were proud of what you'd done."

Aunt Jessie piped up. "Speak for yourself, Mom. All I was, was dog-tired," she said, trading her tempered southern accent for full country twang. "Y'all had Rosemary and me working that store since we were knee-high to a grasshopper."

Mom laughed. "If Mom and Dad had a nickel for every time you threatened child labor laws on them, they wouldn't have needed to run a grocery store. They would have been millionaires."

Nan smiled, a faraway expression in her eyes. "I didn't know it then, but those were the days."

Sarah pulled her knees up under her chin, feeling the swell in her lower abdomen. "It'd be nice if there was some magical way to know when 'those days' were happening while you were living them instead of recognizing it in hindsight."

"Do you want to know my favorite memory of Old Depot Grocery?" Aunt Jessie's lilting voice broke into Sarah's musing. Aunt Jessie nudged Mom with a mischievous grin.

"No. Please. Jessie, do not tell this story." Mom's hands went to her cheeks, horror and repressed laughter contorting her features.

"One day, when we were walking to the store from school — I think Rosemary was eleven and I was nine — Rosemary saw this little gray squirrel just lying on the ground near the road —"

"Rosemary Jimson Clearwater Anderson, that was you? You little imp." Nan's eyes were wide, but a smile teased at the corners of her mouth.

Sarah narrowed her eyes. *Jimson?* Her mother had always signed her name with C as her middle initial. Jimson? Jimmy? What was up with Nan naming her daughter after her first love?

Aunt Jessie, bubbling with laughter, pulled Sarah to the present once more. "At first we thought the little thing was dead, but she noticed it was breathing and scooped it up and put it in her backpack. I don't know what she thought she was going to do with it, but apparently she'd hatched some cockamamie plan. But when we got to the store, Mom put us straight to work.

"Well, we were out back, stacking up the recyclables. All of the sudden we heard shrieks and screams coming from inside the store. Rosemary and I raced back inside to absolute pandemonium." She was doubled over from laughing through her words. "That little squirrel must've been stunned or knocked out or something when we found it, but now it was darting all over the place like a fuzzy rocket. Climbing aisles, leaping across them. It sprang off Miss Claudia's shoulder, and I think that was the shock of my life, hearing the preacher's wife let a cuss word fly. At least, whatever she yelped sounded like a cuss word the way she said it."

Sarah wrapped her arms around her middle, laughing at the mental image, and her mother, Miss Responsibility, being the cause of it all. Tears leaked out the corners of her eyes. "What did y'all do?"

"Daddy finally caught the poor thing. Threw a jacket over it, scooped it up, and deposited it outside. By that time, most of the customers had fled for the parking lot." Aunt Jessie snorted with laughter.

Nan pointed to her daughters. "You. And you. You two were as wide-eyed innocent as could be. Told me it must have snuck through the back door somehow." She laughed. "I can't believe you two kept that secret all this time. Usually y'all tattled on each other first chance you got."

Mom laughed. "You know that Bee Gee's patch I had on my backpack all those years? It wasn't because I was a superfan. Cathy gave it to me to cover up the hole that squirrel chewed."

Nan covered her mouth laughing. "Well,

that explains why you were never as thrilled as I expected you to be when I bought you their albums for Christmas."

"All right, you've all heard my favorite memory. Your turn, Rosemary." Aunt Jessie bit into her fried apple pie.

Mom inhaled and then took a long drink of her sweet tea. "Momma, Jessie, do you remember when Dad used to sing? Saturday mornings, bellowing out 'It Is Well with My Soul' at the top of his lungs?"

Nan smiled. "He had the voice of a bawling basset hound, but he sure made up for it with all the passion in his voice."

Sarah blinked back tears. Not so much for this man who she'd never met, but because Mom had spoken of Granddad Clarence. Opening up things she'd shut away.

Mom studied her hands in her lap. "It was one of the things I missed the most when he was gone."

Nan smiled softly. "I think that was his wish for all of us. That no matter what we faced, it would be well with our souls."

Sarah took a deep breath and stood. It was now or never. "I have some news. A . . . an announcement I'd like to make —"

Nan stood, squinting at the front of the store. "Did you see that man out there?"

The parking lot beyond the glass was

vacant of all but a few cars.

Aunt Jessie shook her head. "There's nobody there. Momma, are you feeling all right?"

Nan headed to the door. "He was there just a moment ago, looking through the glass. And I . . . I can't place him, but I swear I know him somehow."

As Nan exited, the man stepped into view. Sarah clapped her hand over her mouth to stifle a moan and hurried after her. The bells jangled as the door swung shut behind her. She stopped short behind Nan.

Jimmy backstepped, his attention flicking to Sarah and then locking back on Nan. He swallowed. "I'm sorry, I didn't mean to interrupt. I didn't know there was a party going on. I shouldn't've . . ." He turned away.

"Wait." Nan's voice rang clear as she stepped forward. "Do I know you?"

Jimmy faced her, sucked in a breath, and held it. His gaze found Sarah's over the top of Nan's head. The pain in his eyes pierced her soul, a silent plea for help. Sarah lifted one corner of her mouth and shrugged.

He opened his mouth and closed it, then took another shuddering breath. "Glory Ann, it's me. Jimmy. Jimmy Woodston."

Nan swayed. Sarah rushed forward, gripping Nan's arm to steady her.

"No . . . no, you can't be." Nan blinked. "You're not . . ."

"Mother? What's the matter?" Mom's voice sounded from behind Sarah. "Who is this man? Is he upsetting you?"

Sarah turned to her. "It's okay. This is an old friend of Nan's. Jimmy Woodston."

Mom's eyes widened, and she took a step back. Her jaw dropped. "You're . . . you're the one who wrote my mother letters."

Nan's gaze darted between Jimmy and her daughter, her brow furrowed. "Letters?" Her voice sounded as a quaking whisper. "What letters?"

Mom's hands trembled as she wrung them.

"Rosemary, what letters?"

48

Present Day

Glory Ann pressed a hand over her heart, staring at the man across from her in the dimly lit office. His chair made a piercing screech against the floor as he shifted in his seat.

He couldn't be Jimmy. War had stolen her blue-eyed farmer boy with a poet's soul decades ago.

Beyond the office her daughters still waited for an explanation.

From his shirt pocket he pulled a tiny drawstring bag of wildflower seeds that matched the one Glory Ann still kept in a hatbox in the back of her closet.

"My Jimmy is dead."

The man ran a thumb over the burlap fabric in his hand. "I suppose you're right about that."

Glory Ann stared at the floor between her feet as if it somehow held answers. "I saw the officer's car pull up to his parents' house. I clutched a red rose in my hand at his memorial, wishing the whole time it was yellow instead because yellow was for the missing. And the missing still had hope. But I . . ."

Glory Ann blinked rapidly. "It's been fifty-six years. Why —" She shook her head. How?

The walls of the old office seemed to tighten in. Those walls that knew her story better than most. When was this man going to explain how he could possibly be Jimmy? Why he'd disappeared so long? "Why did you come here?"

The man ran his hand over his face and through his hair until the white curls stood tall and wild. "I wanted the . . . the chance to explain. To see you again."

"Now?"

He lifted his head. "I thought you knew I was alive. I thought you just didn't want to see me."

Glory Ann shook her head. "I attended your funeral."

"I sent letters. One asking your parents to break the news to you. The other I sent to you here at the store. Sarah was the one who contacted me. She didn't think you received them. And maybe it's wrong, coming to you after so much time has passed, but it was hard enough believing you knew I was alive and didn't want to see me. But to realize you might not know . . . that . . . that the memory of your sweet face kept me going on some of the darkest days of my life." He ducked his head. "I don't want anything from you, Glory Ann. I just needed you to know."

Jimmy stood and handed her a yellowed envelope. "This is the letter. Sarah said she found it in your daughter Rosemary's keepsakes. I'm not sure what happened to the one I sent to your parents. Must've gotten lost in the mail."

Glory Ann knew exactly what had happened to the letter to her parents. But Rosemary? Why would Rosemary, who knew nothing about any of this, keep something so private, so personal, from her?

She reached for the envelope, staring at the hand that held it — a hand so different from the ones she remembered. This one was liver-spotted and wrinkled. But then she saw the scar on his index finger, just above the knuckle closest to his palm. Still holding the envelope between them, she looked into his eyes. The same shocking sky blue she remembered that shimmered with light and hope, but now there were shadows there too. Shadows that expressed more pain than words ever could. A knot tightened in her throat. Even though this man named Jimmy sat across from her, that starry-eyed boy on the verge of manhood was still gone.

Glory Ann slipped the sheet of paper free from the envelope, and her eyes roved over the familiar handwriting. She held up the letter. "This was from 1986. That's what, twenty-one years since you left for Vietnam? And you said you sent another letter to my parents letting them know that you survived five years prior? That's 1981. Help me understand, Jimmy. Your own parents died without knowing."

"You kept in touch?" Tears shimmered in his eyes.

She nodded.

The tension on his face relaxed a fraction. "That was kind of you."

Years and years and years she'd ached for the tall boy in the cornfields. Who stood with his hands in his pockets and wore a dimpled smile. With his white-blond curls that refused to be tamed. And eyes the color of the sky. With gentle hands that coaxed tiny green things to sprout up from the earth. Who had been stolen from her by something dark and ugly. Far away and far beyond their control.

But now he was back. Stoop-shouldered and gray.

Jimmy bowed his head. "Through some clerical mix-up when I loaned a dying brother-in-arms my jacket, they thought he was me and I was him. After years as a prisoner of war, I was released. But the person who landed back on American soil could still feel the grit of dirt spray from the explosions grating his skin. Like a fine coating of death and destruction." He stared into his palms as though he could still see the stains. "I could've never brought that to you. I would've destroyed you." There was so much weight in his words, she knew they held truth.

"After I worked really hard at destroying what was left of me, and failed at even that, I looked you up. I wanted to make sure life had been kinder to you than it had me. I saw your girls. Said hello to them. Saw evidences of your beautiful life here at this store, and I was happy for you."

Glory Ann's jaw went slack at his words. He'd been to the store? Met her daughters? She snapped her mouth closed, determined to let Jimmy finish his story.

"But it hurt. Because an empty grave in Humboldt held the memory of that boy and that girl sneaking kisses in the cornrows. And it ripped my heart in two — the unfairness of it all." He drew a shuddering breath.

She shook her head, trying to quiet all that buzzed within. "You met my girls?"

He nodded.

A corner of her mouth curled upward, and she bit her lip. "You didn't see it? Rosemary's blonde curls? Her eyes, so like yours?"

His mouth moved, but no sound would come. "Are you saying . . . ?"

Her hands went to her cheeks, and she nodded.

Beyond the office came the squawk of the bathroom door closing, and the creak of floorboards just outside the office door.

"R-Rosemary is our . . . our daughter? H-how?"

The retreating footsteps froze, and then the wood floors complained as they hurried away, followed by the slam of the rear exit door.

Jimmy's brow furrowed at the sudden racket. Glory Ann stood, clasping her hands against her chest. How could she ever make this right?

The rev of an engine sounded in the back lot where Rosemary always parked. Glory Ann stifled a groan and squeezed her eyes shut for a moment.

A tear broke free from the pools in her eyes and trickled down her face. "She didn't know." She heaved a breath. "What a mess I've made."

His head tipped sideways. "That's . . . that's why you married so soon."

Glory Ann nodded. Unable to form words, she held up a finger to tell him to wait, then stepped out of the office.

Clay and Jessamine stood in the empty store, heads bent in quiet conversation. Clay stepped toward her. "Are you all right, Ms. Glory Ann?"

"Yes." She cleared her throat to rid her voice of its rasp. "Rosemary?"

"Sarah and Bo went after her."

Glory Ann nodded. "Good." They were exactly who Rosemary needed at a time like this. Her heart squeezed. Rosemary would never speak to her again. With the store gone, why would she need to?

Jessamine's brow furrowed. "What's going on, Momma? Who is that man? Why did Rosemary tear out of here like that?"

"I promise to tell you everything later. I just need a little more time." Glory Ann walked to the back corner of the store. The darkened place that never could seem to get enough light, no matter how many changes they made to the fixtures over the years. She found that loosened board. One that people walked over all the time and never knew. That concealed something that had become so much a part of the fabric of this place she'd almost forgotten about its existence. With her fingernails she lifted the board and retrieved that yellowed, tear-stained envelope. She walked back into the office and placed it in Jimmy's hands. "I wrote this when I found out I was pregnant, but they told me you died before I'd worked up the courage to send it."

49

Present Day

Sarah sat beside her father on the bench seat of his pickup. She held the grab handle as he took the winding curves in a hurry. He glanced at Sarah. "You found the letters? You're the one who reached out to this Jimmy fellow?"

Sarah bit the inside of her cheek. "I didn't mean for it to turn out this way. I know I shouldn't have been snooping in Mom's things, but when I read those letters to Nan, there was so much longing and regret. And I . . . I know something about what that feels like. So I did a little digging and met Jimmy. He was supposed to have called before he came. I thought I would have had the chance to prepare Mom and Nan. To explain why I did what I did."

Dad sighed. "Any idea why your mother tore out of the store like that?"

Sarah shook her head.

Dad turned off the main road onto a gravel lane.

Curved wrought iron came into view. "The graveyard?" she asked.

Dad gave her a sad-eyed smile. "Sometimes she comes here when she's really upset."

"Granddad Clarence?"

He nodded. "This place has always been sacred space for her."

Together they exited the truck and passed through the iron gate, traveling the well-worn path. Her mother sat at the graveside bench, spine straight, eyes focused on some distant thing. When they drew close, Sarah's foot cracked a twig and her mother startled out of her trancelike state.

"Mom, are you okay?" It was such a stupid question, but she couldn't think of anything else to say.

Mom shrugged and blinked. "I don't know. I . . ." Her words fell away, and she buried her face in her hands. Sarah and Dad sat, hemming her in like a pair of bookends.

In the silence, Sarah stared out over the neat rows of headstones. A cardinal landed on her grandfather's marker and let out a series of trills and chirps. His mate answered overhead, perched on the limb of a cherry tree.

Mom lifted her head, peering into Sarah's eyes. "Did you know?"

Sarah's mouth opened and closed. "I . . ."

Mom's face twisted as she gestured to the grave. "I wonder if *he knew* I wasn't his, or if she lied to him too."

Dad drew in a sharp breath. Sarah blinked, replaying the words, unable to string them together into anything coherent. "Mom?"

Her mother's shoulders drooped. "I can't believe she had an affair. She seemed to love Clarence so much."

Dad reached and took Mom's hand and squeezed.

Sarah shook her head. "Mom, what are you talking about?"

Eyes shut tight, she said, "Jimmy is my father."

Sarah's heart stutter stepped. An unexpected warmth bloomed in her chest, competing with the ache of her mother's pain. *Jimmy is my grandfather?*

"I overheard them talking in the office. I don't think he knew about me. But Momma knew. Did Da— Clarence?"

Dad placed his arm around Mom. "No matter what the situation, this doesn't make Clarence any less your father. He filled that role to the utmost."

Her mother looked from Dad to Sarah and back, a look of desperation crumpling her face. "I don't know which is worse. Him knowing, or my mother lying to him. Because if D-Daddy knew, then he lied to me too."

Sarah chewed her lip. Did she dare step deeper into these uncertain waters? "I don't know what Granddad Clarence knew. Or why Nan would have kept such a secret from you. I can't speak with complete certainty, but from listening to his story, Nan and Jimmy's relationship ended before she married Granddad Clarence. She thought Jimmy died in Vietnam. Though she loved Granddad Clarence deeply, she's been mourning Jimmy since the news of his death."

"And I hid his letter." She stared vacantly ahead.

Sarah scuffed her shoe against the gravel at her feet. "I'm sorry I went through your things. I know digging up this history has caused a lot of pain, but I can't be sorry about contacting Jimmy."

Sarah gripped the edge of the concrete bench. "When Aaron died, I was so angry and ashamed."

Mom's gaze shot to her, brows knit.

"I couldn't bring myself to tell you that

my marriage to Aaron wasn't happy. I don't know why. I guess I knew how hard you worked to make sure I could have this fabulous life, and I felt like I let you down."

"Oh, honey . . ." Mom placed her hand over Sarah's.

"All this time I thought my anger came from the way Aaron traded our present for a future he couldn't promise. All to gain the approval of a father who refused to give it." She drew a shaky breath and plowed through the pain. "At some point I stopped believing his promises because no matter what he achieved, it would never be enough to fill the hole his father had left. And I couldn't fill it either. And that hurt."

Dad rose from the bench and stood behind Sarah, resting his hands on her shoulders.

She tried to swallow past the tightness in her throat. "The night he died, I planned to leave him. For a day, for forever, I didn't know. I just couldn't be in that house alone anymore. After his death, the condolences made me feel so guilty. I thought I felt that way because I wanted to leave him. I didn't know it until I read Jimmy's letter, but I was wrong." She pressed the heels of her palms against her eyes and then regripped the edge of the bench, holding herself to the moment, pushing the words from the buried places inside her.

"You see, there was this moment as Aaron was walking out the door, trading our anniversary for a work emergency. Words were hanging on the tip of my tongue that I didn't speak. My guilt wasn't really about me wanting to leave, it was because I didn't ask him to stay. And if he'd stayed, he'd . . ." She blinked her burning eyes and shook her head.

"Instead, I drowned in my own silence, fearing that if I finally told him I was tired of waiting for someday, if I fought for us, he still wouldn't choose me."

Sarah dared a glance sideways. Mom's eyes were squeezed tight, her arms clasped around her middle like she was trying to keep her body in one piece. Maybe her mother would never understand her wanting to leave Aaron, but Sarah knew from that old trunk in the attic that the woman beside her knew what it was to live in regret.

"While I was angry at Aaron, it was the things I left unsaid that hurt the most. Jimmy's letter made me see that. When I read his words, his pain was my pain. The longing. The ache of not knowing. I couldn't change what happened with Aaron, but for Jimmy, I knew that it wasn't too late."

Tears that had dammed since Aaron's death spilled over and she took her mother's hands, gently tugging so that Mom no longer clasped her arms around herself. Instead mother and daughter held on to each other — linked by their hands and so much more. "I know this is messy. And its's hard. And it hurts. But you, me, Nan, Jimmy, we've all still got breath in our lungs. And it's not too late for us to find a way forward. We still have time to say what needs to be said. We don't have to be left not knowing."

Mom lifted her gaze and nodded. "You're right, Sarah. We don't."

They sat together as the sun approached the horizon, and then Mom headed for home while Dad drove Sarah to retrieve her car from Old Depot. On that winding lane, Sarah inhaled. Something had shifted. That ache weighing her every breath had lifted.

Dad pulled to a stop in front of the store and let Sarah out. Jimmy stood in the lot, running his hand over his face.

Sarah walked to him. "Where's Nan?"

He thumbed behind him. "In there. I was just about to head home, but I couldn't make myself leave just yet."

A grin stole over her face, and she wrapped him in a hug, squeezing tight. A manic giggle burbled up inside her. "I have a grandfather."

She pulled back and looked into his watery eyes.

He laughed under his breath, staring at her like she was a cool drink of water on a hot day. "I have a granddaughter."

Sarah took his hand and pressed it to her middle. "And a great-grandchild."

He swallowed convulsively, his hand trembling beneath Sarah's. "A child, a grandchild, and a great-grandchild. M-me?"

Sarah nodded and smiled. "You're a little late to the party." She winked. "But not too late."

Jimmy's chin quivered. "Well, praise the Lord for that."

Maybe all their paths were littered with mistakes and secrets that never should have been kept, but Sarah had faith that in the end, the truth would set them free.

50

Present Day

The next morning, Rosemary drove up to her mother's house and knocked on the door. If what she'd overheard was true and that man really was her father, shouldn't she have felt something at the sight of him? Like the similarity in their DNA calling to each other. But his sudden appearance had only left her spiraling. Threatened by this sudden trespasser in a space that belonged to Clarence Clearwater.

Jessamine opened the door and pulled her into a hug without a word.

"Is Momma home?" asked Rosemary.

"Yeah, she just finished up some breakfast. We talked a long time last night. I hope you'll hear her out."

Easy enough for Jessamine to say. "How is she?"

Jessamine shook her head. "I don't know. Shocked, I think. It's been a lot to process

— that someone she mourned for nearly sixty years was alive all this time. Most of all she's worried about you. She wants to explain."

Rosemary stepped inside and slid off her shoes by the door. "She's had my whole lifetime for that."

Jessamine laid her hand on Rosemary's shoulder. "You have every right to be angry, but be gentle. You kept secrets too." She picked up an overnight bag.

"You're leaving? Now?"

"I have to be back at work. But if you need me here, I'll cancel my flight. Mom and I have made our peace. It's not . . . as complicated for me."

Rosemary's mouth curled in a half grin. "I guess not. I love you, sister."

"Still?"

"Of course. Always, Jessie."

"Mom never wanted you to feel trapped here."

"I know that now. I really do. Forgive me for all the times I was so hard on you for living life your own way?" Rosemary sighed. "I wish Daddy were here. He'd know what to do — to say to mend this mess. He always did."

Jessamine scrunched her face. "You remember that hound dog I broke?"

Rosemary smiled. “And Daddy put it back together for me. Best he could, anyway. I still have it.”

Jessamine put her hand on her shoulder. “That’s the thing. You always gave him the credit for every good thing in our lives, but he didn’t do it alone, Rosemary. Any of it. Not even putting that little dog back together.

“I couldn’t sleep that night, thinking about what I’d done, breaking that dog just to hurt you. The instant I let it fall from my hands I knew what a horrible thing I’d done, but I was a stubborn little pain in the butt and it wasn’t until the quiet of the night that I listened to that still voice prodding at my heart.”

She readjusted the bag on her shoulder. “I wandered out of bed and found Mom and Dad both bent over the pieces, gluing it back together. Thought I’d get a spanking for sure when I told them I did it on purpose, but they prayed with me instead and told me about the importance of confessing and repenting for the wrong I’d done. And they used that broken ceramic of all things to teach me about what Jesus had done for me through his sacrifice.” Jessamine squeezed her hand. “I know you never believed I was sincere when I told you sorry the next morning, but I meant every word."

"Mom helped?" Rosemary blew out a hollow laugh. "I always thought she didn't care about it as much as I imagined she did."

"She always cares when we're hurting, sis. I think she just struggles to show it sometimes."

Rosemary nodded, thinking back to rigid Grandma Hawthorne. It certainly wasn't a trait Momma would've learned from her own raising.

Jessamine threw her free arm around Rosemary and squeezed tight. Into her hair, she said, "You really should come visit me sometime when Bo is out on the road. You'd love the Pacific Northwest."

"I . . ."

"Your diagnosis is not a cage any more than the store was."

Rosemary's jaw dropped a fraction.

"Live, Rosemary. Do the things you want to do. That can mean staying here in Brighton and never leaving. Or it can mean seeing the whole world. Living is about seeing past the challenges and not letting fear or false guilt be the decider for your life. Listen to the passions in your heart that your Creator put there. Maybe it's to stay. Maybe it's to go. Just listen for once instead of coming up with a list of reasons why you can't."

She brushed a quick kiss to Rosemary's cheek. "Love ya, sis. Hang in there. And call me if you need to talk."

With that, Jessamine went out the door and bounced down the steps with a tread too light and free for a woman her age.

And then Rosemary was alone in the entryway, left reflecting on how wise her younger sister had become. She squared her shoulders, unsure of what to make of all she said, but determined to take the first bit of advice. To be gentle. To listen.

She walked to the kitchen where family meals and family meetings happened. Around a kitchen table where they were always fed. Always loved. Even if she hadn't always understood that love at the time.

Her mother stood beside that table with her mouth bent downward and her fists clenched at her sides like she was trying to stay strong while the weight of her burdens threatened to crumple her.

Momma sank into a dining chair across the table. Her eyes bore into Rosemary's. "Go ahead and say it."

Rosemary took the chair across from her. "I can't believe you kept this from me my whole life." But if anything, Rosemary's secret had been more life-altering than

Momma's. She released a heavy breath. "Now you go." She clutched the edge of the chair, bracing herself for what Momma would say.

"I can't believe you hid that letter from me all these years. All this time he's been alive. Years he could have been in your life. And in mine. I'm not saying in what way. I don't know how Jimmy fits in our lives but —"

"Did you have an affair?"

Momma shook her head, eyes wide. She reached across the table and gripped Rosemary's hand. "No. Never. I was engaged to Jimmy. We were supposed to get married, but he was called up for service in Vietnam instead. Shortly after he'd shipped out, I heard he'd died. I was pregnant and I had to tell my parents that Jimmy and I made choices that I wasn't proud of." She studied Rosemary's face. "But I've never once regretted you.

"My father drove me to Brighton and introduced me to your daddy. Told me that I'd ruin mine and their lives if I didn't marry him and pretend Jimmy's baby was his. Honestly, at the moment, I was so angry at my father, that he could assume he could make this kind of decision for me, that I didn't care if mine and Jimmy's moment of passion burned me and my family to the ground. But I did care about what it would mean for my child." She squeezed Rosemary's hand. "For you. Maybe that's hard to understand, but I was just nineteen and times were so different then than they are now."

Rosemary's insides crawled imagining a wedding night contrived to cover up that Rosemary was another man's baby. "Did he know? Or did you lie to Clarence too?"

"Rosemary, call him Daddy like you always did. That's who he was. Nothing could change that. He went into it all with eyes wide open. And I resented him and his no-strings-attached kindness. He always encouraged me to see him as a friend and expected nothing more. But I was so deep in grief I couldn't see the gift I'd been given in marrying that man. And then one day, a few years later, I saw him with new eyes."

Rosemary chewed her bottom lip. "Why?"

"Because even though I was hurting too much to receive his love for myself, I saw the way he loved you. It opened up a crack in the walls I'd built around my heart. And love bloomed in those cracks. Like dandelions in springtime."

"You always seemed to love each other so much."

"It took time for me to catch up to how he felt about me. But I eventually did. I was scared when I was pregnant with Jessamine that he'd feel differently about her. But he didn't entertain my concerns for a second. He'd just smile and start singing 'My Girl' and dance through the empty aisle with you on his hip."

Rosemary tried to swallow past the lump in her throat. "When I opened that letter, I was in shock. It held such longing. And it talked about mistakes. Dad had died, and I thought this man, this lover of yours, was just sweeping in to take advantage of the life my father had built. And I couldn't stand the thought of you loving someone else. I had intended to confront you. Almost did a hundred times. But the fact was, I'd rather live with my version of the truth, that you and Daddy loved each other, than take the chance of finding out that hadn't been true."

Tears trailed down Momma's face. "I'm so sorry, Rosemary. If I had told you about Jimmy a long time ago then you would have known exactly who he was when you read that letter. You just loved your daddy so much, worshipped the ground he walked on, and I was afraid that telling you about Jimmy would somehow damage your relationship with him. Jimmy was supposed to be dead, after all, and as more and more time passed, I couldn't see how it mattered, you knowing about him. At least not enough to risk changing the way you felt about the man who had raised you."

Voices inside Rosemary's head screamed that of course it mattered. But then she tried to see it through her mother's eyes. This life that she'd built to protect her daughter. And ultimately to protect them all. How would the community have responded to find out that this family they so respected wasn't who they thought they were?

Momma peered at her. "Will you . . . do you ever think you could . . . forgive me?" Rosemary could see her own pain in the reflection of her momma's eyes.

Rosemary splayed her hands on her thighs. Thirty-five years. Thirty-five years Rosemary had taken from Jimmy and Momma. At the time, she hadn't believed she was truly stopping anything, maybe delaying the inevitable — that Momma would move on and love again. Cause a wrinkle in some ill-advised love affair. But completely derailing the reunion of her mother and her biological father, the man her mother mourned in secret for decades?

It hit her then. Every choice Rosemary had made since the day Daddy died was all an attempt to freeze time. To somehow preserve some semblance of the life he'd built. Stay in the same place. Do the same things. Marry a man who shared so many of Daddy's finest qualities. And yet she'd pushed Sarah away. Identified Old Depot as a trap when it was supposed to be a symbol of love and family. Just like Momma tried to protect her, she'd tried to protect Sarah. All their efforts to protect had wounded instead.

"It's okay." Momma poked at the placemat on the table in front of her, straightening it. "You don't have to answer now. I . . . I know it's a lot to take in."

"Of course I forgive you, Momma. I'm not sure how to feel about it all. But I think I understand why you did what you did."

Momma's voice held a tremble when she spoke. "Jimmy would like to meet you. He told me to tell you that he understands if you need time, or don't want to at all. But he desperately wanted you to know that he didn't knowingly abandon you."

Rosemary's throat tightened.

"I promise, he didn't know. I never had the chance to tell him."

Sarah had been right. There was no going

back. But every now and then an opportunity arose to mend things and embrace what you've been given, cracks and all.

Momma clasped her hands and held them tight against her chest. "I need to apologize for something else. I never realized you felt second to Jessamine until you said so the other day. That difference you felt, it wasn't because I loved one of you more than the other. I always loved you with my whole heart. But that heart was also carrying around a lot of hurt. You must've felt that. If I would have just told you about Jimmy from the beginning, you might have understood that it wasn't about you. It was about me missing my blue-eyed boy when I should have loved my blue-eyed girl better. Counted the blessing that you looked so much like him instead of fearing that pain. I hope you can forgive me, Rosemary, for all the ways I fell short."

Rosemary stood and took her mother's wrinkled hand, tugging her to her feet. Questions filled her deep brown eyes. Rosemary pulled her mother tight to her chest. "We've all fallen short, Momma. You, me, Sarah — we've worked so hard to fix our brokenness ourselves and then hide the cracks we've left behind. I'm sorry I took your letter. No matter who wrote it or why, it was never mine to take."

Momma leaned back from the embrace, tears running rivers down her aged cheeks. "What did I offer you, but my own broken path to follow? Our efforts to fix and mend have left a wake of pain, no matter how unintentional."

Rosemary nodded, the tightness in her chest easing. "It's high time all three of us come out of hiding and let the light come in."

51

Present Day

Three days after Jimmy's sudden appearance, Sarah's father hoisted Mom's trunk and brought it down the attic ladder and into the living room. Mom sat in front of the trunk, heaved a sigh, and then wiped away dust that wasn't there. She fitted the key into the lock and opened the hinged lid that didn't squeak.

She turned to Sarah. "I go up there every so often to look through all of this. If I get to missing Daddy. Or feeling guilty. Hidden away in that dark attic, I've reread all these articles, wallowing in my shame. I kept it a secret because I knew better than the way I was behaving, but that shame was an addiction I couldn't kick. And if anyone knew, they'd force me to acknowledge what I was doing to myself every time I opened this box. I wasn't there to remember. I was punishing myself."

Sarah sat beside her on the ottoman and placed a hand on her knee.

Her mother looked at her with a watery grin. "I oughta wring your neck for going through my things without permission, young lady. But I guess I'll thank you instead. I'm sorry I barely spoke about Granddad Clarence." She smiled at her husband, who sat across the room. "And I need to apologize to you, Bo. You knew about the way I hurt, but I hid the way I tortured myself. Twisting the knife deeper when nobody was watching." She sat straighter. "It's time to choose a new way forward."

Sarah nodded. Peace settled over her like a warm blanket.

Mom pulled out the picture of Granddad Clarence with little Rosemary perched on his shoulder. "This man right here was my hero. When I learned that the man I idolized wasn't my biological father, I didn't know if I should feel angry or hurt or deceived. But the more I think about it, the more him choosing to be my father to protect me from cruel people makes sense for the man he was."

Sarah leaned against her mother's shoulder, listening to her talk about growing up in the store. Through her stories, it became clear how Mom had become the woman sitting in front of her today. And why she so deeply feared Sarah following in her footsteps.

Mom sighed. "Now that the store is gone, selling feels like a mistake."

The words Sarah had been holding back since her first meeting with Jimmy burst forth. "I bought Old Depot." She bit her lip shut.

Mom blinked and shook her head. "An investment company bought it."

Sarah nodded and her shoulders crept higher, uncertain of the effect her words would bring. "Yes, a company my lawyer set up."

"Honey, why? Why would you do this? The store is a money pit. You're about to have a child. And you're alone."

"I'm not alone, Mom. I have you and Dad and Nan." *And Clay and Libby. Jimmy.* "And yes, my husband is gone. And maybe he worked away what little time we had together, but he also went to great lengths to make sure that I would never want for anything. His company is still run by a board of directors. A check still comes to my account every quarter. And that's beside the insurance money and sale of the ridiculously expensive house we lived in."

Mom lifted her empty hands, "So, you're what? Going to run a little grocery store for the rest of your life?"

Sarah gave her a wry smile. "I seriously considered it. I know you don't think much about what you did for a living, but I always saw a family who worked hard to serve their community. Built bonds with people. And lent a helping hand when it was needed. The care and service you and Nan and Granddad provided went above and beyond."

Mom averted her eyes and sniffled.

"But no, I'm not continuing the store. I had an idea." Sarah took a steadying breath before plowing on, no doubt trampling on her mother's confused emotions all over again. "Jimmy's life, and Clay's actually, inspired the plan. I bought the store and the adjacent field. I'll need a lot of help, but what I want to do is convert the store into three to four apartments for soldiers who have recently returned from combat. Maybe they are struggling with PTSD or maybe they just are having a hard time knowing how to fit back into civilian life. Like Jimmy and Clay, they can have the chance to work with their hands. Bring forth life in those fields. Growing crops. Having a sense of closeness that they are missing from their brothers- and sisters-in-arms in the community-style housing."

"Sarah, that sounds like an awfully big undertaking. Something that requires expertise in specialized fields."

"I know I'm not equipped for this, but I know how to find the people who are. And I have the means to fund it. You were right. This little town is changing, and maybe they don't need Old Depot in the same way. So, I thought we could change Old Depot. To serve those in need. And to create a space for community. Just in a different way."

Her words having dried up, she waited for her mother's response. She worried her hands.

"Well, it sounds like you've put a lot of thought into it. I wish you would have just told us. We'd have never sold it to you for such a high price."

"I know. It was important to me that the store sell for what you needed from it. I hope you can understand."

Mom let out a breath and smiled softly. "Whether this was the best decision of your life or the worst, you have my full support."

The next morning, Rosemary tucked the breakfast leftovers into her repurposed margarine containers. Sarah always fussed about them, complaining that a person had to open every container to find what they were looking for. But it was what frugal southern women did. Make full use of whatever they had on hand.

She closed the refrigerator and wrung her trembling hands. Jimmy should be there any minute. She'd wrestled with the idea of meeting this unwittingly absentee father. An absence her interference prolonged. She'd made amends with Momma, but she owed Jimmy an apology too. She'd done a lot of apologizing lately. But it wasn't like in the times gone by. Where she said she was sorry but continued to carry the weight of guilt and shame. She was learning to hold out her regret and pain, make it known, and then place it into the hands of her heavenly Father.

Maybe she'd sometimes pick it back up again when she shouldn't, but she was determined to live in a new way. One in which she let the pain heal and let the people around her live their own lives without fearing so much they'd repeat her mistakes. Mistakes were a part of each person's story. And she needed to let Momma and Sarah write their own.

A knock sounded at the door.

She opened it to a gray-haired man, who

stood on her stoop with his head bowed.

"Good morning, Mr. Woodston."

He winced. "Please, call me Jimmy."

She inhaled past the tightness in her chest. "Well . . . Jimmy . . . would you like to come inside?"

He nodded and she made way for him to enter her home. "Bo is out trying to retrain his reprobate duck hunting dog. Which I'm pretty sure is just an excuse to give the two of us a little time to get acquainted. He's eager to meet you though."

Jimmy followed her down the hall to the living room. He paused, pointing to the pictures she'd hung last night after opening her trunk with Sarah and Bo. "Is that Clarence?"

She nodded.

He bowed his head a moment and then looked into her eyes. "He was good to you?"

Warmth filled her chest at the thought of Clarence Clearwater. Her daddy. "The very best."

He brushed his shaky fingertips across the bottom of the frame. "I'm so grateful."

Rosemary nodded, unsure of what to say. "Come on in. Let's have a seat."

They settled across from each other.

"Rosemary, please, please know that I never knew I was a father."

"I know."

"I would like to believe that had I known, I would have done things differently when I returned to the States. But I wasn't well. I wouldn't have been a good father to you. Not then. And I don't expect you want a father now. But I do want you to know that it is an honor to have met you." He fidgeted on the couch. "Goodness, you are so like Glory Ann."

Rosemary smiled. "From what I hear, I was the spitting image of you when I was a little girl. Did Momma tell you that she snuck me back to visit with your parents when they still lived in Humboldt? I remember them a little bit. They were kind people."

"I'm so thankful to her for that. I can't imagine what it must have been like for them, thinking I'd died in Vietnam." He shook his head, staring at the floor, and then lifted his gaze. "Your daughter, Sarah, is just wonderful. She told me about her new purpose for Old Depot Grocery. I think it could really help people step off the battlefield. I plan to assist her with it, if I have your blessing. I don't want my presence to disturb your life. And I know you might have some mixed feelings about me interfering at the store."

Her eyes went to her daddy's picture on

the wall. He would have been proud of Sarah's new purpose for Old Depot. And after the things Momma had told her about why Clarence had chosen to be her surrogate father in Jimmy's stead, it brought a sense of completeness, Jimmy working there too. Carrying on a legacy that Clarence Clearwater would have championed if he'd been alive to do it.

Eyes full of moisture, she stood then sat beside him on the ottoman. "I'd be honored if you'd help Old Depot Grocery find its new purpose. And I'm blessed, getting the chance to know you, even after all this time."

52

Present Day

Sarah stepped over the train tracks, Old Depot behind her, her favorite view in front of her. The sinking sun filtered through the tall maple in the center of the field. In a few minutes that golden glow would become the dusky purples and blues she loved so much. She smiled. It was hers now. And in this long fallow field, new things would grow.

"Good *night,* that's a beautiful view."

Sarah turned, heart hammering at the unexpected sound of Clay's voice. He tapped his battered hat in a steady rhythm on his thigh.

She smiled. "One of my favorite places on earth."

He drew to her side, looking over the land. "I can see why."

"I know it's just a field. A dime a dozen around here, but I love it."

Clay placed his hat on his head, tipping it

at an angle. "You know, sometimes it is the simplest things that seem to hold the most magic."

She couldn't argue with that. "Before we know it, there will be people working in those fields, finding new purpose.

"Jimmy's going to help too. Not only around here but we also talked about some plans to partner with the organization he founded. Fresh fruit and vegetables we grow here can help fill his mobile grocery trucks that go into areas that lack proper grocery stores."

Clay smiled. "How are Ms. Glory Ann and Ms. Rosemary reacting to Jimmy being involved?"

Sarah shrugged. "I know they each have their own emotions to work through, but all in all, I think they're supportive of it."

He nodded, a solemn look taking over his face. "It's been great to see the changes that have come about in just these few weeks. All because you had the courage to speak up."

She scrunched her nose. "Well, I know I didn't go about all of it in the right way, but I've learned that it's better to try than to become too paralyzed to move."

His hat came off again, and he dusted it against his leg. "You gals have inspired me."

She smiled at him. "Oh yeah?"

"Yes, ma'am. So in the spirit of speaking the truth, there's something I need to tell you."

Sarah's mouth went dry. She wasn't sure she could take any more painful truths, at least, not at the moment. "Oh?"

"I wanted to tell you that I like you."

She laughed under her breath. "Why? I never had the feeling you didn't."

"Nah. I mean I like you like you."

Her cheeks warmed. "You like me like me? Are we in middle school?" She teased to cover her swooping thoughts.

"I know you've got a whole heap of things going on right now. You're about to be a momma, and this new venture with Old Depot. I know the pain of losing Aaron is still so fresh, but should you ever come to the point that you'd entertain romance being a part of your life again, I'd love for you to give us a chance. I just wanted you to know."

She blinked, her heart thudding in her chest. "You just wanted me to know?"

"Yep. Thought we might as well avoid the whole hidden letter, decades of pining sort of thing. And I'd just tell you outright that I think you are a fine woman and I like you, plain and simple."

She bit the corners of her cheeks to keep her smile at bay. "Clay, I can't make you any sort of promises that I'll ever be in a place where I'm ready for more than anything but friendship. And the way I've heard Ms. Paulette talking, there's something brewing between you and Lissie Baker. Something about her sitting with you at church." She choked on her laugh. "I don't want to get in the way of that."

He cut her a mock glare. "Nothing but foolish gossip. There is nothing going on between me and Lissie. She's not my type."

"So, what is your type, Clay? Mentally rocky widows who dig into family history, resurrecting ghosts and turning lives upside down while buying the family store out from under their mother and grandmother without their knowledge?"

He tapped his chin. "You know, I've never really thought about it, but now that you mention it, that oddly specific description is exactly my type."

She shook her head and laughed.

He hooked his thumbs in the pockets of his jeans. "And I'm not in any hurry. I'm quite content with my life, thank you very much. But I'm inclined to believe it'd be a whole lot better with you in it." He placed a hand on her shoulder, the pair of them looking over the field now bathed in blue, gray, and purple. "Someday isn't always a bad word, Sarah."

She breathed a sigh in the comfortable silence. Life had taken some turns, but Nan had been right, in front of her there was nothing but a field of verdant possibility. And in a way she'd never imagined, Old Depot Grocery continued to be at the center of it all.

Epilogue

Nine Months Later

Sarah ran her hand over the front of the filmy chiffon, trying to still the butterflies. Sometimes it was still a shock to find her stomach flat. Well, almost flat. She thought of her little boy. Hopefully little Luke Aaron Ashby was on his best behavior for the ceremony.

After all, it was the perfect day for a June wedding.

Sarah picked up her bouquet that looked like a handheld English garden. After losing Aaron, she'd never anticipated a day in which she'd relish all the details and hopeful excitement that went along with a wedding, but every moment of planning this day had filled her with joy. It was even healing in a way.

Strains of Handel's "Largo" filtered through the air, and she stepped away from the oval mirror and prepared to take her place. Part of Clay's barn had been converted into a dressing area for the ladies of the wedding party. Sarah smiled at the time and attention Clay had put into what had once been an unused tack room. The full-length mirrors. Accordion changing partitions. Refreshments. Rugs on the newly polished concrete floors. All the animals had been put out to pasture for the week, and the barn fairly sparkled. It was silly, really, for him to go to so much trouble for one day. But she couldn't deny that she was touched by his efforts.

When she exited the tack room her mother, Aunt Jessie, and Nan waited. They melted into a hug.

"You look beautiful, Sarah." Her grandmother put her hand on her cheek.

Sarah looked into her wrinkle-creased eyes. There was such a joy. "So do you."

She'd been so afraid her grandmother would be angry when she'd found out that she bought Old Depot. But instead she simply smiled when she heard the plans and said, "Your granddad Clarence would have been so pleased. He always saw Old Depot as a way to serve his country in his own way, and now you're carrying that on."

"Well, we'd better get going or the groom is going to think that he's being left at the altar." Mom tilted her head toward the exit to the barn. A pathway lined with a white aisle runner led out to where the guests and groom waited.

Sarah stepped forward, blinking in the morning sun. Immediately her eyes found Clay's. Her partner at The Depot. They should be ready for their first residents in a couple months, just in time for the first harvest on the field next door.

Baby Luke squirmed in his arms. The sight of Clay holding her baby boy, Aaron's baby boy, pricked her heart. But her heart was learning this gentle waltz that swayed between grief and joy, and her steps weren't as uncertain as they'd once been.

Sarah's eyes went then to Jimmy. Her grandfather. His eyes glistened, and his chin quivered a bit. She took her place at the front and looked over the crowd. The opening notes of "Here Comes the Bride" played, and the crowd of people stood.

The whole world could have stopped turning, and nothing would have stopped Glory Ann from reaching the end of that aisle where a man waited for her, endless rows of young cornstalks growing behind him.

She'd wondered when Jimmy asked her to dinner, nine months ago, if it was sheer foolishness, but she'd said yes anyway.

They'd spent that entire first meal in stilted conversation, their words tripping all over each other. It was so odd, having such an entwined history so completely severed by circumstance. But even though war had stolen Jimmy from her once, the Lord had seen fit to bring him back. Before long Glory Ann and Jimmy grew back together again.

Her daughters on each side of her squeezed her arms.

At the sight of her, Jimmy's face softened as if he were caught in a dream. Maybe a lifetime had been taken from them by the ugliness of war and kept secrets, but no matter how long they'd have together, they were determined to squeeze every drop out of life and shower love on all the people around them in hopes that their love could help beauty grow where pain had been sown.

Her gaze went to Sarah, who watched Clay holding squirming baby Luke. That girl might not know it yet, but she was absolutely smitten. Sure as shootin', there would be another wedding on this farm before too long.

Just before they reached the end of the aisle, Glory Ann slipped an envelope into

Rosemary's hand. Rosemary and Cathy had spent days planning the perfect honeymoon for the happy couple. Glory Ann couldn't wait to see Rosemary's face when she realized it had been for her and Bo all along.

Rosemary looked at her in surprise and took the envelope. She pressed a kiss to Glory Ann's cheek and Jessamine did the same to her opposite cheek. Glory Ann squeezed their hands, and the two of them joined Sarah.

Glory Ann took the final steps alone. The stolen years melted away.

"Dearly beloved, we are gathered here today to join this man and this woman . . ."

Once again, she was his lovestruck bride and he was her blue-eyed boy.

AUTHOR'S NOTE

Though the characters and happenings of this story are a work of my imagination, Old Depot was a real grocery store that was a part of my own family's heritage. This small grocery store in Camden, Tennessee, was owned by my maternal grandparents. Many of my family members, on both my mother's and father's side of the family, worked there at one time or another. As a little girl, whenever I would come for a visit, I loved running up and down those store aisles and playing hide-and-seek with my brother. I can still remember the sound of the floorboards and the way the place just seemed to have a life of its own. Even though the store closed back when I was a young girl, there is something about it that always held a sense of home to me. I hope I did it justice in these pages. On another note, if any characters resemble anyone in real life, it is purely by coincidence. Although, if you worked at Old Depot, you might recognize some of the anecdotes, like the prank calls and stolen ice and forgotten money bags.

ACKNOWLEDGMENTS

Thank you to the entire team at Revell for the opportunity to publish another book with you. The support and expertise I've received from this team of people blows me away. I am so grateful for the time and talent you have invested to help my work shine and to get it into the hands of readers.

A special thank-you to my mom, my dad, and my grandmother Irene Hyatt, who filled out my murky childhood memories of Old Depot and who helped me better understand the ins and outs of running a grocery in a small town. I loved hearing all the stories.

To Patti and Crystal, thank you for giving your time to this story and helping me to work through the kinks to make these characters come alive.

To Caleb, Ellie, and Levi, I appreciate your patience. You always have such grand adventures planned for me. Thanks for understanding when I had to take a rain check. I know it wasn't easy dealing with a writing momma in the middle of a pandemic.

To my husband, thanks for always cheering me on and sharing in the joys of my writing life. And even though I know you are secretly laughing at me when I'm being an angsty writer, you let me moan about how awful my writing is before you kiss me on the forehead and tell me that it's going to be great.

To my chief writing partner, here is another story "in the books." I pray this novel serves whatever purpose You have in store for it and finds its way into the hands of those who would be blessed by the relational healing that takes place in these pages. Jesus, I hope I get to write many more stories with You by my side.

ABOUT THE AUTHOR

Amanda Cox is the author of *The Edge of Belonging.* A blogger and a curriculum developer for a national nonprofit youth leadership organization, she holds a bachelor's degree in Bible and theology and a master's degree in professional counseling, but her first love is communicating through story. Her studies and her interactions with hurting families over a decade have allowed her to create multidimensional characters that connect emotionally with readers. She lives in Chattanooga, Tennessee, with her husband and their three children. Learn more at AmandaCoxWrites.com.

The employees of Thorndike Press hope you have enjoyed this Large Print book. All our Thorndike, Wheeler, and Kennebec Large Print titles are designed for easy reading, and all our books are made to last. Other Thorndike Press Large Print books are available at your library, through selected bookstores, or directly from us.

For information about titles, please call:
(800) 223-1244

or visit our website at:
gale.com/thorndike

To share your comments, please write:

Publisher
Thorndike Press
10 Water St., Suite 310
Waterville, ME 04901